LITTLE *Vampire* WOMEN

LOUISA MAY ALCOTT
AND LYNN MESSINA

HARPER TEEN

An Imprint of HarperCollinsPublishers

HarperTeen is an imprint of HarperCollins Publishers.

Little Vampire Women

Adaptation copyright © 2010 by Lynn Messina

www.harperteen.com

Library of Congress Cataloging-in-Publication Data
Messina, Lynn (Lynn Ann), 1972-
Little vampire women / by Louisa May Alcott and [adapted by] Lynn Messina. — 1st ed.
p. cm.
Summary: In this twist on Louisa May Alcott's classic tale that chronicles the joys and sorrows of the four March sisters as they grow into young women in mid-nineteenth-century New England, the girls are vampires and neighbor Laurie wants to join them.
ISBN 978-0-06-197625-4
[1. Vampires—Fiction. 2. Sisters—Fiction. 3. Family life—New England—Fiction. 4. New England—History—19th century—Fiction.] I. Alcott, Louisa May, 1832-1888. Little women. II. Title.
PZ7.M556Lit 2010   2009053449
[Fic]—dc22   CIP
                                                          AC

Typography by Ray Shappell
10 11 12 13 14   CG/RRDH   10 9 8 7 6 5 4 3 2
❖
First Edition

PART
ONE

PLAYING PILGRIMS

"Christmas won't be Christmas without any corpses," grumbled Jo, lying on the rug.

"It's so dreadful to be poor!" sighed Meg, looking down at her old dress.

"I don't think it's fair for some vampires to have plenty of pretty squirming things, and other vampires nothing at all," added little Amy, with an injured sniff.

Being so poor, the Marches customarily dined on quarts of pig's blood, goat's blood, and, on very special occasions, cow's blood, but they rarely had the luxury of a living, breathing animal to feast on, and when they did, it was usually a small creature hardly more than a snack. Most of their meals had to be warmed over the fire to be brought up to the proper temperature, which was particularly humiliating for the young girls. Gone were the days when they could sink their fangs into a wiggling beaver, let alone a writhing cow. A human had never been on the menu, even when the family was wealthy and lived in a large, well-appointed house, for the Marches were humanitarians who believed the consumption of humans unworthy of the modern vampire. Humans were an inferior species in many ways, but they deserved to be pitied, not consumed.

"We've got Father and Mother, and each other," said Beth contentedly from her corner. She was the shy, domestically inclined sister.

"We haven't got Father, and shall not have him for a long time," Jo said sadly. She didn't say "perhaps never," but each silently added it, thinking of Father far away, where the fighting was.

The war was the reason they were to be denied even a field mouse this Christmas. It was going to be a hard winter for all humans, and their mother thought they ought not spend money for pleasure, when so many were suffering in the army. That the suffering was limited to mortal men did not concern Mother, for her commitment to the human race was steadfast, despite the criticism of her neighbors, who found both the Marches' beliefs and behavior baffling. Typically, vampires didn't concern themselves with the petty wars of humans. They had roamed the earth long before people and would continue to roam it long after they were gone.

"We can't do much, but we can make our little

sacrifices, and ought to do it gladly. But I am afraid I don't," and Meg shook her head, as she thought regretfully of all the pretty corpses she wouldn't get to eat.

"But I don't think the little we should spend would do any good. We've each got a dollar, and the army wouldn't be much helped by our giving that. I agree not to expect any gifts from Mother or you, but I do want to buy *Mr. Bloody Wobblestone's Scientifical Method for Tracking, Catching, and Destroying Vampire Slayers.*[1] I've wanted it so long," said Jo, who yearned to join the league of defenders, brave and gallant vampires who protected their fellow creatures from those humans who would destroy them by any means possible. In the last century, the noble profession had undergone a vast change, adopting modern techniques to battle an ancient threat. Relying on one's instincts, which had always been an imperfect process at best and a guessing game at worst, had been supplanted by steadfast science. Now, instead of spending three months learning the antiquated art of filtering out the smothering scent of garlic, one simply could put on an allium mask,[2] which accomplished the task for you.

---

[1] Bestselling how-to that introduced the so-called scientifical method of slayer hunting, by Clifford Farmer (b. 1685).

[2] Invented by Willis Whipetten (1750–1954) for his son, John, who suffered from dysgeusia garlisima, a chemosensory disorder that makes everything smell like garlic.

"I planned to spend my dollar in new music," said Beth, who loved to play music on the Marches' very old, poorly tuned piano. Mrs. March believed in a liberal education and strove to cultivate an interest in the arts in all her children.

"I shall get a nice box of Faber's fang enhancements," said Amy decidedly. Her fangs, though long, were blunt and did not come to an aristocratic point like her sisters'. No one minded the dullness save herself, but Amy felt deeply the want of a pair of killer-looking fangs.

"Mother didn't say anything about our money, and she won't wish us to give up everything. Let's each buy what we want, and have a little fun; I'm sure we work hard enough to earn it," cried Jo.

"I know I do—teaching those tiresome children nearly all night, when I'm longing to enjoy myself at home," began Meg, in the complaining tone again.

"You don't have half such a hard time as I do," said Jo, who served as companion and protector to their 427-year-old aunt. "How would you like to be shut up for hours with a nervous, fussy old lady who's convinced every tradesman who comes to the door is there to slay her?"

"It's naughty to fret, but I do think washing dishes and keeping things tidy is the worst work in the world. It makes me cross," Beth said.

"I don't believe any of you suffer as I do," cried

Amy, "for you don't have to go to school with impertinent girls who plague you if you don't know your lessons, and laugh at your dresses, and label your father if he isn't rich, and insult you when your fangs aren't nice."

"If you mean libel, I'd say so, and not talk about labels, as if Papa was a pickle bottle," advised Jo, laughing.

As young readers like to know "how people look," we will take this moment to give them a little sketch of the four sisters, who sat knitting away in the near dawn, while the December snow fell quietly without, and the fire crackled cheerfully within. It was a comfortable room, though the carpet was faded and the furniture very plain, for a good picture or two hung on the walls, books filled the recesses, chrysanthemums and Christmas roses bloomed in the windows, and a pleasant atmosphere of home peace pervaded it.

Margaret, the eldest of the four, looked to be about sixteen, and very pretty, being plump and fair, with large eyes, plenty of soft brown hair, a sweet mouth, and white hands, of which she was rather vain. A year younger, Jo was very tall, thin, and brown, and reminded one of a colt, for she never seemed to know what to do with her long limbs, which were very much in her way. She had a decided mouth, a comical nose, and sharp, gray eyes, which appeared to see everything and were by turns fierce, funny, or thoughtful. Her long, thick hair was her one beauty, but it was usually bundled into a net, to be out of her way. Round shoulders had Jo, big hands and feet, a flyaway look to her clothes, and the uncomfortable appearance of a girl who was rapidly shooting up into a woman and didn't like it. (Although her transformation to vampire brought an abrupt end to the growth spurt, the awkwardness of her appearance remained a permanent fixture.) Elizabeth, or Beth, as everyone called her, appeared to be an ashen-faced, smooth-haired, bright-eyed girl of thirteen, with a shy manner, a timid voice, and a peaceful expression which was seldom disturbed. Her father called her "Little Miss Tranquility," and the name suited her excellently, for she seemed to live in a happy world of her own, only venturing out to meet the few whom she trusted and loved. Amy, though the youngest, was a most important person, in her own opinion at least. A regular snow maiden, with blue eyes, and yellow hair curling on her shoulders, pale and slender, and always carrying herself like a young vampire lady mindful of her manners.

Each girl looked as if she'd been alive for scarcely more than a decade, especially Amy, whose pallid complexion could do little to mute her youthful energy, but they had all undergone the Great Change thirty-two years previous, which made them vampires of some experience. However, they were still considered adolescents, for vampires lived very long lives indeed and thirty-odd years was scarcely a fraction of it. Therefore, in all the ways that mattered, the March girls, although chronologically older than their mortal counterparts, were perched just as precariously on the edge of womanhood.

The clock struck six. Mother was coming, and everyone brightened to welcome her.

"I'll tell you what we should do," said Beth, "let's each get Marmee something for Christmas, and not get anything for ourselves."

"That's like you, dear! What will we get?" exclaimed Jo.

Everyone thought soberly for a minute, then Meg announced, "I shall get her a rabbit to feed on."

"A squirrel," cried Jo.

"A bunny," said Beth.

"I'll get a little mouse. It won't cost much, so I'll have some left to buy my fang enhancements," added Amy.

"How will we give the things?" asked Meg.

"Put them on the table, and bring her in and see her open the bundles. Don't you remember how we used to do on our birthdays?" answered Jo.

Having decided how to present their gifts, the girls discussed where to buy them, for the only store on Main Street that sold small animals was a pet shop and they didn't know how Mr. Lewis would feel about providing tasty delicacies for their mother. Concord was an integrated town, where vampires could live peacefully in the open, but there were still moments when reminders of a vampire's particular lifestyle could make the locals uncomfortable.

Though they were eager to buy presents, they had to stay indoors, for the sun was about to rise. Jo suggested they practice hunting vampire slayers, her favorite occupation, and the girls complied reluctantly, for they didn't share Jo's passion. Meg was the slayer and Jo tracked her to the attic closet, where her quarry had already chopped the heads off Beth's poor, blameless doll. Beth protested the unfair abuse and attached a neat little cap to the poor invalid's neck. As both arms and legs had been removed during a previous field exercise, she had to wrap the deformed doll in a blanket.

Her sisters laughed at the makeshift hospital ward she assembled.

"Glad to find you so merry, my girls," said a cheery voice at the door, and the girls turned to welcome a tall, motherly lady with a "can I help you" look about her which was truly delightful. She was not elegantly dressed, but a noble-looking woman of forty biological years, and the girls thought the gray cloak and unfashionable bonnet covered the most splendid mother in the world.

"Well, dearies, how have you got on tonight? There was so much to do that I didn't come home to dinner. Has anyone called, Beth? How is your cold, Meg? Jo, you look tired to death. Come and kiss me, baby."

While making these maternal inquiries, Mrs. March took off her artificial teeth to reveal her well-appointed fangs. Some vampire ladies in the community thought it was just the thing to walk around with their teeth hanging out, but Marmee thought naked fangs were an indecency on par with naked ankles.

As they gathered about the table, Mrs. March said, with a particularly happy face, her fangs gleaming white in the firelight, "I've got a treat for you."

A quick, bright smile went round like a streak of moonshine. Beth clapped her hands, and Jo cried, "A letter! A letter! Three cheers for Father!"

"Yes, a nice long letter. He is well, and thinks he shall get through the cold season better than we feared. He sends all sorts of loving wishes for Christmas, and an especial message to you girls," said Mrs. March.

"I think it was so splendid of Father to go at all when the war has nothing to do with vampires," said Meg warmly.

The War Between the States was over the moral issue of slavery, which was indeed of little interest to vampires. However, slave quarters were verdant feeding grounds for vampires south of the Mason-Dixon Line, for their inhabitants were often too tired from days of backbreaking, abusive labor to put up a fight, and the slaves who disappeared were often mistakenly assumed to have fled north with the help of abolitionists. Being an ethical vampire with implacable morals,

Mr. March felt he should do his part to help win the war his kind had unintentionally started by making it seem as though the North was interfering extensively in private Southern business.

"Don't I wish I could go as a drummer, a vivan—what's its name? Or a nurse, so I could be near him and help him," exclaimed Jo, who would rather do anything than work for her awful aunt March.

"When will he come home, Marmee?" asked Beth, with a little quiver in her voice.

"Not for many months, dear. He will stay and do his work faithfully as long as he can, and we won't ask for him back a minute sooner than he can be spared. Now come and hear the letter."

They all drew to the fire, Mother in the big chair with Beth at her feet, Meg and Amy perched on either arm of the chair, and Jo leaning on the back, where no one would see any sign of emotion if the letter should happen to be touching.

Very few human letters were written in those hard times that were not touching, especially those which fathers sent home, and this vampire letter was no different. In it little was said of the hardships endured, the dangers faced, or the homesickness conquered. It was a cheerful, hopeful letter, full of the comical lengths Mr. March often had to go to in order to avoid sunshine. He'd joined the army as a chaplain and tried very hard to stay inside his tent during daylight hours, but this was not always practical, as war followed no schedule. Only at the end did the writer's heart over-flow with fatherly love and longing for the little vampire girls at home.

"Give them all of my dear love and a kiss. Tell them I think of them by night, pray for them by day, and find my best comfort in their affection at all times. A year seems very long to wait before I see them, but remind them that while we wait we may all work, so that these hard days need not be wasted. I know they will remember all I said to them, that they will be loving children to you, will do their duty faithfully and fight their bosom enemy bravely," he said, referring to the demon beast that lived inside them all. It was a daily challenge to overcome their vampire natures, but Mr. March knew his girls could do it and from afar he urged them to "conquer themselves so beautifully that when I come back to them I may be fonder and prouder than ever of my little vampire women." Everybody sniffed when they came to that part. Jo wasn't ashamed of the great bloody tear[3] that dropped off the end of her nose and landed in a bright red splatter on her otherwise pristine dress, and Amy never minded the rumpling of her

---

[3] Paulson Dillywither (1834–1897) argues convincingly in *Vampire Habits and Customs: The Beastly True Nature of Nature's True Beast* that lacrimal hemoglobin emissions, also known as blood tears, are caused by an infiltration of blood into the nasolacrimal duct.

curls as she hid her face on her mother's shoulder and sobbed out, "I am a selfish girl! But I'll truly try to be better, so he mayn't be disappointed in me by-and-by."

"We all will," cried Meg. "I think too much of drinking cow and deer blood and wearing beautiful silk gloves, but I won't anymore, if I can help it."

"I'll try and be what he loves to call me, 'a little vampire woman,' and not be rough and wild, but do my duty here instead of wanting to be somewhere else," said Jo, thinking that keeping her temper at home was a much harder task than facing a rebel or two down South.

Beth said nothing, but wiped away tears with the blue army sock and began to knit with all her might, losing no time in doing the duty that lay nearest her, while she resolved in her quiet little soul to be all that Father hoped to find her when the year brought round the happy coming home.

Mrs. March broke the silence that followed Jo's words, by saying in her cheery voice, "Do you remember how you used to play *Vilgrim's Progress*[4] when you were young things? Nothing delighted you more than

---

[4] Seminal text that first suggested vampires were children of God and therefore worthy of entrance into heaven; by William Swinton (1321–1569). Swinton cited the gift of immortality as proof of God's preference for vampires over their mortal counterparts and even hinted that humanity itself might be damned. John Bunyan's *The Pilgrim's Progress* is largely thought to be an almost verbatim rip-off of the book, although defenders have argued it is a pastiche.

to have me tie my piece bags on your backs for burdens, give you hats and sticks and rolls of paper, and let you travel through the house from the cellar, which was the City of Destruction, up, up, to the housetop, where you had all the lovely things you could collect to make a Celestial City."

"What fun it was, especially going by the lions, fighting Apollyon, and passing through the valley where the hobgoblins were," said Jo, for all the challenges that poor Vilgrim, the vampire pilgrim, had to overcome in his quest for heaven greatly resembled a course for the training of vampire defenders.

"I liked the place where the bundles fell off and tumbled downstairs," said Meg.

"I don't remember much about it, except that I was afraid of the sunlight that poured into the attic. If I wasn't too old for such things, I'd rather like to play it over again," said Amy, who really was too old for childish games despite her persistently youthful appearance.

"We never are too old for this, my dear, because it is a play we are playing all the time in one way or another. Our burdens are here, our road is before us, and the longing for goodness is the guide that leads us through many troubles, mistakes, and uncontrollable feeding frenzies to inner peace which is the true Celestial City. Now, my little vilgrims, suppose you begin again, not in play, but in earnest, and see how far on you can get before Father comes home," Marmee suggested, concerned now, as always, with the preservation of her daughters' souls, for it had not been that many years past since vampires were thought to have no soul at all. For centuries, they were considered minions of the devil and were forced to hide in shadow, fearful that any seemingly harmless gathering of people would quickly become an angry, stake-bearing mob. But thanks to the Camp Moldovenească Accords[5] that was all in the past.

"Really, Mother? Where are our bundles?" asked Amy, who was a very literal vampire.

"Each of you told what your burden was just now, except Beth. I rather think she hasn't got any," said her mother.

"Yes, I have. Mine is dishes and dusters, and envying vampires with nice pianos, and being afraid of people."

Beth's bundle was such a funny one that everybody

---

[5] The international meeting held in 1767 that officially established vampires as naturalized citizens of heaven and granted them full inalienable rights. Out of the Accords came the groundbreaking Swift Nourishment Act, which reclassified the vampiric method of attaining sustenance as commerce, thereby making the consumption of humans who fell below the poverty level a safe and legal option for hungry vampires, as long as said vampires met the asking price and filled out the appropriate paperwork. Named for Jonathan Swift, who first proposed the arrangement in his famous 1729 essay "A Modest Proposal," in which he recommended that Ireland's poor solve their economic woes by selling their children for food.

wanted to laugh, but nobody did, for it would have hurt her feelings very much.

"Let us do it," said Meg thoughtfully. "It is only another name for trying to be good, and the story may help us, for though we don't want to feed on humans, it's hard work resisting our basic demon natures."

They talked over the new plan while old Hannah cleared the table, then out came the four little work baskets, and the needles flew as the girls made blackout curtains for Aunt March, who didn't trust the store-bought article to keep out the light. At nine, they stopped work and went to their coffins.

Chapter Two

A MERRY CHRISTMAS

Jo was the first to wake in the gray twilight of Christmas night. No little creatures hung at the fireplace squirming, and for a moment she felt disappointed. Then she remembered her promise to her mother and resolved not to mind a corpse-free holiday.

"Where is Mother?" asked Meg, as she and Jo ran down a half an hour later.

"Goodness only knows," replied Hannah, who had lived with the family since the girls were sired, and was considered by them all more as a friend than a servant.

"She will be back soon, I'm sure, warm the blood and have everything ready," said Meg.

Meg counted the gift bundles in the basket under the sofa and noticed Amy's was missing. A moment later, the youngest March came into the house and looked rather abashed when she saw her sisters all waiting for her.

"Where have you been, and what are you hiding behind you?" asked Meg, surprised to see, by her hood and cloak, that lazy Amy had been out so early.

"Don't laugh at me, Jo! I didn't mean anyone should know till the time came. I only meant to change the little mouse for a big rat, and I gave all my money to get it, even though I had to break into the shop, for the store was closed on account of the holiday, and I'm truly trying not to be selfish anymore."

As she spoke, Amy showed the plump rat which replaced the slight mouse, and looked so earnest and humble in her little effort to forget herself that Meg hugged her on the spot, and Jo pronounced her "a trump," while Beth ran to the window, and picked her finest rose to ornament the stately vermin.

"You see I felt ashamed of my present, so I ran to the shop and changed it the minute I was up, and I'm so glad, for mine is the most delicious one now."

Another bang of the street door announced the arrival of their mother.

"Merry Christmas, Marmee! Many of them!" they all cried in chorus.

"Merry Christmas, little daughters! I'm sorry I'm late," she said. "But not far away from here lies a poor woman with a newborn baby. Six children are huddled into one bed to keep from freezing, for they have no fire. There is nothing to eat over there, and the oldest boy came to tell me they were suffering hunger and cold. Being a vampire means I have to work doubly hard to be good, so I immediately went to them to offer my services."

The girls were all unusually hungry, having waited nearly an hour, and their breakfast was more tempting than they imagined. Rather than the usual helping of pig's blood, Hannah, in defiance of Mrs. March's orders, had served up a lovely little feast of dainty creatures. There were sparrows and chipmunks and a bashful opossum. The girls' fangs throbbed in expectation, for it had been such a long time since any of them had sunk her teeth into a recently pulsing vein.

For a minute no one spoke, only a minute, for Jo exclaimed impetuously, "I'm so glad you came before we began!"

"Yes," said Meg. "Let's give them our breakfast as a Christmas present."

"May I go and help carry the things to the poor little children?" asked Beth eagerly.

"I shall take the sparrows," added Amy, heroically giving up the article she most liked.

Meg was already covering the chipmunks and piling a vole into one big plate.

When all the food was packed up, the March family proceeded enthusiastically to the door. Jo opened it and said, "But the Hummels are human."

"We know that," said Amy impatiently.

"Shouldn't we bring human food?" Jo said.

Marmee and the girls agreed that human food would probably be more appropriate.

"Let's bring cream and muffins," said Amy, listing two foods she'd loved dearly when she'd had mortal taste buds.

"And buckwheat and bread," added Meg.

Having decided what to bring, they were stymied as to how to accomplish the task. Hannah hadn't made muffins in more than two centuries and in the interim had forgotten the recipe. Even if she could recall the specific ingredients, it was Christmas night, so all of the shops were closed. They had nowhere to purchase provisions. For ten minutes, the girls stood in the doorway wrestling with the problem. Then Beth suggested that they bring the animals to the Hummels' house and advise Mrs. Hummel to make some sort of stew, which she should know how to do, being a poor human and all.

Marmee thought it was an excellent plan and the procession set out for the Hummel abode. A poor, bare, miserable room it was, with broken windows, no fire, ragged bedclothes, a sick mother, wailing baby, and a group of pale, hungry children cuddled under one old quilt, trying to keep warm.

How the big eyes stared and the blue lips smiled as the girls went in.

"*Ach, mein Gott!* It is good angels come to us!" said the poor woman, crying for joy, even as she examined the offerings with a curious eye. She did not recognize the vole but accepted it gratefully, as well as the suggestion that she throw it, along with the other animals, in a pot with some water and salt.

"Funny angels with fangs," said Jo, wearing a heavy winter coat despite the fact that vampires couldn't feel cold. The Marches believed in fitting in as much as possible with the community and always wore season-appropriate attire.

When they returned home, they put the bundled gifts on the table and presented them to Marmee. Beth played her gayest march while Meg conducted Mother to the seat of honor. Mrs. March was both surprised and touched, and smiled with her eyes full as she examined her presents and read the little notes which accompanied them. The bunny bun-bun was sucked dry immediately, followed swiftly by the squirrel and the rabbit. Prior to eating the rat, she paused a moment to smell it deeply before pronouncing it delightful. Bright red blood trickled down her chin.

There was a good deal of laughing and kissing and explaining, in the simple, loving fashion which makes these home festivals so pleasant at the time, so sweet to remember long afterward. Jo looked down at her mother's feet and saw the remains of their gifts scattered like dead things.

Oh, how lovely to have Christmas corpses after all!

Chapter Three

THE
LAURENCE BOY

"Jo! Jo! Where are you?" cried Meg at the foot of the garret stairs.

"Here!" answered a husky voice from above, and, running up, Meg found her sister deeply engrossed in a well-worn copy of *The Seven Signs of a Vampire Slayer and How to Spot One*,[6] curled up in an old three-legged sofa by the window. This was Jo's favorite refuge, and here she loved to retire with a nice book, to enjoy the quiet and the society of a pet rat who lived nearby and didn't mind her a particle. As Meg appeared, Scrabble

---

[6] International bestseller by Dimitri Strinsky (b. 1294), translated into thirty-seven languages, including Swahili. Its sequel, *Seven More Signs of a Vampire Slayer and How I Missed Them the First Time*, is also a classic.

whisked into his hole. This Scrabble was in fact the eighteenth such one, for Jo could never long resist the easy lure of a close-by snack when feeling peckish. The kitchens were several floors below, and despite her superior vampire strength she could rarely bestir herself to make the long journey downstairs.

"Such fun! Only see! A regular note of invitation from Mrs. Gardiner for tomorrow night!" cried Meg, waving the precious paper and then proceeding to read it with girlish delight.

"'Mrs. Gardiner would be happy to see Miss March and Miss Josephine at a little dance on New Year's Eve.' Marmee is willing we should go, now what shall we wear?"

"What's the use of asking that, when you know we shall wear our poplins, because we haven't got anything else?" answered Jo.

"If I only had a silk!" sighed Meg.

"I'm sure our pops look like silk, and they are nice enough for us. Yours is as good as new, but I forgot the burn in mine. Whatever shall I do? The burn shows badly."

"You must sit still all you can and keep your back out of sight. The front is all right. I shall have a new ribbon for my hair, and Marmee will lend me her little pearl pin, and my new slippers are lovely, and my gloves will do, though they aren't as nice as I'd like."

"Mine are spoiled with blood, and I can't get any

new ones, so I shall have to go without," said Jo, who never troubled herself much about dress.

"You must have gloves, or I won't go," cried Meg decidedly. "Gloves are more important than anything else. You can't dance without them, and if you don't I should be so mortified."

"Then I'll stay still. I don't care much for company dancing. It's no fun to go sailing round. I like to fly about and cut capers."

"You can't ask Mother for new ones, they are so expensive, and you are so careless. She said when you spoiled the others that she shouldn't get you any more this winter. Can't you make them do?"

"I can hold them crumpled up in my hand, so no one will know how stained they are. That's all I can do. No! I'll tell you how we can manage, each wear one good one and carry a bad one. Don't you see?"

"Your hands are bigger than mine, and you will stretch my glove dreadfully," began Meg, whose gloves were a tender point with her.

"Then I'll go without. I don't care what people say!" cried Jo, taking up her book.

"You may have it, you may! Only don't stain it, and do behave nicely."

On New Year's Eve the parlor was deserted, for the two younger girls played dressing maids and the two elder were absorbed in the all-important business of "getting ready for the party." Simple as the toilets were, there was a great deal of running up and down, laughing and talking.

After various mishaps, Meg was finished at last, and by the united exertions of the entire family Jo's hair was got up and her dress on. They looked very well in their simple suits, Meg's in silvery drab, with a blue velvet snood, lace frills, and the pearl pin. Jo in maroon, with a stiff, gentlemanly linen collar, and a white chrysanthemum or two for her only ornament. Each put on one nice light glove, and carried one soiled one, and all pronounced the effect "quite easy and fine." Meg's high-heeled slippers were very tight and awkward to walk in, though she would not own it, and Jo's nineteen hairpins all seemed stuck straight into her head. This was not at all comfortable but necessary should vampire slayers attack the party, for the hairpins were dipped in poison and doubled as paralyzing darts.

"Have a good time, dearies!" said Mrs. March, as the sisters went daintily down the walk. "Don't eat much supper, and come away at five when I send Hannah for you."

Down they went, feeling a trifle timid, for they seldom went to parties, and informal as this little gathering was, it was an event to them. Mrs. Gardiner, a stately old vampire lady, greeted them kindly as they passed through the area set apart for the screening of weapons. The March girls were from an old and established family, but even they had to submit to an examination by Pinkerton agents.[7] Everyone did, as the company was mixed and no hostess wanted to inadvertently admit a slayer to her party, for not only was it personally mortifying for a vampire to be slain at your soiree, it was very damaging socially.

Like all society matrons, Mrs. Gardiner welcomed nonvampires into her drawing rooms, for some of the oldest families in the neighborhood were human, making interaction unavoidable. The two groups rubbed together tolerably well, united by a common purpose to keep newcomers out of their circle, and disagreements over a missing servant or an unfair accusation of colluding with slayers broke out only rarely. Although Mrs. Gardiner considered humans to be inferior to her in every way, those of exceptional social standing at the party had nothing to fear from her and her kind. It was the height of rudeness to dine on your guests, particularly if they were your social equal. Likewise, it was unforgivably vulgar to stake your host.

The poor were not afforded the same courtesy and frequently fended off attacks from vampires and nonvampires alike, both of whom fed on them, the former literally, the other metaphorically. For centuries,

---

[7] The Pinkerton National Detective Agency, established in 1850 by Allan Pinkerton, who became famous after foiling an attempt to assassinate President-elect Abraham Lincoln. Pinkerton was the first personal-security agency to hire vampires to screen for slayers.

vampire philosophers had argued that their treatment of humans was kinder; they took only the blood in their veins. Nonvampires took the sweat of their brow, the fire in their belly, and the joy in their heart.

Slayers swore nobly to protect the desperate and the destitute from predators, but in targeting vampires only, they revealed their bigotry. Some vampires were indeed the cruel and thoughtless killing machines that many in the sensationalistic press[8] portrayed them to be, but what of the factory owner or the slave holder? Were they not also cruel and thoughtless? Yet they were exempt from retribution.

Jo, like her mother, knew vampire slayers were mere vigilantes. They dispensed justice as they saw fit, which naturally made it the opposite of just. Marmee's way of helping the poor, providing them with food and shelter and solace, was the only method to save them from their despair. If the system itself was broken, it needed to be changed from the inside; randomly selecting vampires to assassinate wasn't the answer.

When the March girls were cleared by the security agents, Mrs. Gardiner handed them over to the eldest of her six daughters. Meg knew Sallie and was at her ease very soon, but Jo, who didn't care much for girls or girlish gossip, stood about, with her back carefully

---

[8] For an example, see "Vampires Are Thoughtless Killing Machines," *New York Times*, January 23, 1856.

against the wall, and felt as much out of place as a colt in a flower garden. A big redheaded youth approached her corner, and fearing he meant to engage her, she slipped into a curtained recess, intending to peep and enjoy herself in peace. Unfortunately, another bashful person had chosen the same refuge, for, as the curtain fell behind her, she found herself face-to-face with the "Laurence boy."

"Dear me, I didn't know anyone was here!" stammered Jo, preparing to back out as speedily as she had bounced in.

But the boy laughed and said pleasantly, though he looked a little startled, "Don't mind me, stay if you like."

"Shan't I disturb you?"

"Not a bit. I only came here because I don't know many people and felt rather strange at first, you know."

"So did I. Don't go away, please, unless you'd rather."

The boy sat down again and looked at his pumps,[9] till Jo said, trying to be polite and easy, "I think I've had the pleasure of seeing you before. You live near us, don't you?"

"Next door, Miss March."

---

[9] Type of shoe said to be worn by men in olden times; however, this detail has been pointed to by several radical feminist scholars as proof that Laurie's desire to be a vampire is really a repressed desire to be a woman. See Karen Thomapolis's *Unmasking Gender in Little Vampire Women*.

"Oh, I am not Miss March, I'm only Jo," returned the young lady.

"I'm not Mr. Laurence, I'm only Laurie."

"Laurie Laurence, what an odd name."

"My first name is Theodore, but I don't like it, for the fellows called me Dora, so I made them say Laurie instead."

"I hate my name, too, so sentimental! I wish everyone would say Jo instead of Josephine. How did you make the boys stop calling you Dora?"

"I thrashed 'em."

"I can't thrash Aunt March," Jo said, although of course technically she could, for she led her sisters in the study of boxing and karate every morning in the attic room. "So I suppose I shall have to bear it."

"Don't you like to dance, Miss Jo?" asked Laurie, looking as if he thought the name suited her.

"I like it well enough if there is plenty of room, and everyone is lively. In a place like this I'm sure to upset something, tread on people's toes, or do something dreadful. I'd much rather stay apart and watch for slayers."

"Do slayers typically disrupt house parties? I've been abroad a good many years, and haven't been into company enough yet to know how you do things here."

"Not too often," she said. "Thorough screening usually ensures peaceful evenings. But it does happen upon occasion. Just last month, the Phillipses' party was brought to a premature close when the host, Mr. Phillips, was staked in his own ballroom. It was during the dancing, so everyone was very upset, especially his daughter Leticia, as she was about to have her first waltz."

"Did they catch the culprit?"

"He escaped through the window while everyone was watching poor Mr. Phillips's guts explode all over the carpet. I don't know if you've seen many stakings, but it's a dreadful business. The maids always complain about how difficult it is to get molted flesh out of the curtains."

At the words *molted flesh*, the boy's eyes glowed. "I've never seen a staking. What's it like?"

"Very unpleasant all around," she said. "Staking is a terrible way to go. I'd much rather be decapitated. It still makes an awful mess but it's a lot more dignified than your limbs twittering all over the place." She shook her arms in approximation and Laurie laughed, appreciating her humor. Jo liked him tremendously, for most of the human boys she knew were particular about vampires and would rather be slayers than friends, which is why she counted so few of them among her acquaintance.

"I've never thought about it before, but I suppose I'd like to be decapitated, too," Laurie said. "One nice clean chop!"

"Oh, but the chops are rarely clean. Usually it takes several whacks before the connection is cut. You have to have a really sharp battle-ax."

"I'll remember that," he said, then paled and

stuttered, "N-not . . . th-that I plan on decapitating any vampires. I like them immensely. I'd love to be one myself."

"Oh, don't worry. I won't bite you. I'm a strict humanitarian, so it's against my religion to eat humans. We stick to pig's blood and have small animals only on very special occasions. My sister Beth loves kittens."

"I've never met a humanitarian before. There aren't any in Europe."

"There aren't a lot around here either. Just me and my sisters and my parents. It's no big deal. I don't even crave human flesh. Maybe if I'd gone without food for days on end, standing this close to you would give me ideas, but I had a snack an hour ago," Jo said, with a smile to put him at ease. "Tell me about Europe. I love dearly to hear people describe their travels."

Laurie didn't seem to know where to begin, but Jo's eager questions soon set him going, and he told her how he had been at school in Vevay, where the boys never wore hats and had a fleet of boats on the lake, and for holiday fun went on walking trips about Switzerland with their teachers.

"Don't I wish I'd been there!" cried Jo. "Did you go to Paris?"

"We spent last winter there."

"Can you talk French?"

"We were not allowed to speak anything else at Vevay."

"Do say some! I can read it, but can't pronounce."

"*Quel nom a cette jeune demoiselle en les pantoufles jolis?*"

"How nicely you do it! Let me see . . . you said, 'Who is the young lady in the pretty slippers,' didn't you?"

"*Oui, mademoiselle.*"

"It's my sister Margaret, and you knew it was! Do you think she is pretty?"

"Yes, she makes me think of the German vampire girls, she looks so pale and quiet, and dances like a lady."

Jo quite glowed with pleasure at this boyish praise of her sister, and stored it up to repeat to Meg. Both peeped and criticized and chatted till they felt like old acquaintances and didn't even seem to notice the differences between them, which is precisely how Marmee said it should be for humans and vampires. Jo liked the "Laurence boy" better than ever and took several good looks at him, so that she might describe him to the girls, for human boys were almost unknown creatures to them.

"Curly black hair, brown skin, big black eyes, handsome nose, fine teeth, small hands and feet, taller than I am, very polite, for a boy, and altogether jolly. Wonder how old he is?"

By and by, the band struck up a splendid polka and Laurie insisted that they dance.

"I can't, for I told Meg I wouldn't, because . . . " There Jo stopped, and looked undecided whether to tell or to laugh.

"Because, what?"

"You won't tell?"

"Never!"

"Well, I have a bad trick of standing near the window at sunrise, and so I burn my frocks, and I scorched this one. Though it's nicely mended, it shows, and Meg told me to keep still so no one would see it. You may laugh, if you want to. It is funny, I know."

But Laurie didn't laugh. He only looked down a minute, and the expression of his face puzzled Jo when he said very gently, "So it's true that sunlight does you great harm?"

"Only those thoughtless enough to expose themselves. I know I should pull the drapes and go to sleep but I love seeing the first rays peek over the horizon," she said softly.

"Never mind that," Laurie said. "I'll tell you how we can manage. There's a long hall out there, and we can dance grandly, and no one will see us. Please come."

Jo thanked him and gladly went, wishing she had two neat gloves when she saw the nice, pearl-colored ones her partner wore. The hall was empty, and they had a grand polka, for Laurie danced well, and taught her the German step, which delighted Jo, being full of swing and spring. When the music stopped, they sat down on the stairs, and Laurie was in the midst of an account of a vampires' festival at Heidelberg when Meg appeared in search of her sister. She beckoned, and Jo reluctantly followed her into a side room, where Meg sat on a sofa and held her foot.

"I've twisted my ankle. That stupid high heel turned

and gave my foot a sad wrench," she said, glancing down at the unfortunate appendage, which now pointed inward at a most severe angle. "It doesn't ache and I can stand fine but the cracking sound the bones make every time I step is disturbing the other dancers. I think we should leave."

"I knew you'd hurt your feet with those silly shoes. I'm sorry. But I don't see what you can do, except get a carriage, or stay here all night," answered Jo, tugging on the bent limb, which would not straighten despite her considerable efforts. The vampire ability to regenerate would heal the appendage soon, but not so quickly that Meg could rejoin the dancing.

"Can I help you?" said a friendly voice. And there was Laurie, with a full cup in one hand and a plate of ice in the other.

"It's nothing," Meg assured. "I turned my foot a little, that's all."

But Laurie could see for himself that she'd turned her foot a lot and immediately offered to take her home in his grandfather's carriage.

"It's so early! You can't mean to go yet?" began Jo, looking relieved but hesitating to accept the offer.

"I always go early, I do, truly! Please let me take you home. It's all on my way, you know, and it rains, they say."

That settled it. Jo gratefully accepted and they rolled away in the luxurious closed carriage, feeling very festive and elegant.

"I had a capital time. Did you?" asked Jo, rumpling up her hair, and making herself comfortable.

Meg agreed that she did up until the moment she twisted her ankle and had to leave. Laurie went on the box so Meg could keep her foot up, and the girls talked over their party in freedom.

"Sallie's friend, Annie Moffat, took a fancy to me, and asked me to come and spend a week with her when Sallie does. She is going in the spring when the opera comes, and it will be perfectly splendid, if Mother only lets me go," Meg said, cheering up at the thought.

Jo told her adventures, and by the time she had finished they were at home. With many thanks, they said good night and entered the house. The instant the door creaked, two little heads bobbed up and eager voices cried out . . .

"Tell about the party! Tell about the party!"

"I declare, it really seems like being a fine young lady, to come home from the party in a carriage and sit in my dressing gown with a maid to wait on me," said Meg.

"I don't believe fine young ladies enjoy themselves a bit more than we do, in spite of our burned gowns, one glove apiece, and tight slippers that sprain our ankles when we are silly enough to wear them." And I think Jo was quite right.

Chapter Four

BURDENS

With the holidays over, the girls had to take up their packs, which, after the week of merrymaking, seemed heavier than ever. Beth lay on the sofa, trying to comfort herself with a cat and three juicy kittens she'd found hiding in the basement. Amy was fretting because her lessons were not learned and she couldn't find her rubbers. Meg, whose burden consisted of four spoiled vampire children, had not heart enough even to make herself pretty as usual by putting on a blue neck ribbon and dressing her hair in the most becoming way.

"Where's the use of looking nice, when no one sees me but those cross midgets, and no one cares whether I'm pretty or not?" she muttered, shutting her drawer with a jerk as she thought of Mrs. King and her family. "I shall have to toil and moil all my days, with only little bits of fun now and then because I'm poor and can't enjoy my life as other girls do. It's a shame!"

"Well, that's just the way it is, so don't let us grumble but shoulder our bundles and trudge along as cheerfully as Marmee does. I'm sure Aunt March is a regular Old Man of the Sea[10] to me, but I suppose when I've learned to carry her without complaining, she will tumble off, or get so light that I shan't mind her," said Jo, whose resolute speech didn't match her dejected attitude. She had been so despondent that she didn't try to marshal the girls into their usual sunset training session of karate, calisthenics, and boxing, with which they complied with varying degrees of enthusiasm.

Jo happened to suit Aunt March, who was lame and needed an active person to protect her. The childless old lady had offered to adopt one of the girls when the troubles came, and was much offended because her offer was declined. Other friends told the Marches that they had lost all chance of being remembered in the rich old vampire's will, but the unworldly Marches only said . . .

"We can't give up our girls for a dozen fortunes.

---

[10] A reference to the old man from the story "Sinbad the Sailor" in *The Thousand and One Nights*, which some critics argue is coded text about systemic vampire oppression by citing the fact that the Persian king killed his bride every morning as proof that the virgins were vampires. In referencing it here, Jo could be referencing her own systemic oppression.

Rich or poor, we will keep together and be happy in one another."

As well, they knew Aunt March was a tough old broad who had been around for more than four hundred years and would likely be around for another four hundred. Their chances for inheritance were already decidedly slim.

The Marches, in their fondness for family over fortune, were not that unusual amongst their contemporaries. Vampire affection, though not as heartwarmingly sentimental as human affection, was deep and sincere. Parents sired their children and kept them close until they reached their majority at fifty chronological years, at which point they could sire a lifemate and settle down. Freshly sired children usually followed.

Mr. and Mrs. March had themselves followed that path, with Mr. March siring Mrs. March and then a century later siring the four sisters, whom he found in an orphanage about to be separated by an unfeeling proprietress. Marmee's kind heart went out to the benighted foursome and she knew upon seeing them that they were meant to be hers. Her husband complied to her request, feeling, too, that these unfortunate children needed a strong hand and a stronger soul to lead them, and twenty-four hours later, the giddy new mother stood over the four little graves from which her newborn daughters would emerge. It was the happiest day of her life.

Since then, the Marches had come down in the world, for Mr. March had lost his property in trying to help an unfortunate friend. The friend turned out to be a slayer who stole Mr. March's money through an elaborate counterfeit stock scheme.

That Mr. March allowed himself to be swindled out of ownership of his ancestral home disgusted Aunt March, who urged him to hunt down the cowardly slayer and consume him in a fiery fit of rage. Her nephew resisted her counsel, for he believed strongly in his humanitarian principles and was happier to let the villain live than to compromise himself.

His stubbornness made his aunt so angry she refused to speak to them for a time, but when her husband was beheaded by one of his own servants, she was forced to reevaluate her connections and decided the only associates she could trust were family. It was beyond shocking that Uncle March, the premier vampire defender in New England, was slain in his very own home. Well schooled in stealth and an experienced practitioner of the scientifical method, he should never have fallen for the cartoonish pratfalls of the Buffoonish Butler Hoax,[11] a well-known ruse in which a deadly opponent infiltrates a household by pretending to be a harmless servant who is forever

---

[11] Also known as the Silly Servant Stratagem and the Volatile Valet Ploy.

tripping over the silver and spilling the china.

Terrified, Aunt March immediately dismissed the entire staff (after, of course, they removed her husband's gooey remains) and recruited her niece Jo, who hoped to one day be a defender, to look after her. The Concord police inquiry into the unfortunate affair concluded that the slayer had worked alone. But Jo's aunt did not accept the findings because she assumed that the team of human investigators was part of the conspiracy. She therefore remained convinced that a worldwide cabal watched her daily, waiting for its moment to attack.

Being her aunt's protectress wasn't all Jo had hoped it would be, for the job provided little opportunity for her to use, let alone hone, her defender skills, but she accepted the place since nothing better appeared. The work was tedious and dull, but it gave her full access to the large training study, which had been left to dust and spiders since Uncle March's decapitation. Jo remembered the fierce old gentleman who used to let her play with his dart gun and told her thrilling stories of do-or-die hunts. He nurtured her love of adventure but stopped short of teaching her the mechanisms and techniques of modern-day slayer hunting, for he thought it a most unsuitable profession for any woman, especially his niece. The dim, dusty room, with its potions cabinet, investigative instruments, strategical maps, and, best of all, the wilderness of books in which she could now wander where she liked, made the study a region of bliss to her.

The moment Aunt March took her nap, Jo hurried to this well-equipped place, and curling herself up in the easy chair, studied the many tactical guides and first-person accounts of successful apprehensions of vicious slayers. But, like all happiness, it did not last long, for as sure as she had just reached the heart of the story, the pivotal part of a stratagem, or the most perilous adventure of her defender, a shrill voice called, "Josy-phine! Josy-phine!" and she had to leave her paradise to secure the perimeter, check the points of entry, or wind yarn.

Jo's ambition was to do something very splendid. What it was, she had no idea as yet, but left it for time to tell her, and meanwhile, found her greatest affliction in the fact that she couldn't read, run, and ride as much as she liked. A quick temper, sharp tongue, and restless spirit were always getting her into scrapes, and her life was a series of ups and downs, which were both comic and pathetic. But the training she received at Aunt March's was just what she needed, and the thought that she was doing something to support herself made her happy in spite of the perpetual "Josy-phine!"

Chapter Five

BEING
NEIGHBORLY

"What in the world are you going to do now, Jo?" asked Meg one snowy evening, as her sister came tramping through the hall, in rubber boots, old sack, and hood, with a broom in one hand and a shovel in the other.

"Going to hunt vampire slayers," answered Jo.

"I should think two treks at twilight would have been enough! It's wet out, and I advise you to stay dry by the fire, as I do," said Meg.

"Never take advice! Can't keep still all night, and not being a pussycat, I don't like to doze by the fire. I like adventures, and I'm going to find some."

Meg went back to reading *Ivanhoe*,[12] and Jo began

---

[12] Critics disagree as to the source of the reference. The most widely credited source is *Ivanhoe* by Sir Walter Scott (1771–1832).

to search the paths with great energy. A garden separated the Marches' house from that of Mr. Laurence. Both stood in a suburb of the city, which was still countrylike, with groves and lawns, large gardens, and quiet streets, all of which provided excellent cover for a slayer. A low hedge parted the two estates, offering additional concealment. On one side was an old, brown house, looking rather bare and shabby, robbed of the vines that could further hide a predator. On the other side was a stately stone mansion, plainly betokening every sort of comfort and luxury, from the big coach house and well-kept grounds to the conservatory and the glimpses of lovely things one caught between the rich curtains.

Yet it seemed a lonely, lifeless sort of house, for no children frolicked on the lawn, no motherly face ever smiled at the windows, and few people went in and out, except the old gentleman and his grandson.

"That boy is suffering for society and fun," Jo said to herself. "His grandpa does not know what's good for him, and keeps him shut up all alone. He needs a party of jolly boys to play with, or somebody young and lively. I've a great mind to go over and tell the old

---

However, scholars of vampire literature point to *Ye Olde Tale of Ivanhoe the Eternal* by Sir Wilfred Ivanhoe (1173–1879), a first-person account of the adventure tale on which Scott based his famous story. In 1865, the vampire-author embarked on a much-celebrated reading tour of North America to mark the release of a new illustrated edition of his classic, and the Marches would have been sure to have seen him in Concord.

gentleman so!"

The idea amused Jo, who liked to do daring things and was always scandalizing Meg by her queer performances. The plan of "going over" was not forgotten. And when the snowy evening came, Jo resolved to try what could be done. She saw Mr. Laurence drive off, and then sallied out to the hedge, where she paused and took a survey. All quiet, curtains down at the lower windows, servants out of sight, and nothing human visible but a curly black head leaning on a thin hand at the upper window.

"There he is," thought Jo, "poor boy! All alone and sick this happy night. It's a shame! I'll toss up a snowball and make him look out, and then say a kind word to him."

Up went a handful of soft snow, which cracked the window, as Jo frequently forgot how powerful her vampire strength made her, and the head turned at once, showing a face which lost its listless look in a minute, as the big eyes brightened and the mouth began to smile. Jo nodded and laughed, and flourished her broom as she called out . . .

"How do you do? Are you sick?"

Laurie opened the window, and croaked out as hoarsely as a raven . . .

"Better, thank you. I've had a bad cold, and been shut up a week."

"I'm sorry. What do you amuse yourself with?"

"Nothing. It's dull as tombs up here."

"Don't you read?"

"Not much. They won't let me."

"Can't somebody read to you?"

"Grandpa does sometimes, but my books don't interest him, and I hate to ask Brooke, my tutor, all the time."

"Have someone come and see you then."

"There isn't anyone I'd like to see. Boys make such a row, and my head is weak."

"Isn't there some nice girl who'd read and amuse you? Girls are quiet and like to play nurse."

"Don't know any."

"You know us," began Jo, then laughed and stopped.

"But you're not girls, you're vampires," cried Laurie.

"I'm not quiet and nice either, but I'll come, if Mother will let me. I'll go ask her. Shut the window, like a good boy, and wait till I come."

With that, Jo shouldered her broom and marched into the house, wondering what they would all say to her. Marmee did not protest the visit, for she firmly believed that the only way to improve vampire-human relations was to increase vampire-human interaction, and, after fortifying her daughter against any unbecoming urges with a tall glass of pig's blood, sent her to the neighbor's house with her blessing.

Laurie was in a flutter of excitement at the idea of having company, and flew about to get ready, for as Mrs.

March said, he was "a little gentleman," and did honor to the coming guest by brushing his curly pate, putting on a fresh collar, and trying to tidy up the room, which in spite of half a dozen servants, was anything but neat. Presently there came a loud ring, then a decided voice, asking for "Mr. Laurie," and a surprised-looking servant came running up to announce the vampire.

"All right, show her up, it's Miss Jo," said Laurie, going to the door of his little parlor to meet Jo, who appeared with a covered dish in one hand and three kittens in the other.

"Here I am, bag and baggage," she said briskly. "Mother sent her love, and was glad if I could do anything for you. Meg wanted me to bring some of her blanc mange,[13] and Beth thought cats would be comforting. I knew you'd laugh at them because you don't suck the blood out of living animals or even dead ones, but I couldn't refuse, she was so anxious to do something."

It so happened that Beth's funny loan was just the thing, for in laughing over the fact that, no, he did *not* suck the blood out of living animals or even dead ones, Laurie forgot his bashfulness, and grew sociable at once.

"That looks too pretty to eat," he said, smiling with pleasure, his manners unfailingly polite, as Jo

[13] Literally "white food"; as no edible products were traditionally kept in a vampire household, Meg is presumed to have made the blanc mange out of plaster and water.

uncovered the dish, and showed the blanc mange, surrounded by a garland of green leaves, and the scarlet
flowers of Amy's pet geranium.

"It isn't anything. Meg has no idea how to cook so
she just put something white in a saucer. I don't know
what it is but I'm sure it's inedible. What a cozy room
this is!"

"How kind you are! Yes, please take the big chair
and let me do something to amuse my company."

"No, I came to amuse you. Shall I read aloud?" and
Jo looked toward some books nearby.

"Thank you! I've read all those, and if you don't
mind, I'd rather talk," answered Laurie.

"Not a bit. I'll talk all night if you'll only set me
going. Beth says I never know when to stop."

"Is Beth the one who stays at home a good deal and
sometimes goes out with a little basket?" asked Laurie
with interest.

"Yes, that's Beth. She's my girl, and a regular good
one she is, too."

"The pretty one is Meg, and the curly-haired one is
Amy, I believe?"

"How did you find that out?"

Laurie colored up, but answered frankly, "Why, you
see I often hear you calling to one another, and when
I'm alone up here, I can't help looking over at your
house, you always seem to be having such good times. I
beg your pardon for being so rude, but sometimes you

forget to put down the curtain. And when the lamps are lighted, it's like looking at a picture to see you all around the table with your mother, taking turns draining every last little drop of blood out of a beaver or other small mammal. I haven't got any mother, you know." And Laurie poked the fire to hide a little twitching of the lips that he could not control.

The solitary, hungry look in his eyes went straight to Jo's heart. She had been so simply taught that there was no nonsense in her head. Laurie was sick and lonely, and feeling how rich she was in home and happiness, she gladly tried to share it with him. Her face was very friendly and her sharp voice unusually gentle as she said . . .

"We'll never draw that curtain anymore, and I give you leave to look as much as you like. I just wish, though, instead of peeping, you'd come over and see us. Mother is so splendid, she'd do you heaps of good, and Beth would sing to you if I begged her to, and Amy would dance. Meg and I would make you laugh over our hunts, and we'd have jolly times. Wouldn't your grandpa let you?"

"He's very kind, though he does not look so, and he lets me do what I like, pretty much, only he's afraid of vampires," began Laurie.

"We are not only vampires, we are neighbors, too, and he needn't think we'd eat you. We are strict humanitarians!"

"You see, Grandpa lives among his books, and doesn't

mind much what happens outside, so he doesn't know there are good vampires like your family out there."

"That's a shame."

"Do you like your school?" asked the boy, changing the subject, after a little pause, during which he stared at the fire and Jo looked about her, well pleased.

"Don't go to school, I'm a vampire defender—well, right now I'm in training. I protect my great-aunt from imagined assassins, and a dear, cross old soul she is, too," answered Jo.

Laurie opened his mouth to ask another question, but remembering just in time that it wasn't manners to make too many inquiries into vampires' affairs, he shut it again, and looked uncomfortable.

Jo liked his good breeding, and didn't mind having a laugh at Aunt March, so she gave him a lively description of the paranoid old lady, her aunt's parrot that talked Spanish, and the study where she reveled.

Laurie enjoyed that immensely, so she told him about the prim old gentleman vampire who came once to woo Aunt March. In the middle of his fine speech, Poll tweaked his wig off to his great dismay, so the suitor bit the head off the bird in retribution. But the parrot was itself of a special avian vampire species, so its head grew immediately back to insult the gentleman anew. The boy was so amused, he lay back and laughed till the tears ran down his cheeks, and a maid popped her head in to make sure the young master wasn't being consumed by his guest.

"Oh! That does me no end of good. Tell on, please," he said, taking his face out of the sofa cushion, red and shining with merriment.

Much elated with her success, Jo did "tell on," all about her famous defender uncle, her plans to follow in his footsteps, and her fond wish to someday invent a clever instrument that would improve the method by which one caught slayers—though what that was, she couldn't imagine. Then they got to talking about books, and to Jo's delight, she found that Laurie loved adventure tales as well as she did and had read more than herself.

"I wish I could be a vampire so I could go on grand hunts, too," he said.

"Oh, you don't have to be a vampire to go on hunts. Anyone can do it."

"But you have special powers," pointed out Laurie.

Jo shrugged. "Not really. I know people go on about our special vampire strength and senses, but it's a lot of work to develop those things and nobody bothers anymore. Now we use clever instruments like the one I'm going to invent. The new method employs the many modern advances of science and is far superior to the old method of relying on natural skill and instinct. All you need is a daily regimen of calisthenics and barbell lifting to be strong. I'd be happy to train you myself."

"But you can see in the dark and hear and smell

things from far away."

Jo admitted that these were advantages of her race but insisted that devoted study could go a long way to compensate for their lack.

Laurie's eyes glowed with excitement. "Really?"

"Absolutely! It's simply a matter of hard work."

"My grandfather would never agree. Couldn't you just turn me into a vampire? That way, I don't need his permission."

"I couldn't possibly," said Jo earnestly, not sure if he was teasing but also not caring, for she hated the thought of turning any mortal man. She knew all vampires did it eventually, for that was how they mated, but she couldn't bear the thought of doing it herself. Although there were many reasons to sire that didn't include finding a lifemate, such as friendship, whimsy, fondness, or spite, the act always created some kind of connection and Jo loved her independence too well to be tied to anybody on such a deep and abiding level. She knew her sisters would do it one day, though perhaps not Beth, who was far too shy. But that was a long way off—a decade, at least—so she wouldn't have to think about it for ages. "But I'll talk to your grandfather."

"You aren't afraid of him?"

"I'm not afraid of anything," returned Jo, with a toss of the head.

"I don't believe you are!" exclaimed the boy, looking at her with much admiration and desiring the vampire state even more for the courage it seemed to confer.

Laurie led her to the library to wait for his grandfather. It was lined with books, and there were pictures and statues, and distracting little cabinets full of coins and curiosities, and Sleepy Hollow chairs, and queer tables, and bronzes, and best of all, a great open fireplace with quaint tiles all round it.

"What richness!" sighed Jo, sinking into the depth of a velour chair and gazing about her with an air of intense satisfaction. "Theodore Laurence, you ought to be the happiest boy in the world," she added impressively.

"A fellow can't live on books," said Laurie, shaking his head as he perched on a table opposite.

She stood before a fine portrait of the old gentleman and said decidedly, "I'm sure now that I shouldn't be afraid of him, for he's got kind eyes, though his mouth is grim, and he looks as if he had a tremendous will of his own."

"Thank you, ma'am," said a gruff voice behind her, and there, to her great dismay, stood old Mr. Laurence with a wooden stake raised high in his hand.

For a minute a wild desire to run away possessed her, but that was cowardly, and the girls would laugh at her, so she resolved to stay and get out of the scrape as she could. She hated the thought of hurting her new friend's elderly relative but she would gladly knock him down with a scissor kick if necessary to her survival.

The gruff voice was gruffer than ever, as the old

gentleman said abruptly, after the dreadful pause, "So you're not afraid of me, hey?"

"Not much, sir," she said with a glance to the stake.

Mr. Laurence took a threatening step forward. "What have you been doing to this boy of mine, hey?" was the next question, sharply put.

"Only trying to be neighborly, sir." And Jo told how her visit came about.

"You think he needs cheering up a bit, do you?" he asked, his tone suspicious. Everyone knew vampires weren't charitable, so he thought the girl must have an ulterior motive.

"Yes, sir, he seems a little lonely, and young folks would do him good perhaps. We are only girls, but we should be glad to help if we could," said Jo eagerly. "I train my sisters daily in the skills of slayer hunting. Laurie could join us."

Suspecting a trap, the old man raised his stake.

"I could, sir," Laurie said, speaking for the first time since his grandfather appeared. "They could teach me how to defend myself against vampire slayers."

That the human lad had nothing to fear from vampire slayers was an obvious point his grandfather couldn't help but make. Then he added, "And who will teach you how to defend yourself against the vampires?"

Jo laughed. "Us? We're not a threat to anyone!"

Laurie laughed, too, and the change in his grand-son did not escape the old gentleman. There was color, light, and life in the boy's face now, vivacity in his manner, and genuine merriment in his laugh.

"She's right, the lad is lonely," thought Mr. Laurence, but he wasn't sure that allowing him into the company of four deadly creatures was the best solution. He liked Jo, for her odd, blunt ways suited him, but she was a vampire and therefore unworthy of trust.

Laurie knew how implacable his grandfather was in his prejudices and said sorely, "It's just as well. The training would take me away from my study of piano. I plan to be a musician, just like my mother, you know."

"Oh, how marvelous!" cried Jo, clapping her hands. "You will play grand concerts before hundreds and hundreds of people and travel all over the world and see so many—"

"That will do, that will do, young lady," Mr. Laurence said. "Too many sugarplums are not good for him. His music isn't bad, but I hope he will do as well in more important things."

"He doesn't like to hear me play," explained Laurie.

"Then you should let him train with us, sir," Jo said. "We have only a very, very old piano that nobody can get much music out of save my sister Beth, who loves playing."

Mr. Laurence considered the argument. Self-defense was a manly pursuit, even when practiced by vampire girls, and the study of it would leave Laurie less time for inconsequentials like music.

Aware that he wavered, Jo said, "Honestly, sir, we're good folks. My mother helps the poor and my father is fighting the war because he considers it his duty."

The latter hardly recommended the March family to the old man, who thought that the carnage of war was a sideboard buffet with endless appetizing treats for a creature of the night. Nevertheless, he relented and agreed to let Laurie come amongst them for the purposes of strength training and calisthenics.

Delighted, Jo made her good-byes and rushed home to tell her sisters about their new recruit.

Chapter Six

BETH FINDS THE PALACE BEAUTIFUL

To appease Mr. Laurence's concerns, the girls held their training sessions in the large house under the watchful gaze of the old man, who quickly saw that the only one committed to the training itself was Jo, for her sisters laughed and chatted throughout the entire event. All were delighted with the new venue except timid Beth, who thought Laurie's grandfather was as fierce as the lions who protected the Palace Beautiful[14] in their game of Vilgrim's Progress.

Mr. Laurence, although not a lion, did growl when he was displeased, a circumstance that occurred less

---

[14] A rest stop for vilgrims en route to Celestial City, across from Hill Difficulty. Many scholars believe Swinton based the description of the palace on Count Arnold Dracula's castle in Transylvania.

and less as he spent more and more time in the girls' company. He even unwound enough to pay a call on Mrs. March, whose generosity with the Hummels touched his heart.

The new friendship flourished like grass in spring. Everyone liked Laurie, and he privately informed his tutor Mr. Brooke that "the Marches were regularly splendid girls." With the delightful enthusiasm of vampire youth, they took the solitary boy into their midst and made much of him, and he found something very charming in the innocent companionship of these simple-hearted undead girls. Never having known mother or sisters, he was quick to feel the influences they brought about him, and their busy, lively ways made him ashamed of the indolent life he led. He was tired of books, and found vampires so interesting now that Mr. Brooke was obliged to make very unsatisfactory reports, for Laurie was always playing truant and running over to the Marches'.

"Never mind, let him take a holiday, and make it up afterward," said the old man, whose stance on vampires had undergone a sweeping change. "The good lady next door says he is studying too hard and needs young society, amusement, and exercise. I suspect she is right, and that I've been coddling the fellow as if I'd been his grandmother. Let him do what he likes, as long as he is happy. He can't get into mischief in that little nest over there."

What good times they had, to be sure. Meg could walk in the conservatory whenever she liked and revel in bouquets, Jo browsed over the new library voraciously, and convulsed the old gentleman with her criticisms, Amy copied pictures and enjoyed beauty to her heart's content, and Laurie played "lord of the manor" in the most delightful style.

But Beth, though yearning for the grand piano, could not pluck up courage to go to the "Mansion of Bliss," as Meg called it, and so missed out on everything, including the training sessions. She went once with Jo, but the old gentleman, not being aware of her infirmity, stared at her so hard from under his heavy eyebrows, and said "Hey!" so loud, that he frightened her so much her "feet chattered on the floor," she told her mother, and she ran away, declaring she would never go there anymore, not even for the dear piano. No persuasions or enticements could overcome her fear, till, the fact coming to Mr. Laurence's ear in some mysterious way, he set about mending matters. During one of his brief calls, he artfully led the conversation to music, and talked away about great singers whom he had seen, fine organs he had heard, and told such charming anecdotes that Beth found it impossible to stay in her distant corner, but crept nearer and nearer, as if fascinated. At the back of his chair she stopped and stood listening, with her great eyes wide open and her cheeks pale with excitement of this unusual performance. Taking no more notice of her than if she had been a fly, Mr. Laurence talked on about Laurie's lessons and teachers. And presently, as if the idea had just occurred to him, he said to Mrs. March . . .

"The boy neglects his music now, and I'm glad of it. But the piano suffers for want of use. Wouldn't some of your girls like to run over, and practice on it now and then, just to keep it in tune, you know, ma'am?"

Beth took a step forward, and pressed her hands tightly together to keep from clapping them, for this was an irresistible temptation, and the thought of practicing on that splendid instrument would have quite taken her breath away if she had any. Before Mrs. March could reply, Mr. Laurence went on with an odd little nod and smile . . .

"They needn't see or speak to anyone, but run in at any time. For I'm shut up in my study at the other end of the house, Laurie goes to bed early, and the servants leave at nine o'clock."

Here he rose, as if going, and Beth made up her mind to speak, for that last arrangement left nothing to be desired. "Please, tell the young ladies what I say, and if they don't care to come, why, never mind." Here a little hand slipped into his, and Beth looked up at him with a face full of gratitude, as she said, in her earnest yet timid way . . .

"Oh, sir, they do care, very very much!"

"Are you the musical girl?" he asked, without any

startling "Hey!" as he looked down at her very kindly.

"I'm Beth. I love it dearly, and I'll come, if you are quite sure nobody will hear me, and be disturbed," she added, fearing to be rude, and trembling at her own boldness as she spoke.

"Not a soul, my dear. So come and drum away as much as you like, and I shall be obliged to you."

"How kind you are, sir!"

Beth, not frightened now, gave the hand a grateful squeeze because she had no words to thank him for the precious gift he had given her. The old gentleman softly stroked the hair off her forehead, and, stooping down, he kissed her, saying, in a tone few people ever heard . . .

"I had a little girl once, with eyes like these and the same unearthly pale complexion. God bless you, my dear! Good day, madam." And away he went, in a great hurry.

The next evening, Beth, after two or three retreats, fairly got in at the side door, and made her way as noiselessly as any mouse to the drawing room where her idol stood. Quite by accident, of course, some pretty, easy music lay on the piano, and with trembling fingers and frequent stops to listen and look about, Beth at last touched the great instrument, and straightaway forgot her fear, herself, and everything else but the unspeakable delight which the music gave her, for it was like the voice of a beloved friend.

After that, the little brown hood slipped through the hedge nearly every night, and the great drawing room was haunted by a tuneful spirit that came and went unseen. She never knew that Mr. Laurence opened his study door to hear the old-fashioned airs he liked. She never saw Laurie mount guard in the hall to warn the servants away. She never suspected that the exercise books and new songs which she found in the rack were put there for her especial benefit, and when he talked to her about music at home, she only thought how kind he was to tell things that helped her so much.

"Mother, I'm going to work Mr. Laurence a blackout hood,"[15] she said, referring to the heavy garment that provided protection to those vampires who would look outside the window on a sunny day. It was typically made of wool and had narrow eye slits that afforded only a limited view of the world. "He is so kind to me, I must thank him, and I don't know any other way."

"That will please him very much, and be a nice way of thanking him," replied Mrs. March, who took peculiar pleasure in granting Beth's requests because she so seldom asked anything for herself. "But be sure to remove some of the fabric that covers the face so that Mr. Laurence can breathe."

After many serious discussions with Meg and Jo,

---

[15] A primitive version of what is now known as a solar cloak, which makes it possible for vampires to go out in the sun. Filtering out the sun's rays wasn't possible until the invention of Gore-Tex in 1976 by Wilbert L. Gore (1912–1986).

the pattern was chosen, the materials bought, and the hood begun. A cluster of grave pansies on a deeper purple ground was pronounced very appropriate and pretty, and Beth worked away early and late. When it was finished, she wrote a short, simple note, and with Laurie's help, got it smuggled onto the study table one morning before the old gentleman was up.

When this excitement was over, Beth waited to see what would happen. All night passed and a part of the next before any acknowledgment arrived, and she was beginning to fear she had offended her crotchety friend. At midnight of the second day, she went out to do an errand, and give poor Joanna, her armless, legless, headless doll, her daily exercise. As she came up the street, on her return, she saw three, yes, four heads popping in and out of the parlor windows, and the moment they saw her, several hands were waved, and several joyful voices screamed . . .

"Here's a letter from the old gentleman! Come quick, and read it!"

Beth hurried on in a flutter of suspense. At the door her sisters seized and bore her to the parlor in a triumphal procession, all pointing and all saying at once, "Look there! Look there!" Beth did look, and her already white skin somehow turned impossibly whiter with delight and surprise, for there stood a little cabinet piano, with a letter lying on the glossy lid, directed like a sign board to "Miss Elizabeth March."

"For me?" gasped Beth, holding on to Jo and feeling as if she should tumble down, it was such an overwhelming thing altogether.

"Yes, all for you, my precious! Isn't it splendid of him? Don't you think he's the dearest old man in the world? Here's the key in the letter," cried Jo, hugging her sister and offering the note.

"You read it! I can't, I feel so queer! Oh, it is too lovely!" and Beth hid her face in Jo's apron, quite upset by her present.

Jo opened the paper and began to laugh, for the first words she saw were . . .

Miss March:
Dear Madam, I have had many hats in my life, but I never had any that suited me so well as yours. Heartsease is my favorite flower, and this will always remind me of the gentle giver. I like to pay my debts, so I know you will allow "the old gentleman" to send you something which once belonged to the little granddaughter he lost. With hearty thanks and best wishes, I remain
Your grateful friend and humble servant,
JAMES LAURENCE.

"Try it, honey. Let's hear the sound of the baby pianny," said Hannah, who always took a share in the family joys and sorrows.

So Beth tried it, and everyone pronounced it the

most remarkable piano ever heard. It had evidently been newly tuned and put in apple-pie order. Beth lovingly touched the beautiful black and white keys and pressed the bright pedals.

"You'll have to go and thank him," said Jo, by way of a joke, for the idea of the child's really going never entered her head.

"Yes, I mean to. I guess I'll go now, before I get frightened thinking about it." And, to the utter amazement of the assembled family, Beth walked deliberately down the garden, through the hedge, and in at the Laurences' door.

"Well, I wish I may die if it ain't the queerest thing I ever see! The pianny has turned her head! She'd never have gone in her right mind," cried Hannah, staring after her, while the girls were rendered quite speechless by the miracle.

They would have been still more amazed if they had seen what Beth did afterward. If you will believe me, she went and knocked at the study door before she gave herself time to think, and when a gruff voice called out, "come in!" she did go in, right up to Mr. Laurence, who looked quite taken aback, and held out her hand, saying, with only a small quaver in her voice, "I came to thank you, sir, for . . . " But she didn't finish, for he looked so friendly that she forgot her speech and, only remembering that he had lost the little girl he loved, she put both arms round his neck and kissed him.

It was the closest Beth had been to a human since

her own transformation so many years before, and she couldn't get over the warmth of his flesh, the lovely smell of his blood, sweet like metal, as it throbbed through his veins so loudly she could hear it. Gently, she pressed her nose to his neck, feeling his heart so strongly it was as if her own still beat, and slowly, so slowly she hardly knew she was doing it, opened her mouth and wrenched her fangs into his skin so that his blood gushed through her lips and over her tongue and down her throat like a river of life. Yes, it was life she was giving him, eternal life, born of an impulse so wholesome and pure she might as well have been an infant burying her head in her mother's bosom.

The kindly old gentleman was hers now, for always.

Beth ceased to fear him from that moment on and sat there talking to him as cozily as if she'd known him all her life, for love casts out fear, and gratitude can conquer pride. Mr. Laurence, who had drunk Beth's blood when she offered it to him, was too weak and disoriented to follow the conversation. Realizing her dear friend needed immediate planting in the garden so the transformation could be complete, Beth led him gently outside, found a shovel, and began to dig.

When the girls saw that performance, Jo began to dance a jig, by way of expressing her satisfaction, Amy nearly fell out of the window in her surprise, and Meg exclaimed, with up-lifted hands, "Well, I do believe the world is coming to an end."

Chapter Seven

JO MEETS APOLLYON

"Girls, where are you going?" asked Amy, coming into their room early one Saturday evening, and finding them getting ready to go out with an air of secrecy which excited her curiosity.

"Never mind. Little girls shouldn't ask questions," returned Jo sharply.

Now if there is anything mortifying to our feelings when we are young, it is to be told that, especially when we are not really young and have been on this earth for more than forty years, though our appearance, thanks to its vampire nature, doesn't show it. To be bidden to "run away, dear" is still more trying to us. Amy bridled up at this insult, and determined to find out the secret, if she teased for an hour. Turning to Meg, who never refused her anything very long, she said coaxingly, "Do tell me! I should think you might let me go, too, for Beth is fussing over her piano, and I haven't got anything to do, and am so lonely."

"I can't, dear, because you aren't invited," began Meg, but Jo broke in impatiently, "Now, Meg, be quiet or you will spoil it all. You can't go, Amy, so don't be a baby and whine about it."

"You are going somewhere with Laurie, I know you are. You were whispering and laughing together on the sofa last night, and you stopped when I came in. Aren't you going with him?"

"Yes, we are. Now do be still, and stop bothering."

Sitting on the floor with one boot on, Amy began to cry big fat red tears and Meg to reason with her, when Laurie called from below, and the two girls hurried down, leaving their sister wailing. For now and then she forgot her grown-up ways and acted like a spoiled child. Just as the party was setting out, Amy called over the banisters in a threatening tone, "You'll be sorry for this, Jo March, see if you ain't."

"Fiddlesticks!" returned Jo, slamming the door.

They had a charming time, which was a relief, for things between the Marches and Laurie had been a bit awkward of late with Mr. Laurence's transformation into a creature of the night. He was still a kindly old man, but he could not quite control his hunger yet and had thrice tried to dine on his grandson. Now all of Laurie's defender training sessions became useful and he was able to subdue the elderly aggressor until Brooke returned with a portion of cow's blood.

Laurie didn't mind the violent attacks, for he knew his grandfather meant well in his desire to consume an equal rather than prey on the poor. Mrs. March assured him that in a few months, two years on the outside, the old man would gain the upper hand of his new, beastly hunger. And he didn't resent Beth at all for turning the old man. He understood how the timid young vampire had done the only thing possible, overcome with emotion as she was.

No, the unpleasantness stemmed from the fact that the Marches refused to even consider turning him as well. It seemed remarkably unfair that his grandfather should be extended the courtesy but not him. He was the one who longed to have grand adventures and duel with slayers and play music all night and never have to go to college or become a boring old businessman. He wanted super strength and eternal life.

His grandfather had not desired it and yet had been granted it.

Marmee tried to make the lad understand how precious human life was and that it should not be discarded on a whim. He was young yet, she pointed out, and would no doubt feel differently about it in a few years. Laurie insisted his feelings would not change but nobody would listen to him, treating him instead like a little boy who didn't know his own mind. Deciding another tactic might yield better results, Marmee explained that it went against the Marches' principles to change a human for reasons other than love. Of course the girls would sire mates when the time came, but as their mother and a devout humanitarian, she simply couldn't condone their siring for anything less. Naturally, Laurie raised the issue of his grandfather, for they all knew Beth had not sired a mate. Marmee agreed it was highly irregular, but timid Beth was so special and her motive for changing Mr. Laurence so pure that nobody could object.

Laurie conceded the truth of this but thought it was mightily ungenerous of Mrs. March not to volunteer to change him herself. She already treated him like a son; why not make him a real one?

His grandfather was just as bad. Between ravenous assaults on his grandson, he explained to the boy that he was now vitally important to the success of the company, rightly pointing out that much business was conducted during daylight hours and someone who could attend board meetings, lunches, and conferences was an invaluable commodity.

Laurie understood the arguments but thought they were heartily unfair and remained sullen and sulky. His tutor Mr. Brooke tried to cajole him out of his disappointment by listing all the ways he was lucky to be human. Football, for instance, could not be played by the light of the moon.

And now he, Laurie, Meg, and Jo were at the theater

together having a good time, even though Jo was a bit distracted by her fight with Amy. She and her youngest sister had had many lively skirmishes in the course of their lives, for both had quick tempers and were apt to be violent when fairly roused. Amy teased Jo, and Jo irritated Amy, and semioccasional explosions occurred, with both girls showing their fangs and snarling madly and diving into the other like eager, rabid dogs. Although the oldest, Jo had the least self-control, and had hard times trying to curb the fiery spirit which was continually getting her into trouble. Her anger never lasted long, and having humbly confessed her fault, she sincerely repented and tried to do better. Her sisters used to say that they rather liked to get Jo into a fury because she was such an angel afterward. Poor Jo tried desperately to be good, but her bosom enemy was always ready to flame up and defeat her, and it took years of patient effort to subdue it.

When they got home, they found Amy reading in the parlor. She assumed an injured air as they came in, never lifted her eyes from her book, or asked a single question. Perhaps curiosity might have conquered resentment, if Beth had not been there to inquire and receive a glowing description of the play. On going up to put away her best hat, Jo's first look was toward the bureau, for in their last quarrel Amy had soothed her feelings by turning Jo's top drawer upside down on the floor. Everything was in its place, however, and after a hasty glance into her various closets, bags, and boxes, Jo decided that Amy had forgiven and forgotten her wrongs.

There Jo was mistaken, for next day she made a discovery which produced a tempest. Meg, Beth, and Amy were sitting together, late in the evening, when Jo burst into the room, looking excited and demanding breathlessly, "Has anyone taken my notebook?"

Meg and Beth said, "No" at once, and looked surprised. Amy poked the fire and said nothing. Jo saw the look on her face and was down upon her in a minute.

"Amy, you've got it!"

"No, I haven't."

"You know where it is, then!"

"No, I don't."

"That's a fib!" cried Jo, taking her by the shoulders, and looking fierce enough to frighten a much braver child than Amy.

"It isn't. I haven't got it, don't know where it is now, and don't care."

"You know something about it, and you'd better tell at once, or I'll make you." And Jo gave her a shake.

"Scold as much as you like, you'll never see your silly old book again," cried Amy, getting excited in her turn.

"Why not?"

"I burned it up."

"What! My little book in which for years I've been keeping detailed notes about all my slayer-hunting activities? Have you really burned it?" said Jo, her eyes kindling as her hands clutched Amy's throat.

71

"Yes, I did! I told you I'd make you pay for being so cross yesterday, and I have, so . . . "

Amy got no farther, for Jo's hot temper mastered her, and she shook Amy by the neck till her teeth chattered in her head, crying in a passion of grief and anger . . .

"You wicked, wicked girl! I never can write it again, and I'll never forgive you as long as I live."

Meg flew to rescue Amy, who did not need air to breathe so was no worse off for being deprived of it, and Beth to pacify Jo, but Jo was quite beside herself, and with a parting box on her sister's ear, which ejected an upper right molar, she rushed out of the room up to the old sofa in the garret and finished her fight alone, beating up several dozen training figures.

The storm cleared up below, for Mrs. March came home, and, having heard the story, soon brought Amy to a sense of the wrong she had done her sister. Jo's notebook was the pride of her heart, and she was regarded by her family as a vampire defender of great promise. It was only half a dozen little chapters of tactical fighting schemes she'd invented and hoped to implement one day, but Jo had worked over them patiently, recording every detail and thought she'd ever had. She had just copied them with great care, and had destroyed the old notes, so that Amy's bonfire had consumed the loving work of several years. It seemed a small loss to others, but to Jo it was a dreadful calamity, and she felt that it never could be made up to her. Beth mourned as for a kitten that ran away before she could eat it, and Meg refused to defend

Amy. Mrs. March looked grave and grieved, and Amy felt that no one would love her till she had asked pardon for the act which she now regretted more than any of them.

When the supper bell rang, Jo appeared, looking so grim and unapproachable that it took all Amy's courage to say meekly . . .

"Please forgive me, Jo. I'm very, very sorry."

"I never shall forgive you," was Jo's stern answer, and from that moment she ignored Amy entirely.

As Jo received her kiss before sleep, Mrs. March whispered gently, "My dear, don't let the sun come up upon your anger. Forgive each other, help each other, and begin again tonight."

She shook her head, and said gruffly because Amy was listening, "It was an abominable thing, and she doesn't deserve to be forgiven."

With that she marched off to her coffin, and there was no merry or confidential gossip that morning.

That evening, still feeling detestably angry, Jo asked Laurie to go skating with her. He was always kind and jolly and would put her to rights.

Amy heard the clash of skates, and looked out with an impatient exclamation, then, after a flurry to get ready, ran after her friends, who were just disappearing over the hill.

It was not far to the river, but both were ready before Amy reached them. Jo saw her coming, and turned her back. Laurie did not see, for he was carefully skating along the shore, sounding the ice, for a warm spell had preceded the cold snap.

"I'll go on to the first bend, and see if it's all right before we begin to race," Amy heard him say, as he shot away, looking like a young Russian in his fur-trimmed coat and cap.

Jo heard Amy stamping her feet and blowing on her fingers as she tried to put her skates on, but Jo never turned and went slowly zigzagging down the river, taking a bitter, unhappy sort of satisfaction in her sister's troubles. She had cherished her anger till it grew strong and took possession of her, as evil thoughts and feelings always do unless cast out at once. As Laurie turned the bend, he shouted back . . .

"Keep near the shore. It isn't safe in the middle." Jo heard, but Amy was struggling to her feet and did not catch a word. Jo glanced over her shoulder, and the little demon she was harboring said in her ear . . .

"No matter whether she heard or not, let her take care of herself. Besides, a little cold water won't hurt her."

Laurie had vanished round the bend, Jo was just at the turn, and Amy, far behind, striking out toward the smoother ice in the middle of the river. For a minute Jo stood still with a strange feeling in her heart, then she resolved to go on, but something held and turned her round, just in time to see Amy throw up her hands and go down, with a sudden crash of rotten ice, into the river, whose current was suddenly swift and strong and carrying Amy toward a large sharp branch hanging just above the water. Jo's heart stood still with fear. She tried to call Laurie, but her voice was gone. She tried to rush forward, but her feet seemed to have no strength in them, and for a second, she could only stand motionless, staring with a terror-stricken face at the little blue hood careening toward the branch. Something rushed swiftly by her, and Laurie's voice cried out . . .

"Get her. Quick, quick!"

How she did it, she never knew, but for the next few seconds, she worked possessed, blindly obeying Laurie, who was quite self-possessed, and diving into the river and dragging Amy under the branch that would have staked them both, barely missing it by half an inch, then pulling her safely to shore, where Laurie grabbed the child, more frightened than hurt.

"Now then, we must walk you home as fast as we can. Pile our things on, while I get off these confounded skates," cried Laurie, wrapping his coat round Amy, and tugging away at the straps which never seemed so intricate before, aware but unable to fully comprehend in the moment that the girls were immune from cold.

Dripping, and crying, bloody tears mixing with streaming water, they got Amy home, and after an exciting time of it, she fell asleep. During the bustle Jo had scarcely spoken but flown about, looking wild, with her things half off, her dress torn, and her hands blue from immersion in ice. When Amy was comfortably asleep, the house quiet, and Mrs. March sitting by the coffin, she called Jo to her and rubbed her daughter's frozen hands.

"Are you sure she is safe?" whispered Jo, looking

remorsefully at the golden head, which might have been swept away from her sight forever by the treacherous branch.

"Quite safe, dear. She is not hurt, thanks to your swift action," replied her mother cheerfully.

"Laurie did it all. I only let her go, then froze in shock. Mother, if she had died, it would have been my fault." And Jo dropped down beside the coffin in a passion of penitent tears, telling all that had happened, bitterly condemning her hardness of heart, and sobbing out her gratitude for being spared the heavy punishment which might have come upon her.

"It's my dreadful temper! I try to cure it, I think I have, and then it breaks out worse than ever. Oh, Mother, what shall I do? What shall I do?" cried poor Jo, in despair.

"Watch and pray, dear, never get tired of trying, and never think it is impossible to conquer your fault," said Mrs. March, drawing the blowzy head to her shoulder and kissing the wet cheek so tenderly that Jo cried even harder.

"You don't know, you can't guess how bad it is! It seems as if I could do anything when I'm in a passion. I get so savage, I could hurt anyone and enjoy it. I'm afraid I shall do something dreadful some day. Oh, Mother, help me, do help me!" she cried. Never before had she felt so keenly that she had a demon inside her.

"I will, my child, I will. Don't cry so bitterly, but remember this day, and resolve with all your soul that you will never know another like it. Jo, dear, we all have our temptations, some far greater than yours. Every day I wake up with an almost unbearable desire to feed on humans, to crush their soft, pulsing throat between my teeth, and to slake my hunger with their blood so that they would never look at me again with those poor, pathetic eyes so full of need, desperation, and fear. When I feel the hunger means to break out against my will, I just go away for a minute, and give myself a little shake for being so weak and wicked."

"You, Mother? Why, you are never bloodthirsty!" And for the moment Jo forgot remorse in surprise.

"I've been trying to cure myself of it for almost a hundred and seventy-two years, and have only suc-ceeded in controlling it. I am hungry nearly every day of my life, Jo, but I have learned not to show it, and I still hope to learn not to feel it, though it may take me another hundred and seventy-two years to do so."

The patience and the humility of the face she loved so well was a better lesson to Jo than the wisest lecture, the sharpest reproof. She felt comforted at once by the sympathy and confidence given her. The knowledge that her mother had a fault, too, and tried to mend it, made her own easier to bear and strengthened her resolution to cure it.

"How did you learn to control your hunger?"

"Your father, Jo. He never loses patience, never doubts or complains, but always hopes, and works and waits so cheerfully that one is ashamed to do otherwise before him. He helped and comforted me, and showed me that I must try to practice all the virtues I would have my little girls possess, for I was their example. It was easier to try for your sakes than for my own."

"Oh, Marmee. You are so wise. Help me be wise."

"I will, child, for I will repeat this lesson and many others just like it over and over, for I exist only to instruct you."

"Oh, Mother, if I'm ever half as good as you, I shall be satisfied," cried Jo, much touched by her mother's earnestness.

"I hope you will be a great deal better, dear, but you must keep watch over your 'bosom enemy,' as Father calls it, or it may sadden, if not spoil your life. You have had a warning. Remember it, and try with heart and soul to master this quick temper, before it brings you greater sorrow and regret than you have known today."

Amy stirred and sighed in her sleep, and as if eager to begin at once to mend her fault, Jo looked up with an expression on her face which it had never worn before.

"I let the sun come up on my anger. I wouldn't forgive her, and tonight, if it hadn't been for Laurie, it might have been too late! How could I be so wicked?" said Jo, half aloud, as she leaned over her sister softly stroking the wet hair scattered on the pillow.

As if she heard, Amy opened her eyes, and held out her arms, with a smile that went straight to Jo's heart. Neither said a word, but they hugged one another close, in spite of the blankets, and everything was forgiven and forgotten in one hearty kiss.

Chapter Eight

MEG GOES TO VANITY FAIR

It was so nice of Annie Moffat not to forget her promise. A whole fortnight of fun will be regularly splendid," said Jo, looking like a windmill as she folded skirts with her long arms to prepare Meg for her time away.

"And such lovely weather, I'm so glad of that," added Beth, tidily sorting neck and hair ribbons in her best box, lent for the great occasion.

"I wish I was going to have a fine time and wear all these nice things," said Amy with her mouth full of pins, as she artistically replenished her sister's cushion.

"I wish you were all going, but as you can't, I shall keep my adventures to tell you when I come back. I'm sure it's the least I can do when you have been so kind, lending me things and helping me get ready," said Meg, glancing round the room at the very simple outfit, which seemed nearly perfect in their eyes.

"What did Mother give you out of the treasure box?" asked Amy, who had not been present at the opening of a certain cedar chest in which Mrs. March kept a few relics[16] of past splendor, as gifts for her girls when the proper time came.

"A pair of silk stockings, that pretty carved fan, and a lovely blue sash. I wanted the violet silk, but it has three stubborn little blood droplets on the bodice, so I must be contented with my old tarlatan."

"It will look nice over my new muslin skirt, and the sash will set it off beautifully. I wish I hadn't smashed my coral bracelet, for you might have had it," said Jo, "who loved to give and lend, but whose possessions were usually too dilapidated to be of much use. In her enthusiasm, Jo tended to forget her super strength and often abused her belongings by grasping them too tightly or tossing them too roughly.

"There is a lovely old-fashioned pearl fang-enhancement set in the treasure chest, but Mother said a row of gleaming white teeth were the prettiest ornament for a young vampire," replied Meg. "Now, let me see, there's my new gray walking suit, just curl up the

---

[16] Most definitely the description of a cherished family memento, as there is absolutely no proof to substantiate the claim that vampires kept the remains of saints they devoured during the Transylvanian Inquisition (ca. 900–ca. 1550).

feather in my hat, Beth, then my poplin for Sunday and the small party, it looks heavy for spring, doesn't it? The violet silk would be so nice. Oh, dear!"

The next night was fine, and Meg departed in style for a fortnight of novelty and pleasure. Mrs. March had consented to the visit rather reluctantly, fearing that Margaret would come back more discontented than she went. But she begged so hard, and Annie had promised to take good care of her, and a little pleasure seemed so delightful after a winter of irksome work that the mother yielded, and the daughter went to take her first taste of fashionable vampire life.

The Moffats were very fashionable, and simple Meg was rather daunted, at first, by the splendor of the house and the elegance of its occupants. The luxury of Annie's coffin, an ornate affair of solid mahogany polished to an impossibly bright high-gloss sheen and lined with velvet the color of fresh blood, nearly robbed her of speech and she managed only a "very nice," as she pictured the plain pine boxes she and her sisters slept in. But they were kindly people, in spite of the frivolous life they led, and soon put their guest at her ease. Perhaps Meg felt, without understanding why, that they were not particularly cultivated or intelligent vampires, and that all their gilding could not quite conceal the ordinary material of which they were made. It certainly was agreeable to fare sumptuously on fresh blood, drive in a fine carriage, wear her best frock every night, and do nothing but enjoy herself. It suited her exactly, and soon she began to imitate the manners and conversation of those about her, use French phrases, show off her fangs, decorate her dresses with blood splatters, and play parlor games[17] upon vampirists, humans who enjoyed the light-headed thrill of having their blood sucked. Annie taught her a delightful diversion called tic-tac-toe, in which each participant stuck a tack into the human's toe and took bites of all the body parts that twitched in response. The player who made the most puncture marks won. It sounded easy enough to accomplish, but Meg fared dreadfully at first because she lacked the skill of her opponents, who had been sticking pins into humans for years. But once she realized the trick to causing tics was applying appropriate pressure, she became virtually unbeatable.

In comparison to the luxury of the Moffats', her home now looked bare and dismal, but Meg did not have time to repine, for Annie and her sister Belle kept her busily employed in "having a good time."

The evening for the ball came, and Belle insisted Meg wear a "sweet blue silk" dress that, she claimed, she had long since outgrown. Meg knew that was not true because vampires never outgrew anything, but the

---

[17] Such parlor games did not become illegal until 1907, when the Freedom from Vampire Cruelty Despite Personal Preference for Vampire Cruelty Act was passed.

dress was so dear and her morals so easily overcome she readily agreed.

"Now do let me please myself by dressing you up in style," Belle begged. "I admire to do it, and you'd be a regular little beauty with a touch here and there."

Belle shut herself up with her maid, and between them they turned Meg into a fine vampire lady. They crimped and curled her hair, they polished her neck and arms with some fragrant powder, touched her lips with coralline salve to make them redder, and Hortense would have added "a soupçon of rouge," if Meg had not rebelled. They laced her into a sky-blue dress, which was mortifyingly low in the neck to modest Meg. Gold filigree was added to her fangs, bracelets, necklace, brooch, and even earrings, for Hortense tied them on with a bit of pink silk which did not show. A cluster of tea-rose buds at the bosom, and a ruche, reconciled Meg to the display of her pretty, white shoulders, and a pair of high-heeled silk boots satisfied the last wish of her heart. A lace handkerchief, a plumy fan, and a bouquet in a shoulder holder finished her off, and Miss Belle surveyed her with the satisfaction of a little girl with a newly dressed doll.

"Mademoiselle is *charmante, très jolie*, is she not?" cried Hortense, clasping her hands in an affected rapture.

"Come and show yourself," said Miss Belle, leading the way to the room where the others were waiting.

As Meg went rustling after, with her long skirts

trailing, her earrings tinkling and her curls waving, she felt as if her fun had really begun at last, for though she couldn't confirm the notion with a mirror, as she had no reflection, she suspected that she was indeed "a little beauty." Her friends repeated the pleasing phrase enthusiastically, and for several minutes she stood, like a jackdaw in the fable,[18] enjoying her borrowed plumes, while the rest chattered like a party of magpies.

Careful of the unfamiliar heels, Margaret got safely down stairs and sailed into the drawing rooms where the Moffats and a few early guests were assembled, most of whom were vampires but some mortals as well. She very soon discovered that there is a charm about fine clothes which attracts a certain class of people and secures their respect. Several young ladies, who had taken no notice of her before, were very affectionate all of a sudden. Several young gentlemen, who had only stared at her at the other party, now not only stared, but asked to be introduced, and said all manner of foolish but agreeable things to her, and several old ladies, who sat on the sofas, and criticized the rest of the party, inquired who she was with an air of interest. She heard Mrs. Moffat reply to one of them . . .

"Daisy March"—for the Moffats called her Daisy for

---

[18] Cockney for *slack-jaw*, a vampire with a weak mandible who has problems biting. In the famous Aesop fable, the lonely jackdaw longs for beauty and acceptance.

reasons known only to themselves; perhaps because she reminded them of the fresh, spring flower, perhaps because they found her given name repugnant—"father a colonel in the army, one of our first families, but reverses of fortune, you know, and full of unusual ideas about the treatment of humans. That will change soon enough, I don't doubt, as Mrs. M. has made her plans and will play her cards well. The Laurence fortune will be hers as soon as dear Daisy alters the boy. Her younger sister has already gotten her fangs into the grandfather, who seems a little mature for a vampire of only three-and-forty, but the child was always queer."

"Dear me!" said the old lady, putting up her glass for another observation of Meg, who tried to look as if she had not heard and been much disturbed by Mrs. Moffat's shocking lies. Agitated, she tried to forget what she'd heard but could not and kept repeating to herself, "Mrs. M. has made her plans," till she was ready to rush home to tell her troubles and ask for advice. As that was impossible, she did her best to imagine herself acting the new part of fine vampire lady and so got on pretty well, though the dress was too low, the train kept getting under her feet, and she was in constant fear lest her earrings should fly off and get lost or broken. She was flirting her fan and laughing over a game of tic-tac-toe with a young gentleman, when she suddenly stopped laughing and looked confused, for just opposite, she saw Laurie. He was staring at her with undisguised surprise, and disapproval also, she thought, for though he bowed and smiled, yet something in his honest eyes made her wish she didn't have her fangs in the leg of a human girl, even if she was about to win the game.

Determined not to care, she rustled across the room to shake hands with her friend, who looked unusually boyish and shy. "I'm glad you came," she said, with her most grown-up air.

"Jo wanted me to come, and tell her how you looked, so I did," answered Laurie, without turning his eyes upon her, though he half smiled at her maternal tone.

"What shall you tell her?" asked Meg, full of curiosity to know his opinion of her, yet feeling ill at ease with him for the first time.

"I shall say I didn't know you, for you are behaving so unlike yourself, I'm quite afraid of you," he said, fumbling at his glove button.

"How absurd of you! It's all in good fun. Nobody is getting hurt," she insisted, for the girl serving as the game board had enjoyed herself immensely. Even so, Meg knew her parents would not approve of the activity. The Marches did not count vampirists among their acquaintance, as they found their behavior sordid. Thinking it best to change the subject, Meg indicated with a gesture to the opulence of her dress. "Wouldn't Jo stare if she saw me?"

"Yes, I think she would," returned Laurie gravely.

"Don't you like me so?" asked Meg.

"No, I don't," was the blunt reply.

"Why not?" in an anxious tone.

He glanced at the blood dribbling down her chin with an expression that abashed her more than his answer, which had not a particle of his usual politeness in it.

"I don't like cruelty."

That was altogether too much from a lad younger than herself who knew nothing of what it was like to be a vampire out among society folk, being a human and all, and a young one at that. Meg walked away, saying petulantly, "You are the rudest boy I ever saw."

Feeling very much ruffled, she went and stood at a quiet window to reflect, for the room was so noisy, and although she knew it wasn't quite the thing, removed the stream of blood from her chin. She did it discreetly, as if she had something to be ashamed of, which of course only made her feel more ashamed. She leaned her forehead on the cool pane, and stood half hidden by the curtains, never minding that her favorite waltz had begun, till someone touched her, and turning, she saw Laurie, looking penitent, as he said, with his very best bow and his hand out . . .

"Please forgive my rudeness, and come and dance with me."

"I'm afraid it will be too disagreeable to you," said Meg, trying to look offended and failing entirely.

"Not a bit of it, I'm dying to do it. Come, I'll be good. I don't like your behavior, but I do think you look just splendid." And he waved his hands, as if words failed to express his admiration.

Meg smiled and relented, and whispered as they stood waiting to catch the time, "Take care my skirt doesn't trip you up. It's the plague of my life and I was a goose to wear it."

"Pin it round your neck, and then it will be useful," said Laurie, looking down at the little blue boots, which he evidently approved of.

Away they went fleetly and gracefully, for having practiced at home, they were well matched, and the blithe young couple were a pleasant sight to see, as they twirled merrily round and round, feeling more friendly than ever after their small tiff.

"Laurie, I want you to do me a favor, will you?" said Meg.

"Won't I!" said Laurie, with alacrity.

"Please don't tell them at home about the game I was playing. They won't understand the joke, and it will worry Mother."

"Then why did you do it?" said Laurie's eyes, so plainly that Meg hastily added . . .

"I shall tell them myself all about it, and 'fess' to Mother how silly I've been. But I'd rather do it myself. So you'll not tell, will you?"

"I give you my word I won't, only what shall I say when they ask me?"

"Just say I looked pretty and was having a good time."

"I'll say the first with all my heart, but how about the other? You don't look as if you were having a good time. Are you?" And Laurie looked at her with an expression which made her answer in a whisper . . .

"No, not just now. Don't think I'm horrid. I only wanted a little fun, but this sort doesn't pay, I find, and I'm getting tired of it."

"Here comes Ned Moffat. What does he want?" said Laurie, knitting his black brows as if he did not regard his young host in the light of a pleasant addition to the party.

"He put his name down for three dances, and I suppose he's coming for them. What a bore!" said Meg, assuming a languid air which amused Laurie immensely.

He did not speak to her again till suppertime, when he saw her drinking a champagne glass filled with warm human blood with Ned and his friend Fisher, who were behaving "like a pair of fools," as Laurie said to himself, for he felt a brotherly sort of right to watch over the Marches and fight their battles whenever a defender was needed. He himself was dining on the lovely standing rib of beef with Yorkshire pudding provided for the Moffats' human guests.

"I wouldn't drink much more of that, Meg, your mother doesn't like it, you know," he whispered, leaning over her chair, as Ned turned to refill her glass and Fisher stooped to pick up her fan.

"I'm not Meg tonight, I'm a fine vampire lady who does all fine society vampire things. Tomorrow I shall repent these acts and be desperately good again," she answered with an affected little laugh.

"Wish tomorrow was here, then," muttered Laurie, walking off, ill-pleased at the change he saw in her.

Meg danced and flirted, chattered and giggled, as the other girls did. After supper she blundered through a new game called "the German," which consisted of driving one's fangs into the pulse points of a large German man, a skilled player who made scoring almost impossible. The sport was played in teams of two, each earning points for every well-placed tear made, and Meg, little experienced in parlor games of such energetic high zeal, nearly upset her partner with her long skirt. She romped in a way that scandalized Laurie, who looked on and meditated a lecture. But he got no chance to deliver it, for Meg kept away from him till he came to say good night.

"Remember!" she said, trying to smile, for her jaw had begun to ache from exertion, a development she hadn't known was possible.

"*Silence à la mort*," replied Laurie, with a melodramatic flourish, as he went away.

This little bit of byplay excited Annie's curiosity, but Meg was too tired for gossip and went to her coffin, feeling as if she had been to a masquerade and hadn't enjoyed herself as much as she expected. She was sick from too much rich human blood all the next night, and on Saturday went home, quite used up with her fortnight's fun and feeling that she had "sat in the lap of luxury" long enough.

"It does seem pleasant to be quiet, and not have company manners on all the time. Home is a nice place, though it isn't splendid," said Meg, looking about her with a restful expression, as she sat with her mother and Jo on the Sunday evening.

"I'm glad to hear you say so, dear, for I was afraid home would seem dull and poor to you after your fine quarters," replied her mother, who had given her many anxious looks that eve. For motherly eyes are quick to see any change in children's faces.

Meg had told her adventures gaily and said over and over what a charming time she had had, but something still seemed to weigh upon her spirits, and when the younger girls were gone to their coffins, she sat thoughtfully staring at the fire, saying little and looking worried. As the clock struck nine and Jo proposed sleep, Meg suddenly left her chair and, taking Beth's stool, leaned her elbows on her mother's knee, saying bravely . . .

"Marmee, I want to 'fess.'"

"I thought so. What is it, dear?"

"Shall I go away?" asked Jo discreetly.

"Of course not. Don't I always tell you everything? I was ashamed to speak of it before the younger children, but I want you to know all the dreadful things I did at the Moffats'."

"We are prepared," said Mrs. March, smiling but looking a little anxious.

"I told you they taught me games but I didn't tell you we played those games on vampirists. Laurie thought I wasn't proper. I know he did, though he didn't say so. I knew it was wrong, but everyone was so nice and said how well I fit in, and quantities of nonsense, and the humans didn't seem to mind, so I let them convince me it was all right to be cruel."

"Is that all?" asked Jo, as Mrs. March looked silently at the downcast face of her pretty daughter, and could not find it in her heart to blame her little follies.

"No, I drank human blood and romped and tried to flirt, and was altogether abominable," said Meg self-reproachfully.

"There is something more, I think." And Mrs. March smoothed the soft cheek, which remained pale white despite her clear distress as Meg answered slowly . . .

"Yes. It's very silly, but I want to tell it, because I hate to have people say and think such things about us and Laurie."

Then she told the various bits of gossip she had heard at the Moffats', and as she spoke, Jo saw her mother fold her lips tightly, as if ill-pleased that such ideas should be put into Meg's innocent mind.

"Well, if that isn't the greatest rubbish I ever heard,"

cried Jo indignantly. "Why didn't you pop out and tell them so on the spot?"

"I couldn't, it was so embarrassing for me. I couldn't help hearing at first, and then I was so angry and ashamed, I didn't remember that I ought to go away."

"Just wait till I see Annie Moffat, and I'll show you how to settle such ridiculous stuff. The idea of having 'plans' and being kind to Laurie because he's rich and may marry us by-and-by! Won't he shout when I tell him what those silly things say about us poor children?" And Jo laughed, as if on second thought the thing struck her as a good joke.

"If you tell Laurie, I'll never forgive you! She mustn't, must she, Mother?" said Meg, looking distressed.

"No, never repeat that foolish gossip, and forget it as soon as you can," said Mrs. March gravely. "I was very unwise to let you go among vampires of whom I know so little, kind, I dare say, but worldly, ill-bred, and full of these vulgar ideas about young people. I am more sorry than I can express for the mischief this visit may have done you, Meg."

"Don't be sorry, I won't let it hurt me. I'll forget all the bad and remember only the good, for I did enjoy a great deal, and thank you very much for letting me go. I'll not be sentimental or dissatisfied, Mother. I know I'm a silly little vampire girl, and I'll stay with you till I'm fit to take care of myself. But it is nice to have fun and flirt with boys, and I can't help saying I like it," said

Meg, looking half ashamed of the confession.

"That is perfectly natural, and quite harmless, if the liking does not become a passion and lead one to do foolish or unmaidenly things. Learn to know and value the fun worth having and the boys worth admiring, Meg."

Margaret sat thinking a moment, while Jo stood with her hands behind her, looking both interested and a little perplexed, for it was a new thing to hear Meg talking about cruelty, flirting, and things of that sort. And Jo felt as if during that fortnight her sister had grown up amazingly, and was drifting away from her into a world where she could not follow.

"Mother, do you have 'plans,' as Mrs. Moffat said?" asked Meg bashfully.

"Yes, my dear, I have a great many, all mothers do, but mine differ somewhat from Mrs. Moffat's, I suspect. I will tell you some of them, for the time has come when a word may set this romantic little head and heart of yours right, on a very serious subject. You are young, Meg, but not too young to understand me, and mothers' lips are the fittest to speak of such things to girls like you. Jo, your turn will come in time, perhaps, so listen to my 'plans' and help me carry them out, if they are good."

Jo went and sat on one arm of the chair, looking as if she thought they were about to join in some very solemn affair. Holding a hand of each, and watching the two young faces wistfully, Mrs. March said, in her serious yet cheery way . . .

"I want my daughters to be beautiful, accomplished, and good. To be admired, loved, and respected. To have a happy youth, to be well and wisely married, and to lead useful, pleasant lives, with as little care and sorrow to try them as God sees fit to send. To love and sire a good human man is the best and sweetest thing a woman can do, and I sincerely hope my girls may know this beautiful experience. It is natural to think of it, Meg, right to hope and wise to prepare for it, so that when the happy time comes, you may feel ready for the duties and worthy of the joy. My dear girls, I am ambitious for you, but not to have you make a dash in the world, sire rich men merely because they are rich, or have splendid houses, which are not homes because love is wanting. Money is a needful and precious thing, and when well used, a noble thing, but I never want you to think it is the first or only prize to strive for. I'd rather see you poor men's wives, if you were happy, beloved, contented, than queens on thrones, without self-respect and peace."

"Poor girls don't stand any chance, Belle says, unless they put themselves forward," sighed Meg.

"Then we'll be old maids," said Jo stoutly.

"Right, Jo. Better be happy old maids than unhappy wives, or unmaidenly vampire girls, running about to find mates," said Mrs. March decidedly. "Don't be troubled, Meg, poverty seldom daunts a sincere lover. Some of the best and most honored women I know were poor girls, but so love-worthy that they were not allowed to be old maids. Leave these things to time. Make this home happy, so that you may be fit for homes of your own, if they are offered you, and contented here if they are not. One thing remember, my girls. Mother is always ready to be your confidant, Father to be your friend, and both of us hope and trust that our daughters, whether married or single, will be the pride and comfort of our lives."

"We will, Marmee, we will!" cried both, with all their hearts, as she bade them good night.

Chapter Nine

CAMP LAURENCE

L aurie set up a post office in the hedge in the lower corner of the garden, a fine, spacious building with padlocks on the doors and every convenience for the mails (also the females). It was the old martin house, but he stopped up the door and made the roof open, so it would hold all sorts of things, and save them valuable time. Beth was postmistress, for, being most at home, she could attend to it regularly, and dearly liked the nightly task of unlocking the little door and distributing the mail. One July night she came in with her hands full, and went about the house leaving letters and parcels like the penny post.

"Here's your posy, Mother! Laurie never forgets that," she said, putting the fresh nosegay in the vase that stood in "Marmee's corner," and was kept supplied by the affectionate boy.

"Miss Meg March, one letter and a glove," continued Beth, delivering the articles to her sister, who sat near her mother, stitching wristbands.

"Why, I left a pair over there, and here is only one," said Meg, looking at the gray cotton glove. "Didn't you drop the other in the garden?"

"No, I'm sure I didn't, for there was only one in the office."

"I hate to have odd gloves! Never mind, the other may be found. My letter is only a translation of the German song I wanted. I think Mr. Brooke did it, for this isn't Laurie's writing."

Mrs. March glanced at Meg, who was looking very pretty in her gingham morning gown, with the little curls blowing about her forehead, and very womanly, as she sat sewing at her little worktable, full of tidy white rolls, so unconscious of the thought in her mother's mind as she sewed and sang, while her fingers flew and her thoughts were busied with girlish fancies as innocent and fresh as the pansies in her belt, that Mrs. March smiled and was satisfied.

"Two letters for Doctor Jo, a book, and a funny old hat, which covered the whole post office and stuck outside," said Beth, laughing as she went into the study where Jo sat studying.

"What a sly fellow Laurie is! I said I wished bigger hats were the fashion, because I burn my face looking out the window on sunny mornings. He said, 'Why mind the fashion? Wear a big hat, and be safe!' I said I would if I had one, and he has sent me this, to try me. I'll wear it for fun, and show him I don't care for the fashion." And hanging the antique broad-brim on a bust of Plato, Jo read her first letter. In a big, dashing hand, Laurie wrote . . .

Dear Jo, What ho!
Some English girls and boys are coming to see me
tomorrow and I want to have a jolly time. If it's fine,
I'm going to pitch my tent in Longmeadow, and row up
the whole crew to lunch and croquet—have a fire, make
messes, gypsy fashion, and all sorts of larks. They are
nice people, and like such things. Brooke will go to keep
us boys steady, and Kate Vaughn will play propriety for
the girls. I want you all to join us for games as soon as
dusk falls, can't let Beth off at any price, and nobody
shall worry her. My friends have never met vampires but
they know better than to bother you with pesky questions.
Don't bother about rations, I'll see to that and everything
else, only do come, there's a good fellow!
In a tearing hurry, Yours ever, Laurie.

"Here's richness!" cried Jo, flying in to tell the news to Meg.

"Of course we can go, Mother?"

Marmee agreed easily, for she knew her daughters

were delightful emissaries of the humanitarian way of life and the more people they met, the more people they would win over.

"I hope the Vaughns are not fine grown-up people. Do you know anything about them, Jo?" asked Meg.

"Only that there are four of them. Kate is older than you, Fred and Frank (twins) about my age, and a little girl (Grace), who is nine or ten. Laurie knew them abroad, and liked the boys. I fancied, from the way he primmed up his mouth in speaking of her, that he didn't admire Kate much."

"I'm so glad my French print is clean, it's just the thing and so becoming!" observed Meg complacently. "Have you anything decent, Jo?"

"Scarlet and gray boating suit, good enough for me. I shall row and tramp about, so I don't want any starch to think of. You'll come, Bethy?"

"If you won't let any boys talk to me."

"Not a boy!"

"I like to please Laurie, and I'm not afraid of Mr. Brooke, he is so kind. But I don't want to play, or sing, or say anything. I'll work hard and not trouble anyone, and you'll take care of me, Jo, so I'll go.

"And I got a note from Mr. Laurence, asking me to come over and play to him tonight," added Beth, whose friendship with the old gentleman had prospered finely in the months since his Great Change. Many of the servants had left his employ for fear of being consumed, so the timid girl could now roam freely around the house without worrying about running into humans.

On the evening of the fete, the sky was bright and clear, and the girls eagerly prepared for the big event. Moonlight and laughter were good omens for a pleasure party, and soon a lively bustle tramped enthusiastically out of the house to board the boat that would take them to Longmeadow, where those guests for whom the direct light of the sun did not serve as a match for a giant conflagration had gathered many hours previous.

"Welcome to Camp Laurence!" said the young host, as they landed with exclamations of delight. The tent was pitched and wickets were arranged on a pleasant green field, with three wide-spreading oaks in the middle and a smooth strip of turf for croquet.

Laurie presented them to his friends in the most cordial manner. The lawn was the reception room, and for several minutes a lively scene was enacted there. Meg was grateful to see that Miss Kate, though twenty, was dressed with a simplicity which American girls would do well to imitate. Jo understood why Laurie "primmed up his mouth" when speaking of Kate, for that young lady had a standoff, don't-touch-me air, which contrasted strongly with the free and easy demeanor of the other girls. Beth took an observation of the new boys and decided that Frank, who was lame, was not "dreadful," but gentle and feeble, and she would be kind to him on that account. Amy found Grace a well-mannered, merry, little person, and after staring dumbly at one another for a few minutes, they suddenly became very good friends, despite being of different species.

"Brooke is commander in chief," Laurie announced cheerfully. "I am commissary general, the other fellows are staff officers, and you, ladies, are company. The tent is for your especial benefit and that oak is your drawing room, this is the messroom, and the third is the camp kitchen. Now, let's see about dinner."

The commander in chief and his aides soon spread the tablecloth with an inviting array of eatables and drinkables, prettily decorated with green leaves and appropriate for vampires and nonvampires alike. A very merry supper it was, for everything seemed fresh and funny, especially the frogs, for they ribbitted furiously whenever a fang touched their thorny backs, and frequent peals of laughter startled a venerable horse who fed nearby. There was a pleasing inequality in the table, which produced many mishaps to cups and plates, acorns dropped in the milk, little black ants partook of the refreshments without being invited, and fuzzy caterpillars swung down from the tree to see what was going on.

When they could not eat any more, they all adjourned to the drawing room to play games.

"Do you know Truth?" Laurie asked.

"I hope so," said Meg soberly.

"The game, I mean?"

"What is it?" said Fred.

"Why, you pile up your hands, choose a number,

and draw out in turn, and the person who draws at the number has to answer truly any question put by the rest. It's great fun."

"Let's try it," said Jo, who liked new experiments.

Everyone piled and drew, and the lot fell to Laurie.

"Who are your heroes?" asked Jo.

"Grandfather and Napoleon."

"Which lady here do you think prettiest?" said Kate.

"Margaret."

"Which do you like best?" from Fred.

"Jo, of course."

"What silly questions you ask!" And Jo gave a disdainful shrug as the rest laughed at Laurie's matter-of-fact tone.

"Try again. Truth isn't a bad game," said Fred.

Jo's turn came next.

"What do you most wish for?" said Laurie.

"A pair of boot lacings," returned Jo, guessing and defeating his purpose.

"Not a true answer. You must say what you really do want most."

"Genius. Don't you wish you could give it to me, Laurie?" And she slyly smiled in his disappointed face.

"What virtues do you most admire in a man?" asked Kate.

"Courage and honesty."

"How many people have you devoured?" asked Fred.

Meg gasped as Laurie jumped to his feet, personally

offended by the insult, for everyone knew the March girls were out-of-the-ordinary vampires and did not deserve such vile suspicion. Also, he'd assured them on his honor that his friends would not ask vulgar questions about their feeding habits, and here one was at the very first opportunity.

Jo felt her bosom enemy stir and rise slowly, anger coursing through her veins much in the way blood once had. Her eyes, always a sharp gray, glowed violently orange as she imagined tearing out Fred's throat. Her fangs throbbed with thirst. One movement, a slight one at that, and the smug smile would be removed from his face forever. Just a few inches . . .

But Marmee's voice, calm and wise and never far from her heart, warned her to control her temper. "Go on, dear," it said, "patiently and bravely, and always believe that no one sympathizes more tenderly with you than your loving mother."

Jo leaned back and said calmly, "Well, I think Truth is a very silly game. Let's have a sensible game of croquet."

Frank, Beth, Amy, and Grace sat down to watch the game played by the other six. Mr. Brooke chose Meg and Fred. Laurie took Kate and Jo. All proceeded smoothly until the last wicket, which Jo was through and had missed the stroke. Fred was close behind her and his turn came before hers. He gave a stroke, his ball hit the wicket, and stopped an inch on the wrong side. No one was very near, and running up to examine, he gave it a sly nudge with his toe, which put it just an inch on the right side.

"I'm through! Now, Miss Jo, I'll settle you, and get in first," cried the young gentleman, swinging his mallet for another blow.

"You pushed it. I saw you. It's my turn now," said Jo sharply.

"Upon my word, I didn't move it. It rolled a bit, perhaps, but that is allowed. So, stand off please, and let me have a go at the stake."

"We don't cheat in America, but you can, if you choose," said Jo angrily.

"Vampires are a deal the most tricky, everybody knows. There you go!" returned Fred, croqueting her ball far away.

Jo opened her lips to say something rude, but checked herself in time and stood a minute, hammering down a wicket with all her might, while Fred hit the stake and declared himself out with much exultation. She went off to get her ball, and was a long time finding it among the bushes, but she came back, looking cool and quiet, and waited her turn patiently. It took several strokes to regain the place she had lost, and when she got there, the other side had nearly won, for Brooke's ball was the last but one and lay near the stake.

"By George, it's all up with us! Good-bye, Mr. Brooke. Miss Jo owes me one, so you are finished," cried Fred excitedly, as they all drew near to see the finish.

"Vampires have a trick of being generous to their enemies," said Jo, with a look that made the lad redden, "especially when they beat them," she added, as, leaving the tutor's ball untouched, she won the game by a clever stroke.

Such gentlemanly behavior from a parasitic creature inferior to him in every way offended the Englishman to such a degree that, with a deep-hued cry of fury, he pulled a stake from the ground, lifted it high in the air, and threw it directly at Jo's chest.

To Jo's everlasting disgust, she didn't move. All her fine training as a vampire defender, the many hours of study, the pile of books she'd read, all the feints and maneuvers she'd memorized, came to naught in this moment when she needed them most, the stake sailing through the air intent on its target. It was Beth, amazing Beth who tiptoed upon the earth as if afraid to disturb the grass, who engaged her super vampire speed and saved Jo from certain annihilation by catching the stake a mere half inch from its mark.

Nobody could believe it, least of all Beth, who sank softly to her knees, the stake clutched in her hand, then slipping from her fingers as her clenched fist opened almost by compulsion. The company stared first at Beth, who was too shocked to shrink from the attention, then Fred, a foreigner surrounded by hostiles.

Although much alarmed by the astounding turn of events, Meg tried to smooth things over as she imagined a fine vampire lady like Mrs. Moffat might, by introducing a new topic as if nothing untoward had happened. "How beautifully you do it!" she said, with a look at Kate's sketch pad, which was open on the blanket. "I wish I could draw."

The rest of the company remained frozen, unsure of how to proceed. Laurie thought Fred should be brought up on charges of assault and attempted murder and was happy to drag the villain to the local magistrate himself. Jo thought they should re-create the entire episode so she could attempt to handle it in a way befitting an aspiring defender. Fred rather thought he should run.

Kate was scared for her brother and worried for her siblings, innocent little Grace and lame Frank. Keeping one eye on Fred, she replied graciously to Meg, though her voice was stretched thin with fear, "Why don't you learn? I should think you had taste and talent for it."

"I haven't time," explained Meg.

"Your mamma prefers other accomplishments, I fancy. So did mine, but I proved to her that I had talent by taking a few lessons privately, and then she was quite willing I should go on," Kate said, relaxing just a bit as the territory grew more familiar. "Can't you do the same with your governess?"

"I have none."

"I forgot young ladies in America go to school more than we. Very fine schools they are, too, Papa says. You go to a private one, I suppose?"

"I don't go at all. I am a governess myself."

"Oh, indeed!" said Miss Kate, but she might as well have said, "Dear me, how dreadful!" for her tone implied it, and something in her face made Meg cringe, and wish Jo would attack Miss Kate rather than Fred.

Mr. Brooke, who had been wondering how to handle the situation, which, as the only authority figure present, was his responsibility, observed the change in Meg's expression and said quickly, "Young ladies in America love independence as much as their ancestors did, and are admired and respected for supporting themselves."

Realizing her unintentional slight might make her brother's life forfeit, Kate rushed to make amends. "Oh, yes, of course it's very nice and proper in them to do so. We have many most respectable and worthy young women who do the same and are employed by the nobility, because, being the daughters of gentlemen, they are both well bred and accomplished, you know."

But her patronizing tone only made matters worse for it hurt Meg's pride, and made her work seem not only more distasteful, but degrading.

An awkward pause followed in which everyone present, including innocent little Grace, expected Jo to bite Kate's neck for this fresh insult to her sister or at the very least bleed the brother like a leech. But in fact Jo was not attending to the exchange, which seemed to her wholly incomprehensible at a time such as this, when she had very nearly allowed herself to be staked. The shame was almost unbearable and she occupied her mortified mind by running through the five steps of the Grosengauer Gambit: leap, somersault, pike dive, cartwheel, round kick.[19]

She'd practiced it a dozen times in her attic garret and knew the moves as intimately as her own hand. And yet she'd stood there like a bubble waiting to be popped!

"Did the German song suit, Miss March?" inquired Mr. Brooke, breaking the uncomfortable moment with yet another new topic.

"Oh, yes! It was very sweet, and I'm much obliged to whoever translated it for me." And Meg's downcast face brightened as she spoke.

"Don't you read German?" asked Miss Kate with a look of surprise.

"Not very well. My father, who taught me, is away, and I don't get on very fast alone, for I've no one to correct my pronunciation."

"Try a little now. Here is Schiller's *Mary Stuart* and a tutor who loves to teach." And Mr. Brooke retrieved his book from the blanket and handed it to her with an inviting smile.

"It's so hard I'm afraid to try," said Meg, grateful, but so bashful in the presence of the accomplished young lady beside her that she had completely forgotten Fred's attempted murder of Jo.

---

[19] Originally developed by famed naturalist Georg Grosengauer (1793–1817) as a technique for fending off wildebeest in the Serengeti.

Kate volunteered to read a bit to encourage Meg, and, hoping to provide a distraction so her unfortunate brother could make his escape, she read one of the most beautiful passages in a perfectly correct but perfectly expressionless manner.

Mr. Brooke made no comment as she returned the book to Meg, who said innocently, "I thought it was poetry."

"Some of it is. Try this passage."

"Enough," cried Frank, who couldn't bear the tension any longer. "Either kill him or let him go, but let's not have any more of this polite, vacuous chatter."

"Amen," said Laurie, who knew which of the two he'd rather do.

"Please," Kate said, her manner full of expression now. "Please. He's just a boy and he doesn't always think before he acts. Forgive him. His dislike of vampires runs deep and strong, for his twin was made lame by one, you see, and even though the assailant was apprehended and punished for acts unbecoming an Englishman, the damage was done. My brother will never walk without the crutch. Fred only acted overzealously in his love for his brother. Must you punish him for that?"

Jo, who was by far the most abused, thought it only fair and square to let Fred off the hook. He was a scoundrel and a cheat, which were terrible things to be, but she was a coward, which was a dozen times worse. "Let him go, Laurie. It's all right with me. I don't want to play croquet with him or Truth but I don't think he needs to be run into town or strung up on a gibbet. The gentlemanly thing to do is to shake on it and think about it no more." So saying, she held out her milky white hand.

It was galling for Fred to accept the offer, for in proposing they let bygones be bygones, the vampire had once again shown him up as an Englishman. But a look at Grace's scared face had him acquiescing immediately.

Brooke suggested another game of croquet, which everyone save Jo complied with after the stake was reinserted into the ground, but the joy had gone out of the night. Fred sulked something awful and Kate brooded over the fact that she was playing croquet with a governess. The game ended with a listless victory for Laurie's team, and everyone agreed it was time to go.

On the lawn where it had gathered, the little party separated with cordial good nights and good-byes, for the Vaughns were going to Canada. As the four sisters went home through the garden, they marveled again at Beth's remarkable midair catch. Amy couldn't wait to relay the events to Marmee and ran ahead. Beth trailed after her, anxious to downplay her part in the affair, lest she receive credit of which she wasn't worthy.

Meg linked her arm through Jo's and shook her head. "I always said she was a little saint," claimed Meg, as if there could be no further doubt of it.

Chapter Ten

SECRETS

Jo was very busy in the garret, for the October evenings were long and comfortable. For two or three hours the moon shone brightly through the high window, showing Jo seated on the old sofa, writing busily, with her papers spread out upon a trunk before her, while Scrabble XXI, the latest pet rat in a long succession, promenaded the beams overhead, accompanied by his oldest son, a fine young fellow, who was evidently very proud of his whiskers. Quite absorbed in her work, Jo scribbled away till the last page was filled, when she signed her name with a flourish and threw down her pen, exclaiming . . .

"There, I've done my best! If this won't suit I shall have to wait till I can do better."

Lying back on the sofa, she read the application

carefully through, making dashes here and there, and putting in many exclamation points, which looked like little balloons. Then she tied it up with a smart red ribbon, and sat a minute looking at it with a sober, wistful expression, which plainly showed how earnest her work had been. Jo's desk up here was an old tin kitchen[20] which hung against the wall. In it she kept her papers and a few books, safely shut away from Scrabble, who, being likewise of a literary turn, as were many of his ancestors, was fond of making a circulating library of such books as were left in his way by eating the leaves.

She put on her hat and jacket as noiselessly as possible, and going to the back entry window, got out upon the roof of a low porch, swung herself down to the grassy bank, and took a roundabout way to the road. Once there, she composed herself, hailed a passing omnibus, and rolled away to town, looking very merry and mysterious.

If anyone had been watching her, he would have thought her movements decidedly peculiar, for on alighting, she went off at a great pace till she reached a certain number in a certain busy street. Having found the place with some difficulty, she went into the

---

[20] As vampires do not require kitchens, many converted the room into an additional parlor. Old appliances such as stoves were often removed to the study to be used as desks.

doorway, looked up the dirty stairs, and after standing stock-still a minute, suddenly dived into the street and walked away as rapidly as she came. This maneuver she repeated several times, to the great amusement of a black-eyed young gentleman lounging in the window of a building opposite. On returning for the third time, Jo gave herself a shake, pulled her hat over her eyes, and walked up the stairs, looking as if she were going to have all her teeth out.

There was a dentist's sign, among others, which adorned the entrance, and after staring a moment at the pair of artificial jaws which slowly opened and shut to draw attention to a fine set of teeth, the young gentleman put on his coat, took his hat, and went down to post himself in the opposite doorway, saying with a smile and a shiver, "It's like her to come alone, but if she has a bad time she'll need someone to help her home."

In ten minutes Jo came running downstairs with the general appearance of a person who had just passed through a trying ordeal of some sort. When she saw the young gentleman she looked anything but pleased, and passed him with a nod. But he followed, asking with an air of sympathy, "Did you have a bad time?"

"Not very."

"You got through quickly."

"Yes, thank goodness!"

"Why did you go alone?"

"Didn't want anyone to know."

"You're the oddest fellow I ever saw. How many did you have out?"

Jo looked at her friend as if she did not understand him, then began to laugh as if mightily amused at something. The dear boy thought she'd had teeth removed. How delightfully absurd to believe a vampire needed a dentist!

"What are you laughing at? You are up to some mischief, Jo," said Laurie, looking mystified.

Jo didn't respond but shrugged rather carelessly, as if hoping to throw him off the scent but knowing she only stoked the fire of his curiosity.

"I have some very interesting news," he said. "It's a secret, and if I tell you, you must tell me yours."

"I haven't got any," began Jo, but stopped suddenly, remembering that she had.

"You know you have—you can't hide anything, so up and 'fess, or I won't tell," cried Laurie.

"Is your secret a nice one?"

"Oh, isn't it! All about people you know, and such fun! You ought to hear it, and I've been aching to tell it this long time. Come, you begin."

"You'll not say anything about it at home, will you?"

"Not a word."

"And you won't tease me in private?"

"I never tease."

"Yes, you do. You get everything you want out of

people. I don't know how you do it, but you are a born wheedler."

"Thank you. Fire away."

"Well, I've applied for entrance to Gentleman Jackson's Preparatory Salon for the Training of Vampire Defenders, and he's to give his answer next week," whispered Jo, in her confidant's ear.

"Hurrah for Miss March, the celebrated American defender!" cried Laurie, throwing up his hat and catching it again, to the great delight of two ducks, four cats, five hens, and half a dozen Irish children, for they were out of the city now.

"Hush! It won't come to anything, I dare say, since he's never accepted a female before, but I couldn't rest till I had tried, and I said nothing about it because I didn't want anyone else to be disappointed."

"It won't fail. Why, Jo, you are a born defender compared with half the rabble Gentleman Jackson trains daily. Won't it be fun to see you in the graduating class, and shan't we feel proud?"

Jo's eyes sparkled, for it is always pleasant to be believed in, and a friend's praise is always sweeter than a dozen acceptances.

"Where's your secret? Play fair, Teddy, or I'll never believe you again," she said, trying to extinguish the brilliant hopes that blazed up at a word of encouragement.

"I may get into a scrape for telling, but I didn't promise not to, so I will, for I never feel easy in my mind till I've told you any plummy bit of news I get. I know where Meg's glove is."

"Is that all?" said Jo, looking disappointed, as Laurie nodded and twinkled with a face full of mysterious intelligence.

"It's quite enough for the present, as you'll agree when I tell you where it is."

"Tell, then."

Laurie bent, and whispered three words in Jo's ear, which produced a comical change. She stood and stared at him for a minute, looking both surprised and displeased, then walked on, saying sharply, "How do you know?"

"Saw it."

"Where?"

"Pocket."

"All this time?"

"Yes, isn't that romantic?"

"No, it's horrid."

"Don't you like it?"

"Of course I don't. It's ridiculous, it won't be allowed. My patience! What would Meg say?"

"You are not to tell anyone. Mind that."

"I didn't promise."

"That was understood, and I trusted you."

"Well, I won't for the present, anyway, but I'm disgusted, and wish you hadn't told me."

"I thought you'd be pleased."

"At the idea of a human coming to take Meg away? No, thank you."

"You'll feel better about it when a human comes to take you away."

"I'd like to see a human try it," cried Jo fiercely.

"So should I!" and Laurie chuckled at the idea.

"I don't think secrets agree with me, I feel rumpled up in my mind since you told me that," said Jo rather ungratefully.

Something about Brooke's interest in Meg didn't sit comfortably with her, although she couldn't quite put her finger on it. In word and deed, he was unfailingly polite and courteous, but he had a steady, careful gaze that seemed to take in everything. Sometimes she felt as if he looked at them all like they were strange, foreign creatures.

He had the eyes of a slayer, she realized. That was it exactly. And wouldn't his being a slayer explain the stolen glove as well? Laurie thought his tutor treasured it as a love token, but Jo wasn't so naïve. No, she'd walked the earth decades longer than he, read *Seven Signs of a Slayer* at least seven times, and survived a staking (though, she readily admitted, through no fault of her own). Mr. John Brooke had evil designs on her sister and perhaps her whole family. She knew it to be true with every fiber of her being. She didn't have the scientific proof yet but her instincts told her Brooke was a dangerous threat.

"Race down this hill with me, and you'll be all right," suggested Laurie.

No one was in sight, the smooth road sloped invitingly before her, and finding the temptation irresistible, Jo darted away, soon leaving hat and comb behind her and scattering hairpins as she ran. She reached the goal a good two minutes before Laurie, who was quite satisfied with the success of his treatment, for as he approached he saw no signs of unhappiness in Jo's face. He was, however, perversely unsatisfied with his own performance, even though he knew his own deplorably human legs could in no way compete with Jo's swift vampire limbs.

"That was capital," said Jo, exuberant from the exercise. She adored being able to run miles in the splendid air, and not lose her breath, rather like a horse. Poor humans with their huffing and puffing. "But see what a guy it's made me. Go, pick up my things, like a cherub, as you are." She dropped down under a maple tree, which was carpeting the bank with crimson leaves.

Laurie leisurely departed to recover the lost property, and Jo bundled up her braids, hoping no one would pass by till she was tidy again. But someone did pass, and who should it be but Meg, looking particularly ladylike in her state and festival suit, for she had been making calls.

"What in the world are you doing here?" she asked, regarding her disheveled sister with well-bred surprise.

"Getting leaves," meekly answered Jo, sorting the rosy handful she had just swept up.

"And hairpins," added Laurie, throwing half a dozen into Jo's lap. "They grow on this road, Meg, so do combs and brown straw hats."

"You have been running, Jo. How could you? When will you stop such romping ways?" said Meg reprovingly, as she settled her cuffs and smoothed her hair, with which the wind had taken liberties.

"Never. Don't try to make me grow up before my time, Meg. It's hard enough to have you change all of a sudden. Let me be a little girl as long as I can."

As she spoke, Jo bent over the leaves to hide the trembling of her lips, for lately she had felt that Margaret was fast getting to be a woman, and Laurie's secret made her dread the separation which, even if Brooke proved to be the villain she supposed, must surely come sometime and now seemed very near. Laurie saw the trouble in Jo's face and drew Meg's attention from it by asking quickly, "Where have you been calling, all so fine?"

"At the Gardiners', and Sallie has been telling me all about Belle Moffat's wedding. It was very splendid, and they have gone to spend the winter in Paris. Just think how delightful that must be!"

"Do you envy her, Meg?" said Laurie.

"I'm afraid I do."

"I'm glad of it!" muttered Jo, tying on her hat with a jerk.

"Why?" asked Meg, looking surprised.

"Because if you care much about riches, you will never go and sire a poor man," said Jo, frowning at Laurie, who was mutely warning her to mind what she said.

"I shall never 'go and sire' anyone," observed Meg, walking on with great dignity while the others followed, laughing, whispering, skipping stones, and "behaving like children," as Meg said to herself, though she might have been tempted to join them if she had not had her best dress on.

For a week or two, Jo behaved so queerly that her sisters were quite bewildered. As soon as she woke at dusk, she ran to the door to check the post, was rude to Mr. Brooke whenever they met, would sit looking at Meg with a woebegone face, occasionally jumping up to shake and then kiss her in a very mysterious manner. Laurie and she were always making signs to one another, till the girls declared they had both lost their wits. On the second Saturday after Jo got out of the window, Meg, as she sat sewing at her window, was scandalized by the sight of Laurie chasing Jo all over the garden and finally capturing her in Amy's bower.[21] What went on there, Meg could not see, but shrieks of

---

[21] Shelter in which a vampire defender stores his bows and arrows; many young vampire women of the time kept one for their hairpins and fang enhancements.

laughter were heard, followed by the murmur of voices and a great flapping of papers.

"What shall we do with that girl? She never will behave like a young vampire lady," sighed Meg, as she watched the race with a disapproving face.

"I hope she won't. She is so funny and dear as she is," said Beth, who had never betrayed that she was a little hurt at Jo's having secrets with anyone but her.

In a few minutes Jo bounced in, laid herself on the sofa, and affected to read.

"Have you anything interesting there?" asked Meg, with condescension.

"Nothing but a letter from a salon in town," returned Jo, hiding her face behind the sheet.

"You'd better read it aloud. That will amuse us and keep you out of mischief," said Amy in her most grown-up tone.

With a loud "Hem!" Jo began to read very fast. The girls listened with interest as the writer thanked the candidate for her application to their esteemed institution, congratulated her on her impressive qualifications, and offered her a place among their newly forming squad of vampire defenders.

"You?" cried Meg, dropping her work. "You've been accepted to Gentleman Jackson's salon?"

"They've never taken a girl before," said Amy.

"Oh, my Jo, I am so proud!" and Beth ran to hug her sister and exult over this splendid success.

Dear me, how delighted they all were, to be sure! How Meg wouldn't believe it till she saw the words, "Miss Josephine March, Cadet," actually printed on the invitation to join the class. How graciously Amy complimented the salon's training methods and success rate in tracking and apprehending slayers. How Beth got excited, and skipped and sang with joy. How Hannah came in to exclaim, "Sakes alive, well I never!" in great astonishment at "that Jo's doin's." How proud Mrs. March was when she knew it. How Jo laughed, as she declared she might as well be a peacock and done with it, and how Gentleman Jackson's salon might be said to have established an annex in the House of March, as the girls promised to study with Jo at home.

"Tell us about it." "When did it come?" "When did you do it?" "What will Father say?" "Won't Laurie laugh?" cried the family, all at once as they clustered about Jo, for these foolish, affectionate people made a jubilee of every little household joy.

"Stop jabbering, girls, and I'll tell you everything," said Jo, wondering if her uncle had felt the same excitement when he had gained admittance to the salon. "When I went for an interview, Gentleman Jackson said he liked my qualifications but he didn't accept girls, only let them watch the men training. It was good practice, he said, and when the beginners improved, so did the observer. Well, I thought that was mightily unfair, so I let him know exactly how I felt. I told him all about Uncle March and his library and the training sessions we have here and my job as protectress of my aunt and that it was absurd to exclude a girl whose qualifications he liked just because she was a girl. He listened patiently and said he'd think about it and he must have decided it was unfair because he accepted me, and I'm so happy, for in time, I may be able to support myself and help the girls."

Jo's triumphant tale ended here, and clutching the letter dearly, she pressed soft little kisses on it, for to be independent and earn the praise of those she loved were the dearest wishes of her heart, and this seemed to be the first step toward that happy end.

Chapter Eleven

A TELEGRAM

"November is the most agreeable month in the whole year," said Amy, standing at the window one bright evening, looking out at the frostbitten garden, "for the nights last so long and one can finally finish all of one's errands."

"That's the reason I was born in it," observed Jo cheerfully.

"It's one of those months in which pleasant things happen," said Beth, who took a hopeful view of everything.

"Nothing pleasant ever does happen in this family," said Meg, made suddenly out of sorts by her sister's unfounded optimism. "We go grubbing along day after day, without a bit of change, and very little fun. We might as well be in a treadmill."

"My patience, how blue you are!" cried Jo. "I don't much wonder, poor dear, for you see other girls having splendid times, while you grind, grind, year in and year out. Oh, don't I wish I could manage things for you! You're pretty enough and good enough already, so if I could I'd have some rich relation leave you a fortune unexpectedly. Then you'd dash out as an heiress, scorn everyone who has slighted you, go abroad, and come home my Lady Something in a blaze of splendor and elegance."

Meg laughed, and turned to the frostbitten garden again. Jo smiled and leaned both elbows on the table in a relaxed attitude, but Amy spatted[22] away energetically, and Beth, who sat at the other window, said cheerfully, "Marmee is coming down the street, and Laurie is tramping through the garden as if he had something nice to tell."

In they both came, Mrs. March with her usual question, "Any letter from Father, girls?" and Laurie to say in his persuasive way, "Won't some of you come for a drive? I've been working away at mathematics till my head is in a muddle, and I'm going to freshen my wits by a brisk turn. It's a dull night, but the air isn't bad, and I'm going to take Brooke home, so it will be gay inside, if it isn't out. Come, Jo, you and Beth will go, won't you?"

---

[22] To nibble on a small animal, usually a mouse.

"Of course we will."

"Much obliged, but I'm busy." And Meg whisked out her workbasket, for she had agreed with her mother that it was best, for her at least, not to drive too often with the young tutor, whose interest they'd both observed.

"We three will be ready in a minute," cried Amy, running away to wash her hands.

"Can I do anything for you, Madam Mother?" asked Laurie, leaning over Mrs. March's chair with the affectionate look and tone he always gave her.

"No, thank you, except call at the office, if you'll be so kind, dear. It's our day for a letter, and the postman hasn't been. Father is as regular as the sun, but there's some delay on the way, perhaps."

A sharp ring interrupted her, and a minute after Hannah came in with a letter.

"It's one of them telegraph things, Mum," she said, handling it as if she was afraid it would explode and do some damage.

At the word "telegraph," Mrs. March snatched it, read the two lines it contained, and dropped back into her chair as frail as if the little paper had sent a stake through her heart. Laurie dashed downstairs for pig's blood, while Meg and Hannah supported her, and Jo read aloud, in a frightened voice . . .

Mrs. March:
Your husband is very ill. Come at once.
S. HALE
Blank Hospital, Washington.

How still the room was as they listened breathlessly, how strange the message, and how suddenly the whole world seemed to change, as the girls and their mother tried to comprehend the notion of a sick vampire, for never before in the long history of immortals had one fallen ill. Plenty died in the heat of battle or the sun, but none had ever been stricken with a disease.

"What does that mean?" asked Jo.

"Ill in what manner?" said Beth.

"What kind of sickness could he have caught?" Amy wondered.

"I'm sure we didn't hear that right," Meg insisted.

Mrs. March read the message over, and stretched out her arms to her daughters, saying, in a tone they never forgot, "I shall go at once."

For several minutes there was nothing but the sound of sobbing in the room, mingled with broken words of comfort, tender assurances of help, and hopeful whispers that it may all yet be a mistake.

"Perhaps there's another Mr. March in the army and they sent us his telegram," suggested Jo.

This indeed seemed a rather likely explanation, for there could be as many as four or five Marches, and the family immediately fell into sympathizing for the poor unidentified family who had unknowingly suffered such a devastating blow.

"We should send something," insisted Meg.

"Flowers," said Jo.

"Chocolates," said Amy.

"Black veils," said Beth. "We could sew them ourselves."

"Be calm, girls, and let me think," said Marmee.

They tried to be calm, poor things, as their mother sat up, looking distracted but steady, and put away her puzzlement to think and plan for them.

"Where's Laurie?" she asked presently, when she had collected her thoughts and decided on the first duties to be done.

"Here, ma'am. Oh, let me do something!" cried the boy, hurrying from the next room whither he had withdrawn, feeling that their first sorrow was too sacred for even his friendly eyes to see.

"Send a telegram saying I will come at once to inspect the identity of this so-called Mr. March. The next train goes after midnight. I'll take that."

"What else? The horses are ready. I can go anywhere, do anything," he said, looking ready to fly to the ends of the earth.

"Leave a note at Aunt March's. Jo, give me that pen and paper."

Tearing off the blank side of one of her newly copied pages, Jo drew the table before her mother, well knowing that money for the long, probably unnecessary journey must be borrowed, and feeling as if she could do anything to add a little to the sum for the desperately ill stranger.

"Now go, dear, but don't kill yourself driving at a desperate pace. There is no need of that."

Mrs. March's warning was evidently thrown away, for five minutes later Laurie tore by the window on his own fleet horse, riding as if for his life.

"Jo, get these things. I'll put them down, they'll be needed and I must go prepared for nursing, as it is my duty to care for whatever sad invalid human I find there. Hospital stores are not always good. Beth, go and ask Mr. Laurence for a couple of bottles of old wine. I'm not too proud to beg for this faceless stranger. Amy, tell Hannah to get down the black trunk, and Meg, come and help me find my things, for I'm half bewildered."

Trying to comprehend how an immortal could suffer the illnesses of humanity might well bewilder the poor lady, and Meg begged her to sit quietly in her room for a little while, and let them work. Everyone scattered like leaves before a gust of wind, and the quiet, happy household was broken up as suddenly as if the paper had been an evil spell.

Mr. Laurence came hurrying back with Beth, bringing every comfort the kind old gentleman could think of for the invalid, and friendliest promises of protection for the girls during the mother's absence, which comforted her very much. There was nothing he didn't offer, from his own dressing gown to himself as escort. But the last was impossible. Mrs. March would not hear of the novice vampire undertaking the trip, for he could not know the many challenges a creature of the night faced on a long journey. But he saw the look of relief when he spoke of it, knit his heavy eyebrows, rubbed his hands, and marched abruptly away, saying he'd be back directly. No one had time to think of him again till, as Meg ran through the entry, with a pair of rubbers in one hand and a cup of pig's blood in the other, she came suddenly upon Mr. Brooke.

"I'm very sorry to hear of this, Miss March," he said, in the kind, quiet tone which sounded very pleasantly to her perturbed spirit. "I came to offer myself as escort to your mother. Mr. Laurence has commissions for me in Washington, and it will give me real satisfaction to be of service to her there."

Down dropped the rubbers, and the blood was very near following, as Meg put out her hand, with a face so full of gratitude that Mr. Brooke would have felt repaid for a much greater sacrifice than the trifling one of time and comfort which he was about to take.

"How kind you all are! Mother will accept, I'm sure, and it will be such a relief to know that she has someone to take care of her. Thank you very, very much!"

Meg spoke earnestly, and forgot herself entirely till something in the brown eyes looking down at her made her remember the cooling blood, and led the way into the parlor, saying she would call her mother.

Everything was arranged by the time Laurie returned with a note from Aunt March, enclosing the desired sum, and a few lines repeating what she had often said before, that she had always told them it was absurd for March to go into the army, always predicted that no good would come of it, and she hoped they would take her advice the next time. Mrs. March put the note in the fire, the money in her purse, and went on with her preparations, with her lips folded tightly in a way which Jo would have understood if she had been there.

The evening wore away. All other errands were done, and Meg and her mother were busy at some necessary needlework, while Beth and Amy got blood, and Hannah finished her ironing with what she called a "slap and a bang," but still Jo did not come. They began to get anxious, and Laurie went off to find her, for no one knew what freak Jo might take into her head. He missed her, however, and she came walking in with a very queer expression of countenance, for there was a mixture of fun and fear, satisfaction and regret in it, which puzzled the family as much as did the roll of bills she laid before her mother, saying with a little choke in her voice, "That's my contribution toward making Father or the unknown victim comfortable and bringing him home to us or the other Marches!"

"My dear, where did you get it? Twenty-five dollars!

Jo, I hope you haven't done anything rash?"

"No, it's mine honestly. I didn't beg, borrow, or steal it. I earned it, and I don't think you'll blame me, for I only sold what was my own."

As she spoke, Jo took off her bonnet, and a general outcry arose, for all her abundant hair was cut short.

"Your hair! Your beautiful hair!" "Oh, Jo, how could you? Your one beauty." "My dear girl, there was no need of this." "She doesn't look like my Jo anymore, but I love her dearly for it!"

As everyone exclaimed, and Beth hugged the cropped head tenderly, Jo assumed an indifferent air, which did not deceive anyone a particle, and said, rumpling up the brown bush and trying to look as if she liked it, "It doesn't affect the fate of the nation, so don't wail, Beth. It will be good for my vanity, I was getting too proud of my wig. It will do my brains good to have that mop taken off. My head feels deliciously light and cool, and the barber said I could soon have a curly crop, which will be boyish, becoming, and easy to keep in order. I'm satisfied, so please take the money and let's have supper."

"Tell me all about it, Jo. I am not quite satisfied, but I can't blame you, for I know how willingly you sacrificed your vanity, as you call it, to your love. But, my dear, it was not necessary, and I'm afraid you will regret it one of these days," said Mrs. March.

"No, I won't!" returned Jo stoutly, feeling much relieved that her prank was not entirely condemned.

"Didn't you feel dreadfully when the first cut came?" asked Meg, with a shiver.

"I took a last look at my hair while the man got his things, and that was the end of it. I never snivel over trifles like that. I will confess, though, I felt queer when I saw the dear old hair laid out on the table, and felt only the short rough ends of my head. It almost seemed as if I'd lost an arm or leg off. The woman saw me look at it, and picked out a long lock for me to keep. I'll give it to you, Marmee, just to remember past glories by, for a crop is so comfortable I don't think I shall ever have a mane again."

Mrs. March folded the wavy chestnut lock, and laid it away with a short gray one in her desk. She only said, "Thank you, deary," but something in her face made the girls change the subject, and talk as cheerfully as they could about the good weather for traveling, Mr. Brooke's kindness, and the happy times they would have when Marmee confirmed that the sick man wasn't their father. "What do you mean, Mr. Brooke's kindness?" Jo asked.

"He's going to escort Mother to Washington, as Mr. Laurence has commissions for him to discharge there," Meg explained.

Jo felt a sense of dread come over her and she ran to find her mother. "Marmee, you mustn't do it," she said. "You mustn't."

Her mother smiled softly at her, for she was a little

surprised to find her passionate Jo in a tizzy about something. "Mustn't do what, dear?"

"Go with Brooke. He's a vampire slayer, I just know it."

Marmee ran a gentle hand over her daughter's shorn locks. "My darling girl, it's a distressing time and our thinking processes don't always work as smoothly as they do during peaceful times. I know and have seen how unhappy the young gentleman's courting of your sister has made you, and I understand. You don't want to lose her and our happy family and so you've created a wild fiction in your head to justify this discomfort. It's perfectly natural for someone with your exuberant spirit and nothing to fret about. It will pass soon enough."

Jo protested violently that she wasn't imagining things; that the Russellmacher Ruse No. 4,[23] in which a slayer pretends to be an ardent human suitor, was a classic maneuver she'd read about a dozen times; and that even if one didn't believe in the deadly Russellmacher Ruse, one had to admit there was something deeply suspicious about a human man who—

Here her mother cut her off before she could admit the evidence of the glove, for she knew her daughter's

---

[23] One of ten tricks detailed in the autobiography of former slayer Heinrich Russellmacher (1623–1830), *Memoirs of a Repentant Slayer: How I Learned to Stop Slaying and Love Vampires*.

powerful imagination. "Go to sleep and don't talk."

The girls kissed Marmee quietly, and went silently to their coffins. Beth and Amy soon fell asleep in spite of the great trouble, but Meg lay awake, thinking the most serious thoughts she had ever known in her short life. Jo lay motionless, and her sister fancied that she was asleep, till a stifled sob escaped the casket.

Meg lifted the lid and exclaimed, "Jo, dear, what is it? Are you worried about Father?"

"No, not now."

"What then?"

"My . . . My hair!" burst out poor Jo, trying vainly to smother her emotion in the hard, knotty pine.

It did not seem at all comical to Meg, who kissed and caressed the afflicted heroine in the tenderest manner, although she couldn't help noticing that Jo's hair wasn't quite as short as she'd thought.

"I'm not sorry," protested Jo, with a choke. "I'd do it again tomorrow, if I could."

Meg pulled back and said slowly, "I think that indeed you could."

"Of course I would," insisted Jo. "I've never meant anything more and I don't care who the money is for. It's only the vain part of me that goes and wails in this silly way. Don't tell anyone, it's all over now."

"But, Jo, it *is* over now. Look!" she said, lifting her sister's hand to her own head, so she could feel for herself the freshly grown locks that tumbled over her shoulders. "It's come back."

Shocked, Jo pulled and tugged on the tresses that just hours before she had surrendered for the benefit of her father or an unknown stranger also called Mr. March. But now it seemed as if her grand sacrifice was an empty gesture, for as surely as the moon would rise tomorrow, her body would assume its original formation. No matter what damage she inflicted on herself, it always returned to the way it was on the day she'd changed. She'd lost teeth, broken arms, and knocked eyeballs out of their sockets, and still she woke every evening with her parts intact. But neither she nor her sisters had ever cut off all their hair, for they always assumed it would be lost forever. Hair, unlike, say, an arm, seemed separate and distinct from the body, an embellishment that hung *on* it rather than *from* it. But now she knew that supposition was false. One's hair was as resilient as one's lung.

Far from finding comfort in this development, Jo felt humiliated, for who but she would make such a to-do about an act that would ultimately prove meaningless, and she cried herself to sleep, thoroughly ruining yet another pillowcase with blood-tinged tears.

Chapter Twelve

LETTERS

November 5

My dearest Mother,

*It is impossible to tell you how despondent your letter
made us, for the news was so awful we couldn't do
anything for hours but sit in the parlor and brood. How
dreadful that our dear father is truly ill and suffering from
a fever so high as to make him not know himself! What a
shock you must have had, coming into the hospital room,
so confident that the telegram had reached the wrong
Mrs. March, and seeing the beloved face that you have
adored so constantly for more than a century. I'm sorry
we weren't there to support or defend you when Father
tried to drive a cross through your heart. Thank goodness
Mr. Brooke was there to intervene. I know Father is
too weak in his current condition to do you real harm,
but perhaps you should stay at a safe distance until he*

understands that he himself is a vampire as well.

*You did not say in your letter what the doctors
think of Father's strange illness, and that worries me.
I understand that they do not attend to many vampire
soldiers at the Blank Hospital and that vampire medicine
as a science is nonexistent, for it's never been necessary
before, but the medical officers must have some idea of
treatment for Father's fever if not diagnosis of its cause.
Please write back immediately and tell us all you know.
We are prepared for the worst and, in the absence of
anything more definite, are imagining it constantly.*

*The girls are all as good as gold. Jo helps me with
the sewing, and insists on doing all sorts of hard jobs. I
should be afraid she might overdo, if I didn't know her
"moral fit" wouldn't last long. Beth is as regular about
her tasks as a clock, and never forgets what you told her.
She grieves about Father, and looks sober except when
she is at her little piano. Amy minds me nicely, and I
take great care of her. She does her own hair, and I am
teaching her to make buttonholes and mend her stockings.
She tries very hard, and I know you will be pleased with
her improvement when you come. Mr. Laurence watches
over us like a motherly old hen, as Jo says, and Laurie is
very kind and neighborly. He and Jo keep us merry, for
we get pretty blue sometimes, and feel like orphans, with
you so far away. Hannah is a perfect saint. She does not
scold at all, and always calls me Miss Margaret, which
is quite proper, you know, and treats me with respect. We*

are all well and busy, but we long, day and night, to have
you back. Give my dearest love to Father, and believe me,
ever your own . . .
MEG

November 8
My precious Marmee,
I am on the trail! Gentleman Jackson recalls a similar
occurrence of "vampire fever," as the doctors are now
calling Father's strange disease, during the Transylvanian
Inquisition.[24] He claims to have a vague memory of
another illness striking with similar symptoms, most
particularly the chills that Father suffers daily. As you
well know, vampires are impervious to temperature
and do not as a matter of course experience chills. My
entire squad and many of the instructors are carefully
reading books and journals from that terrible time in
hopes of discovering a vital clue to the fever's origins and
cure. Gentleman Jackson is confident that we will find
something to save Father, so I am, too. You must remain
hopeful as well. We are desperately sorry to hear that the
attacks have worsened and that you cannot dab Father's
brow without fear of losing your arm.

Don't spare too many thoughts for us, for we are
well. Everyone is so desperately good, it's like living in

---

[24] A series of ecclesiastical tribunals (ca. 900–ca. 1550) devoted to purging vampires from Transylvania.

*a nest of turtledoves. You'd laugh to see Meg head the
table and try to be motherish. She gets prettier every day,
and I'm in love with her sometimes. The children are
regular archangels, and I—well, I'm Jo, and never shall
be anything else.*

*Give Father my lovingest hug that ever was, and kiss
yourself a dozen times for your . . .*
TOPSY-TURVY JO

November 10
Dear Mother,
*There is only time for me to send my love, and some
pressed pansies from the root I have been keeping safe
in the house for Father to see. We are delirious with
joy to know that the formula Gentleman Jackson sent is
yielding results. Meg says it's too soon to know for sure,
but I'm positive Father's blood combined with the other
ingredients is the cure we've been so desperately praying
for. How wonderful to hear of him sitting up and reading
our letters to you. Jo was overwhelmed by the news and
tried to thank God for being so good to us but she could
only say, "I'm glad! I'm glad!" I told her that would do
nicely as a regular prayer, for I know she felt a great
many in her heart.*

*I read every morning, try to be good all day, and sing
myself to sleep with Father's tune. Everyone is very kind,
and we are as happy as we can be without you. I wind the
clock and air the rooms every day.*

Kiss dear Father on the cheek he calls mine. Oh, do come soon to your loving . . .
LITTLE BETH

November 12
Ma Chere Mamma,
We are all well I do my lessons always and never corroborate the girls—Meg says I mean contradick so I put in both words and you can take the properest. Meg is a great comfort to me and lets me have an extra warm cup of blood every morning at tea its so good for me Jo says because it keeps me sweet tempered. Laurie is not as respeckful as he ought to be he calls me Chick and hurts my feelings by talking French to me very fast when I say Merci or Bon jour as Sallie Gardiner does. The sleeves of my blue dress were all worn out, and Meg put in new ones, but the full front came wrong and they are more blue than the dress. I felt bad but did not fret I bear my troubles well but I do wish Hannah would put more starch in my aprons. Can't she? Didn't I make that interrigation point nice? Meg says my punchtuation and spelling are disgraceful and I am mortyfied but dear me I have so many things to do, I can't stop. Adieu, I send heaps of love to Papa. It's so lovely that he's no longer trying to stake you. Your affectionate daughter . . .
AMY CURTIS MARCH

November 14

Dear Mis March,

I jes drop a line to say we git on fust rate. The girls is clever and fly round right smart. Miss Meg is going to make a proper good housekeeper. She hes the liking for it, and gits the hang of things surprisin quick. Jo doos beat all for goin ahead, but she don't stop to cal'k'late fust, and you never know where she's like to bring up. She done out a tub of clothes on Monday, but she starched 'em afore they was wrenched, and blued a pink calico dress till I thought I should a died a laughin. Beth is the best of little creeters, and a sight of help to me, bein so forehanded and dependable. She tries to learn everything, and really goes to market beyond her years, likewise keeps accounts, with my help, quite wonderful. We have got on very economical so fur. Amy does well without frettin, wearin her best clothes. Mr. Laurie is as full of didoes as usual, and turns the house upside down frequent, but he heartens the girls, so I let em hev full swing. The old gentleman sends heaps of things, and is rather wearin, but means wal, and it aint my place to say nothin. Dinner iz reddy, so no more at this time. I send my duty to Mr. March, and hope he's seen the last of his fever.

Yours respectful,

Hannah Mullet

November 16
Head Nurse of Ward No. 2,
All serene on the Rappahannock, troops in fine condition,
commissary department well conducted, the Home Guard
under Colonel Teddy always on duty, Commander in Chief
General Laurence reviews the army daily, Quartermaster
Mullet keeps order in camp, and Major Lion does picket
duty at night. A salute of twenty-four guns was fired on
receipt of good news from Washington that Mr. March
had kicked the fever for good, and a dress parade took
place at headquarters. Commander in chief sends best
wishes, in which he is heartily joined by . . .
COLONEL TEDDY

November 18
Dear Madam,
The little girls are all well. Beth and my boy report daily.
Hannah is a model servant, and guards pretty Meg like a
dragon. Glad the fine weather holds. Pray make Brooke
useful, and draw on me for funds if expenses exceed your
estimate. Don't let your husband want anything. Thank
God he is mending.
Your sincere friend and servant,
JAMES LAURENCE

Chapter Thirteen

LITTLE
FAITHFUL

For two weeks the amount of virtue in the old house would have supplied the neighborhood. It was really amazing, for everyone seemed in a heavenly frame of mind, and self-denial was all the fashion. Relieved of their first anxiety about their father, the girls insensibly relaxed their praiseworthy efforts a little, and began to fall back into old ways. They did not forget their motto to "hope and keep busy," but hoping and keeping busy seemed to grow easier, and after such tremendous exertions, they felt that Endeavor deserved a holiday, and gave it a good many.

Jo brought home books on the Inquisition from Gentleman Jackson's salon and settled in on the sofa to read them for clues as to how her father could have caught the fever. The hefty tomes were filled with so many thrilling stories about brave defenders that she barely got through a book a day and sometimes even forgot the purpose of her study. Amy found that housework and art did not go well together, and returned to her mud pies. Meg went nightly to her pupils, and sewed, or thought she did, at home, but much time was spent in writing long letters to her mother, or reading the Washington dispatches over and over. Beth kept on, with only slight relapses into idleness or grieving.

All the little duties were faithfully done each day, and many of her sisters' also, for they were forgetful, and the house seemed like a clock whose pendulum was gone a-visiting. When her heart got heavy with longings for Mother or fears for Father, she went away into a certain closet, hid her face in the folds of a dear old gown, and made her little moan and prayed her little prayer quietly by herself. Nobody knew what cheered her up after a sober fit, but everyone felt how sweet and helpful Beth was, and fell into a way of going to her for comfort or advice in their small affairs.

All were unconscious that this experience was a test of character, and when the first excitement was over, felt that they had done well and deserved praise. So they did, but their mistake was in ceasing to do well, and they learned this lesson through much anxiety and regret.

"Meg, I wish you'd go and see the Hummels. You know Mother told us not to forget them," said Beth, two weeks after Mrs. March's departure.

"I'm too tired to go this afternoon," replied Meg, rocking comfortably as she sewed.

"Can't you, Jo?" asked Beth.

"Too many books yet to read."

"Why don't you go yourself?" asked Meg.

"I have been every day, but the baby is sick, and I don't know what to do for it. Mrs. Hummel goes away to work, and Lottchen takes care of it. But it gets sicker and sicker, and I think you or Hannah ought to go."

Beth spoke earnestly, and Meg promised she would go tomorrow.

"Ask Hannah for some nice little mess,[25] and take it round, Beth, the air will do you good," said Jo, adding apologetically, "I'd go but I want to finish my research."

"I'm tired, so I thought maybe some of you would go," said Beth.

"Amy will be in presently, and she will run down for us," suggested Meg.

So Beth lay down on the sofa, the others returned to their work, and the Hummels were forgotten. An hour passed. Amy did not come, Meg went to her room to try on a new dress, Jo was absorbed in her story, and Hannah was sound asleep before the kitchen fire,

---

[25] Vampires believed in the nineteenth century that poor humans benefited greatly from cleaning and straightening up, and charitable organizations frequently donated untidy packages to be scattered in their homes.

when Beth quietly put on her hood, filled her basket with odds and ends for the poor children, and went out into the chilly air with a heavy head and a grieved look in her patient eyes. It was late when she came back, and no one saw her creep upstairs and shut herself into her mother's room. Half an hour after, Jo went to "Mother's closet" for something, and there found little Beth, looking very grave.

"Christopher Columbus! What's the matter?" cried Jo, as Beth put out her hand as if to warn her off, and said quickly . . .

"Stand back."

"What's wrong?"

"Oh, Jo, the baby's dead!"

"What baby?"

"Mrs. Hummel's. It died in my lap before she got home," cried Beth with a sob.

"My poor dear, how dreadful for you! I ought to have gone," said Jo, taking her sister in her arms as she sat down in her mother's big chair, with a remorseful face.

Beth tore free of her sister's embrace, ran to the other side of the room, and pressed her back against the wall. "Don't touch me. You mustn't. You mustn't. I feel so queer. My throat is sore and my head aches. It actually feels as if someone is driving a stake through it. What's wrong with me, Jo?"

"If Mother was only at home!" exclaimed Jo, suddenly frightened, for her sister's cheeks were bright red and her eyes blazed hotly. Slowly, she crossed the room and gently pressed her hand against Beth's forehead as the girl trembled. "You have the fever."

Beth turned her head away. "Don't touch me. Stay away. You must all stay away. Don't let Amy come. Or Meg."

Although very scared indeed, Jo calmly led her sister to her coffin and closed the lid. "Selfish pib, to let you go and stay reading rubbish myself!" Jo muttered as she went to consult Hannah.

The good soul was wide awake in a minute, and took the lead at once, assuring that there was no need to worry; they had already found the cure and Mr. March was all better now, so recovery was swift, all of which Jo believed and felt much relieved as they went up to call Meg.

"It's not a coincidence," Meg said after she had heard the story of the Hummel baby and Beth's illness, so much like their father's.

"No," Jo said simply, "it's the work of slayers." She knew what had to be done next but first she had to see to the comfort of Beth and the safety of her family.

"I shall stay, of course, I'm oldest," began Meg, looking anxious and self-reproachful, for she knew that Beth would never have fallen ill if she and Jo had done their duty to the Hummels. But if they had, they would've been struck by the fever, too, and what good would it have done for all three of them to be sick? No, it was far better that only one of them suffered the illness. But it was a shame it had to be Beth, for she was so good and kind and gentle. Jo would have been a much better victim, as she was as sturdy as a bull and just as mean.

"We'll send Amy to Aunt March's," Jo said. "There's no telling who they'll go after next and the old lady needs protection. I'll bring her, then get the formula from Gentleman Jackson and procure the ingredients."

Beth would have much preferred to have Jo as her caretaker but she knew her sister had important matters to see to, so she submitted to Meg's administrations.

Amy rebelled outright, and passionately declared that she had rather have the fever than go to Aunt March. Meg reasoned, pleaded, and commanded, all in vain. Amy protested that she would not go, and Meg left her in despair to ask Hannah what should be done. Before she came back, Laurie walked into the parlor to find Amy wrenching with sobs, with her head in the sofa cushions. She told her story, expecting to be consoled, but Laurie only put his hands in his pockets and walked about the room, whistling softly, as he knit his brows in deep thought. Presently he sat down beside her, and said, in his most wheedlesome tone, "Now be a sensible little vampire woman, and do as they say. Someone has to protect your aunt March from assassins. Think on it. She's a cross old curmudgeon and a regular samphire. Who wouldn't want to stake the old bat? There must be legions after her by now."

Amy smiled weakly. "You mean vampire. Samphire is seaweed."

"Oh, do I?" His tone was teasing.

"You're making fun of the way I mix up my words every now and then."

"Maybe. But only in a lighthearted way. I mean nothing by it. Now, shall you be very brave and go protect your aunt March?"

"Well—I guess I will," said Amy slowly.

"Good girl! Call Meg, and tell her you'll give in," said Laurie, with an approving pat, which annoyed Amy more than the "giving in."

Meg and Jo came running down to behold the miracle which had been wrought, and Amy, feeling very precious and self-sacrificing, promised to go.

"How is the little dear?" asked Laurie, for Beth was his especial pet, and he felt more anxious about her than he liked to show.

"She is lying down in Mother's coffin and feels better. The delirium hasn't set in yet," answered Meg.

"What a trying world it is!" said Jo, rumpling up her hair in a fretful way. "No sooner do we get out of one trouble than down comes another. There doesn't seem to be anything to hold on to when Mother's gone, so I'm all at sea."

"Well, don't make a porcupine of yourself, it isn't becoming. Tell me if I shall telegraph to your mother, or do anything?" asked Laurie.

"That is what troubles me," said Meg. "I think we ought to tell her, but Hannah says we mustn't, for Mother can't leave Father, and it will only make them anxious. Beth won't be sick long, and Hannah knows just what to do with the formula, and Mother said we were to mind her, so I suppose we must, but it doesn't seem quite right to me."

"Hum, well, I can't say. Suppose you ask Grandfather after the first dose."

"We will. Jo, go and get the medicine at once," commanded Meg. "We can't decide anything till it's been given."

"Stay where you are, Jo. I'm errand boy to this establishment," said Laurie, taking up his cap.

"I'm afraid you are busy," began Meg.

Laurie insisted he had finished his lessons and was free to serve them in whatever capacity they needed. Grateful, Jo sent him with a note for Gentleman Jackson that explained the entire situation, knowing full well that the noble vampire defender would personally oversee the administration of the medicine. Then she set off for the Hummels'.

The shack, for it couldn't be called anything but that, its walls barely standing and its roof so full of holes that moonlight dappled the dirt floor, was empty. The still-smoldering fire and the tumbled shelves spoke of a hurried departure. The enemy in Jo's bosom snapped and snarled as she searched the room for hints about the Hummels—who they were, where they went, what they did—but they'd left nothing meaningful behind.

Jo paused, closed her eyes, and inhaled deeply, but the only smell that pervaded her nostrils was that of garlic, which hung from the riddled ceiling in large burlap sacks. She tried again, working to sift out the pungency of the herb and get beyond the scent barrier, but it was impossible without an allium mask. How thoughtless of her not to bring one, for she should have anticipated this difficulty. The Hummel gang was clearly an experienced band of ruffians. Of course they would use garlic to throw her off the scent. Now all she could pick up was garlic. That, and the stench of death.

It was very faint, but there and recent. So the baby had really died.

Jo felt the weight of the loss as keenly as Beth, and her bosom enemy rattled and raged at the thought of that poor little innocent being slaughtered to satisfy some unholy crusade against vampires. What a world they lived in! Humans killed helpless babies, then turned around and called vampires monsters.

She was so enraged by what had been done to her father and to Beth and to the unknown infant that she wanted to rip the throat out of the first person she came across and drink, drink, drink. All those years of abstaining, of preserving life, of treating humans better than they treated each other, had left her thirsty, so very thirsty, for the taste of pure human blood, fresh and still pulsing. Pig and cow and beaver and sheep didn't taste the same, no matter what Marmee claimed. Why should she deprive herself any longer? What had humanity ever done to deserve her nobility?

With a ferocious slam of the door, she was off, a predator in the night hunting for justice, for even if the victims she found were innocent of the crimes committed against her, they were still guilty of something. Every human was.

There, she thought, a sound in the distance, a rattle of a carriage, the pounding of hooves. In a flash, she was at the carriage's door, pulling it open and confronting the frightened passengers inside, a man and a woman in simple woolen coats and thick fur-lined gloves. They weren't rich but nor were they poor, falling somewhere in the merchant class, Jo supposed, and although not exactly fair game for a vampire, fair enough, given her mood.

She leaned forward, toward the gentleman, who had nothing to recommend him but his proximity, and flared her fangs, frantic for the taste of blood. She pressed her lips to his throat and tasted his fear, a salty thing with a desperate edge, and heard a sob. Someone was crying, either the man or the woman, and pleading for mercy. Both, Jo realized, as her fangs brushed the soft flesh of his neck. Now that the moment had arrived, she wanted to savor it. Oh, how sweet the taste.

She closed her eyes, opened her jaws wide, and—

A baby cried.

No, Jo thought, shaking her head. Don't listen. Don't hear.

But the high-pitched wail continued and grew stronger until the sound filled the carriage and Jo's head.

She straightened and looked across at the young woman cradling the infant in her arms. The baby was distraught, the mother was distraught, and now, too, was Jo, who could see her own beloved Marmee holding her just as gently all those decades ago, calming her with a soft word and a cheerful promise that everything would be all right. More recently still, Jo had promised her that she would learn to keep her temper in check. How had her mother done it? *When I feel that the hunger means to break out against my will, I just go away for a minute, and give myself a little shake for being so weak and wicked.*

Jo stood up, climbed out of the carriage, and shut the door. One baby had already died that night because of the Marches, and that was more than enough.

Chapter Fourteen

DARK DAYS

Beth did have the fever, and was much sicker than anyone expected. The antidote did not work. Baffled, Gentleman Jackson made another batch, then another and another, taking extra care each time to measure out the ingredients in case a minuscule amount made the difference. He took blood first from Beth's arm, then from her leg, then chest, toe, and ear. It didn't matter what he did. Beth grew worse and worse.

Meg stayed at home, lest she should infect the Kings or their children, and kept house, feeling very anxious and a little guilty when she wrote letters in which no mention was made of Beth's illness. She could not think it right to deceive her mother, but she had been bidden to mind Hannah, and Hannah wouldn't hear of "Mrs. March bein' told, and worried just for such a trifle."

Jo devoted herself to Beth day and night, not a hard task, for Beth was very patient, and bore her pain uncomplainingly as long as she could control herself. But there came a time when during the fever fits she began to talk in a hoarse, broken voice, to play on the coverlet as if on her beloved little piano, and try to sing with a throat so swollen that there was no music left, a time when she did not know the familiar faces around her, but addressed them by wrong names, and called imploringly for her mother. One afternoon, late in the day, when Jo was napping coffin-side, she woke to find Beth's nose a few inches from her own, her eyes wide and kindling with hatred, a pencil gripped tightly in her grasp as she pressed it against her beloved sister's heart.

"Beast," she growled. "Abomination."

Then Jo grew frightened, even though she easily wrested the paltry weapon from the poor invalid's hand. Meg begged to be allowed to write the truth, and even Hannah said she "would think of it, though there was no danger yet." A letter from Washington added to their trouble, for Mr. March had had a relapse, and could not think of coming home for a long while.

How dark the days seemed now, how sad and lonely the house, and how heavy were the hearts of the sisters as they worked and waited, while the shadow of death hovered over the once happy home. Then it was that Margaret, lying unsleeping in her casket, felt how rich she had been in things more precious than any luxuries money could buy—in love, protection, peace, and health, the real blessings of life. Then it was that Jo, living in the darkened room, with that suffering little sister always before her eyes and that pathetic voice sounding in her ears, learned to see the beauty and the sweetness of Beth's nature, to feel how deep and tender a place she filled in all hearts, and to acknowledge the worth of Beth's unselfish ambition to live for others, and make home happy by that exercise of those simple virtues which all may possess, and which all should love and value more than talent, wealth, or beauty. Often, she thanked God that she hadn't slaughtered that family in the carriage, for how could she sit by Beth's side with that hideous sin on her soul? And Amy, in her exile, longed eagerly to be at home, that she might work for Beth, feeling now that no service would be hard or irksome compared with the onerousness of protecting annoying Aunt March, who ordered her about like a servant and jumped at every creak of a floorboard, and remembering, with regretful grief, how many neglected tasks those willing hands had done for her. Laurie haunted the house like a restless ghost, and Mr. Laurence locked the grand piano, because he could not bear to be reminded of the young neighbor who had turned him into an invincible being.

Meanwhile Beth lay in her coffin with old Joanna at her side, for even in her wanderings she did not forget her forlorn protégé. She longed for her cats, but would not have them brought, lest she eat them by mistake, for although she thought herself human, the desire to consume the innocent felines was unbearable. She raged at Jo for holding her prisoner in a house of horrors, and tried to cut Hannah's head off with a letter opener. Soon even these intervals of crazed consciousness ended, and she lay hour after hour, tossing to and fro, with incoherent words on her lips, or sank into a heavy sleep which brought her no refreshment. Gentleman Jackson came twice a night, Hannah sat up during the day, Meg kept a telegram in her desk all ready to send off at any minute, and Jo never stirred from Beth's side.

The first of December was a wintry day indeed to them, for a bitter wind blew, snow fell fast, and the year seemed getting ready for its death. When Gentleman Jackson came an hour before dawn, he looked long at Beth, held the hot hand in both his own for a minute, and laid it gently down, saying, in a low voice to Hannah, "If Mrs. March can leave her husband, she'd better be sent for."

Hannah nodded without speaking, for her lips twitched nervously, Meg dropped down into a chair as the strength seemed to go out of her limbs at the sound of those words, and Jo, standing with a pale face for a minute, ran to the parlor, snatched up the telegram, and throwing on her things, rushed out into the storm. She was soon back, and while noiselessly taking off her cloak, Laurie came in with a letter, saying that Mr. March was mending again. Jo read it thankfully, but the heavy weight did not seem lifted off her heart, and her face was so full of misery that Laurie asked quickly, "What is it? Is Beth worse?"

"I've sent for Mother," said Jo, tugging at her rubber boots with a tragic expression.

"Good for you, Jo! Did you do it on your own responsibility?" asked Laurie, as he seated her in the hall chair and took off the rebellious boots, seeing how her hands shook.

"No. Gentleman Jackson told us to."

"Oh, Jo, it's not so bad as that?" cried Laurie, with a startled face.

"Yes, it is. She doesn't know us, she doesn't even talk about the flocks of green doves, as she calls the vine leaves on the wall. She doesn't look like my Beth, and there's nobody to help us bear it. Mother and Father both gone, and God seems so far away I can't find Him."

As the bloody tears streamed fast down poor Jo's cheeks, she stretched out her hand in a helpless sort of way, as if groping in the dark, and Laurie took it in his, whispering as well as he could with a lump in his throat, "I'm here. Hold on to me, Jo, dear!"

She could not speak, but she did "hold on," and the warm grasp of the friendly human hand comforted her sore heart, and seemed to lead her nearer to the Divine arm which alone could uphold her in her trouble.

Laurie longed to say something tender and comfortable, but no fitting words came to him, so he stood silent, gently stroking her bent head as her mother used to do. It was the best thing he could have done, far more soothing than the most eloquent words, for Jo felt the unspoken sympathy, and in the silence learned the sweet solace which affection administers to sorrow. Soon she calmed down, and looked up with a grateful face.

"Thank you, Teddy, I'm better now. I don't feel so forlorn, and will try to bear it if it comes."

"Keep hoping for the best, that will help you, Jo. Soon your mother will be here, and then everything will be all right."

"I'm so glad Father is better. Now she won't feel so bad about leaving him. Oh, me! It does seem as if all the troubles came in a heap, and I got the heaviest part on my shoulders," sighed Jo.

"I know something that will make your burden lighter," said Laurie, beaming at her with a face of suppressed satisfaction at something.

"What is it?" cried Jo, forgetting her woes for a minute in her wonder.

"I telegraphed to your mother yesterday, and Brooke

answered she'd come at once, and she'll be here tonight, and everything will be all right. Aren't you glad I did it?"

Laurie spoke very fast, and turned red and excited all in a minute, for he had kept his plot a secret, for fear of disappointing the girls or harming Beth. Jo's eyes grew quite red as she flew out of her chair, and the moment he stopped speaking she electrified him by throwing her arms round his neck, and crying out, with a joyful cry, "Oh, Laurie! Oh, Mother! I am so glad!" She did not sob again, but laughed hysterically, and trembled and clung to her friend as if she was a little bewildered by the sudden news.

Laurie, though decidedly amazed, behaved with great presence of mind. He patted her back soothingly, and finding that she was recovering, followed it up by a bashful kiss or two, which brought Jo round at once. Holding on to the banisters, she put him gently away, saying, "Oh, don't! I didn't mean to, it was dreadful of me, but you were such a dear to go and do it in spite of Hannah that I couldn't help flying at you. Tell me all about it."

"I don't mind," laughed Laurie, as he settled his tie. "Why, you see I got fidgety, and so did Grandpa. We thought Hannah was overdoing the authority business, and your mother ought to know. She'd never forgive us if Beth . . . Well, if anything happened, you know. So I got Grandpa to say it was high time we did something, and off I pelted to the office yesterday. Your mother will come, I know, and the late train is in at two A.M. I shall go for her, and you've only got to bottle up your rapture, and keep Beth quiet till that blessed lady gets here."

"Laurie, you're an angel! How shall I ever thank you?"

"Fly at me again. I rather liked it," said Laurie, looking mischievous, a thing he had not done for a fortnight.

"No, thank you. I'll do it by proxy, when your grandpa comes. Don't tease, but go home and rest, for you'll be up half the night. Bless you, Teddy, bless you!"

Jo had backed into a corner, and as she finished her speech, she vanished precipitately into the kitchen, where she sat down upon a dresser and told the assembled cats that she was "happy, oh, so happy!" while Laurie departed, feeling that he had made a rather neat thing of it.

"That's the interferingest chap I ever see, but I forgive him and do hope Mrs. March is coming right away," said Hannah, with an air of relief, when Jo told the good news.

Meg had a quiet rapture, and then brooded over the letter, while Jo set the sickroom in order, and Hannah "brewed up a couple of jugs of bloods in case of company unexpected." A breath of fresh air seemed to blow through the house, and something better than moonlight brightened the quiet rooms. Everything appeared to feel the hopeful change. Beth's bird began to chirp again, and a half-blown rose was discovered on Amy's bush in the window. The fires seemed to burn with unusual cheeriness, and every time the girls met, their pale faces broke into smiles as they hugged one another, whispering encouragingly, "Mother's coming, dear! Mother's coming!" Everyone rejoiced but Beth. She lay in that heavy stupor, alike unconscious of hope and joy, doubt and danger. It was a piteous sight, the once white face so rosy and vacant, the once busy hands so weak and wasted, the once smiling lips quite dumb, and the once pretty, well-kept hair scattered rough and tangled on the pillow. All day she lay so, only rousing now and then to mutter "Water!" piteously, as if the insipid liquid could do anything to slake her thirst, and repelling all attempts to feed her blood. All day Jo and Meg hovered over her, watching, waiting, hoping, and trusting in God and Mother, and all day the snow fell, the bitter wind raged, and the hours dragged slowly by. But night came at last, and every time the clock struck, the sisters, still sitting on either side of the coffin, looked at each other with brightening eyes, for each hour brought help nearer. Gentleman Jackson came in at midnight and took one look at the patient and shook his head sadly, indicating without a word how hopeless the case was. He'd read every book, tried every experiment, used every resource at his disposal, but he simply didn't have a cure for

Beth's vampire fever. Why the antidote worked on Mr. March, he didn't know, and the fact of that one success tortured him. For a moment, he'd thought he'd made a scientific breakthrough, but all he'd created was an anomaly.

Hannah, quite worn out, lay down on the sofa at the coffin's foot and fell fast asleep, Mr. Laurence marched to and fro in the parlor, feeling that he would rather face a rebel battery than Mrs. March's countenance as she entered. Laurie lay on the rug, pretending to rest, but staring into the fire with the thoughtful look which made his black eyes beautifully soft and clear.

The house was still as death, and nothing but the wailing of the wind broke the deep hush. The clock struck one. Weary Hannah slept on, as Meg and Jo watched Beth silently, waiting for the end. An hour went by, and nothing happened except Laurie's quiet departure for the station. Another hour, still no one came, and anxious fears of delay in the storm, or accidents by the way, or, worst of all, a great grief at Washington, haunted the girls.

It was past four, when Jo, who stood at the window thinking how dreary the world looked in its winding sheet of snow, heard a movement by the coffin, and turning quickly, saw Meg kneeling before their mother's easy chair with her face hidden. A dreadful fear passed coldly over Jo, as she thought, "Beth is dead, and Meg is afraid to tell me."

Awakened by the stir, Hannah started out of her sleep, hurried to the coffin, looked at Beth, felt her hands, listened at her lips, and, then, throwing her apron over her head, sat down to rock to and fro, exclaiming, under her breath, "It won't be long now. It won't be long now."

Jo was back at her post in an instant, prepared at any moment to say good-bye to her darling girl.

All three were so intent on their grief and misery that they didn't hear the carriage arrive or Laurie's shout or the hurried footsteps on the stairs or even the door to the room open. But they all saw Marmee's beautiful face, sharply drawn with tension, as she ran to her beloved daughter's side and they all saw her extract a small vial from her bag.

"Antidote, my dears," she said. "Antidote that will surely save her." And she spoke with such simple confidence that nobody in the room could disbelieve her. Jo felt the relief through her entire body and sank to her knees to give thanks that Marmee was home.

Chapter Fifteen

CONFIDENTIAL

When Beth woke from that long nightmare, the first object on which her eyes fell was her mother's face. Too weak to wonder at anything, she only smiled and nestled close in the loving arms about her, feeling that the hungry longing was satisfied at last. Then she slept again, and the girls waited upon their mother, for she would not unclasp the thin hand which clung to hers even in sleep.

Hannah warmed cow's blood for the traveler, who whispered her account of Father's state, Mr. Brooke's promise to stay and nurse him, the delays which the storm occasioned on the homeward journey, and the unspeakable anxiety that she might arrive too late to save her.

"How did you know the antidote would work?" Meg asked.

"I didn't," Marmee said, "but I prayed and hoped that it would, for it wrought miracles with your father. The two formulas were identical, except for the blood used, and that struck me as a difference of some importance. Something about your father's blood made the antidote work for him, and although I know nothing about the science, it seemed reasonable to me that as the patriarch of the line, and Beth's sire, that his blood might save her, too. And now Beth is resting quietly. I've always told you girls that your father is a special man and this surely proves it."

The girls acquiesced with silent nods and looked again at their dear Beth, sleeping naturally once again in her casket. Oh, what a cherished and beautiful sight it was to see her pale and healthy again. With a blissful sense of burdens lifted off, Meg and Jo closed their weary eyes, and lay at rest, like storm-beaten boats safe at anchor in a quiet harbor. Mrs. March would not leave Beth's side, but rested in the big chair, waking often to look at, touch, and brood over her child, like a miser over some recovered treasure.

Laurie meanwhile posted off to comfort Amy, and told his story so well that Aunt March actually "sniffed" herself, and never once said "I told you so." Amy's relief was palpable, as was her desire to rush off and see her mother, but she knew her duty was to stay with Aunt March until the villain who had poisoned Beth and her father was apprehended and she dully retrained herself. Laurie, who was dropping with sleep in spite of manful efforts to conceal the fact, rested on the sofa, while Amy wrote a note to her mother. She was a long time about it, and when she returned, he was stretched out with both arms under his head, sound asleep, while Aunt March sat doing nothing in an unusual fit of benignity.

After a while, they began to think he was not going to wake up till morning, and I'm not sure that he would, had he not been effectually roused by Amy's cry of joy at the sight of her mother. There probably were a good many happy little girls in and about the city that night, but it is my private opinion that Amy was the happiest of all, when she sat in her mother's lap and told her trials, receiving consolation and compensation in the shape of approving smiles and fond caresses.

In due time, Marmee took off again, promising Amy that she could come home soon, but the girl was so distraught at the thought of not seeing her sister immediately, Laurie volunteered to stand guard over the old lady. Aunt March rejected out of hand the idea of a mere human boy being in charge of her safety, and when he diligently described his training regimen with the girls, she rolled her eyes and said she'd just as well have a stuffed poodle protect her.

A solution was arrived at when Amy suggested they all travel to the house together to see Beth, although this created the additional problems of Aunt March not wanting to go and Laurie not wanting to escort the insulting old bat. Eventually, both relented when it became clear that Amy would not stop the great heaving sobs that poured through her body, and the girl had the joy of reuniting with her sister.

That evening while Meg was writing to her father to report the traveler's safe arrival, Jo slipped upstairs into Beth's room, and finding her mother in her usual place, stood a minute twisting her fingers in her hair, with a worried gesture and a decided look.

"What is it, dear?" asked Mrs. March, holding out her hand, with a face which invited confidence.

"I want to tell you something, Mother."

"About Meg?"

"About Mr. Brooke."

"John?"

"Who?" cried Jo, staring.

"Mr. Brooke. I call him 'John' now. We fell into the way of doing so at the hospital, and he likes it."

"Oh, dear! I know you'll take his part. That mean thing! To go petting Papa and helping you, just to wheedle you into liking him." And Jo pulled her hair again with a wrathful tweak.

"My dear, don't get angry about it, and I will tell you how it happened. John went with me at Mr. Laurence's request, and was so devoted to poor Father that we couldn't help getting fond of him. He was perfectly open and honorable about Meg, for he told us he loved her and desired nothing more than her siring him, but would earn a comfortable home before he asked her to do him the honor. He only wanted our leave to love her and work for her, and the right to make her love him if he could. He is a truly excellent young man, and we could not refuse to listen to him, but I will not consent to Meg's engaging herself so young."

"Of course not. It would be idiotic! I knew there was mischief brewing. I felt it, and now it's worse than I imagined. Listen to me, Mother, John isn't all that he seems. He's a slayer."

Now Marmee smiled and patted her daughter on the head. "Yes, dear, so you've said. But I think perhaps you've mistaken your feelings. You dislike the thought of someone carrying Meg away, so you've made her suitor a villain. It's perfectly natural to resist something that will alter the whole rhythm of your life but if you listen to me and trust me to guide you wisely, you will find that change is a natural and even desirable thing."

"It's true I wish I could marry Meg myself, and keep her safe in the family," said Jo, "but my accusation has nothing to do with my personal feelings. It's grounded in pure scientific evidence. I've done extensive research into Father's fever and have found incontestable proof that John Brooke means us harm."

Her mother nodded. "Beth is asleep. Speak low, and tell me all about it."

"You recall that Gentleman Jackson found the

formula for the cure in a journal dating back to the Transylvanian Inquisition?" Jo said. She did not have to pause here and refresh her mother's memory about that dark time, when vampires were considered demons, lived shadowy lives, and feared discovery and death at any moment. Many humans suffered greatly as well, for sometimes the only way to prove one wasn't a vampire was to bleed to death when one's severed leg did not regenerate. "Well, the fever has its roots in the same period. You see, an inquisitor in Sibiu[26] decided that interviewing each suspected vampire was too slow a process and invented a disease that wiped out entire lines in a fell swoop. He created a sickness that could be spread by people. A human was contaminated with the illness, which for him was no worse than a cold, and he passed it to the vampire through close contact. That's how Beth caught it from the Hummel baby, which, being only an infant, did not have the strength to fight the infection and died itself. The disease, called the chilly death, as the body was wracked by chills, was made from, among other things, manganese, hornbeam, chernozem, and essence of vampire. No one knows exactly what essence of vampire is, but historians do know that it can be extracted from seemingly ordinary items like a woman's glove. Then it is mixed with the other components to create the deadly formulation,

[26] City in Transylvania, now part of Romania.

which can be used against any vampire who shares a sire with the glove's owner. This means that the chilly death made from any of the vampires that Father sired would kill *all* the vampires in his line. That connection also explains why Father's blood saved Beth. He's her sire, so his blood was the most vital ingredient in the antidote. And here's the important piece of information you don't know: Last summer Meg left a pair of gloves over at the Laurences' and only one was returned. We forgot about it, till Teddy told me that Mr. Brooke had it," Jo revealed, delivering the coup de grace.

Her mother did not respond for a full minute and when she did speak, it was with all the gravity her daughter expected. "I can readily understand, Jo, why you are so worried and I'm sorry for it, but put your mind at ease. John would never hurt this family. He is smitten with Meg and if he did take her glove, he was merely holding on to a sentimental keepsake. It's harmless, truly, and I don't think I need remind you who in this family is always losing her gloves. If what you say is true, then the slayer could have very easily used one of your many missing gloves to create his concoction."

"I know I can't seem to keep my hands on them or them on my hands, but what of Father's relapse? The event occurred while Brooke was present at his bedside."

"Oh, my dear, you can't imagine what a crowded place the hospital was, hordes of people in and out and about, scattering from one end to the other, comforting the sick and dying, their loved ones hovering and helping and grieving. Any one of a hundred people could have done it."

"But any one of those hundred didn't do it," Jo began.

Her mother interrupted her with a soft shake of her head. "You're tired from lack of sleep and exhausted from worry and not thinking clearly. Go to your coffin and have a nice, long rest. You'll see things differently in the evening when you wake."

"Well, I won't," Jo said, "but I won't plague you with it anymore. It's just that I hate to see things going all crisscross and getting snarled up, when a pull here and a snip there would straighten it out."

"What's that about crisscrosses and snarls?" asked Meg, as she crept into the room with the finished letter in her hand. She'd heard the entire conversation but thought it better not to reveal that, for she was far too tired to argue with Jo.

"Only one of my stupid speeches. I'm going to sleep. Come, Peggy," said Jo, unfolding herself like an animated puzzle.

"Quite right, and beautifully written. Please add that I send my love to John," said Mrs. March, as she glanced over the letter and gave it back.

"Do you call him 'John'?" asked Meg, smiling, with her innocent eyes looking down into her mother's.

"Yes, he has been like a son to us, and we are very

fond of him," replied Mrs. March, returning the look with a keen one.

"I'm glad of that, he is so lonely. Good night, Mother, dear. It is so inexpressibly comfortable to have you here," was Meg's answer.

The kiss her mother gave her was a very tender one, and as she went away, Mrs. March said, with a mixture of satisfaction and regret, "She does not love John yet, but will soon learn to."

Chapter Sixteen

PLEASANT MEADOWS

Like moonlight after a storm were the peaceful weeks which followed. The invalids improved rapidly, and Mr. March began to talk of returning early in the new year. Beth was soon able to lie on the study sofa all night, amusing herself with well-beloved cats at first, and in time with doll's sewing, which had fallen sadly behind-hand. Her once active limbs were so stiff and feeble that Jo took her for a nightly airing about the house in her strong arms. Meg cheerfully blackened and burned her white hands holding the curtains back from the window so "the dear" could see the full blaze of the sun safely from within the deep recess of the room, while Amy celebrated her return by making as many drawings of her sisters as she could prevail on them to accept.

As Christmas approached, the usual mysteries began to haunt the house, and Jo frequently convulsed the family by proposing utterly impossible or magnificently absurd ceremonies, in honor of this unusually merry Christmas. Laurie was equally impracticable, and would have had bonfires, skyrockets, and triumphal arches, if he had had his own way. After many skirmishes and snubbings, the ambitious pair were considered effectually quenched and went about with forlorn faces, which were rather belied by explosions of laughter when the two got together.

Several nights of unusually mild weather fitly ushered in a splendid Christmas Eve. Hannah "felt in her bones" that it was going to be an unusually fine holiday, and she proved herself a true prophetess, for everybody and everything seemed bound to produce a grand success. To begin with, Mr. March wrote that he should soon be with them, then Beth felt uncommonly well that evening, and, being dressed in her mother's gift, a soft crimson merino wrapper, was borne in high triumph to the window to behold the offering of Jo and Laurie. The Unquenchables[27] had done their best to be worthy of the name, for like elves they had worked most of the night and conjured up a comical surprise. Out in the garden stood a stately snow maiden, crowned with

---

[27] Derogatory slang for *vampire*, as if their thirst for blood can never be quenched. Here used as a fond term of affection.

holly, bearing a basket of fruit and flowers in one hand, a great roll of music in the other, a perfect rainbow of an Afghan round her chilly shoulders, and a Christmas carol issuing from her lips on a pink paper streamer.

How Beth laughed when she saw it, how Laurie ran up and down to bring in the gifts, and what ridiculous speeches Jo made as she presented them.

"I'm so full of happiness, that if Father was only here, I couldn't hold one drop more," said Beth, quite sighing with contentment as Jo carried her off to the study to rest after the excitement, and to refresh herself with some of the delicious kittens Santa had brought her.

"So am I," added Jo, slapping the pocket wherein reposed the long-desired *Mr. Bloody Wobblestone's Scientific Method for Tracking, Catching, and Destroying Vampire Slayers*.

"I'm sure I am," echoed Amy, juggling a pair of fang enhancements, which her mother had given her.

"Of course I am!" cried Meg, smoothing the silvery folds of her first silk dress, for Mr. Laurence had insisted on giving it. "How can I be otherwise?" said Mrs. March gratefully, as her eyes went from her husband's letter to Beth's smiling face, and her hand caressed the brooch made of gray and golden, chestnut and dark brown hair, which the girls had just fastened on her breast.

Now and then, in this workaday world, things do happen in the delightful storybook fashion, and what a comfort it is. Half an hour after everyone had said they were so happy they could only hold one drop more, the drop came. Laurie opened the parlor door and popped his head in very quietly. He might just as well have turned a somersault and uttered an Indian war whoop, for his face was so full of suppressed excitement and his voice so treacherously joyful that everyone jumped up, though he only said, in a queer, breathless voice, "Here's another Christmas present for the March family."

Before the words were well out of his mouth, he was whisked away somehow, and in his place appeared a tall man, muffled up to the eyes, leaning on the arm of another tall man, who tried to say something and couldn't. Of course there was a general stampede, and for several minutes everybody seemed to lose their wits, for the strangest things were done, and no one said a word.

Mr. March became invisible in the embrace of four pairs of loving arms. Jo disgraced herself by nearly fainting away, and had to be doctored by Laurie in the china closet. Mr. Brooke kissed Meg entirely by mistake, as he somewhat incoherently explained. And Amy, the dignified, tumbled over a stool, and never stopping to get up, hugged and cried over her father's boots in the most touching manner. Mrs. March was the first to recover herself, and held up her hand with a warning, "Hush! Remember Beth."

But it was too late. The study door flew open, the

little red wrapper appeared on the threshold, joy put strength into the feeble limbs, and Beth ran straight into her father's arms. Never mind what happened just after that, for the full hearts overflowed, washing away the bitterness of the past and leaving only the sweetness of the present.

It was not at all romantic, but a hearty laugh set everybody straight again, for Hannah was discovered behind the door, wrestling with the fat turkey, which she had forgotten to put down when she rushed up from the kitchen. As the laugh subsided, Mrs. March began to thank Mr. Brooke for his faithful care of her husband, at which Mr. Brooke suddenly remembered that Mr. March needed rest, and seizing Laurie, he precipitately retired. Then the two invalids were ordered to repose, which they did, by both sitting in one big chair and talking hard.

Mr. March told how he had longed to surprise them, and how, when the fine weather came, he had been allowed by his doctor to take advantage of it, how devoted Brooke had been, and how he was altogether a most estimable and upright young man. Why Mr. March paused a minute just there, and after a glance at Meg, who was violently poking the fire, looked at his wife with an inquiring lift of the eyebrows, I leave you to imagine. Also why Mrs. March gently nodded her head and asked, rather abruptly, if he wouldn't like to have something to eat. Jo saw and understood the look, and she stalked grimly away to get a carafe of pig's blood, muttering to herself as she slammed the door, "I hate estimable young men with brown eyes who try to kill us all!"

There never was such a Christmas dinner as they had that day. The fat turkey was a sight to behold, when Hannah sent him up, squawking, screeching, and flapping. Mr. Laurence and his grandson dined with them, also Mr. Brooke, at whom Jo glowered darkly. The humans ate plum pudding, which Laurie brought with him, for he knew the reliable old vampire servant wouldn't know the first thing about making plum pudding that melted in one's mouth. Two easy chairs stood side by side at the head of the table, in which sat Beth and her father, feasting modestly on chickens. They drank healths, told stories, sang songs, "reminisced," as the old folks say, and had a thoroughly good time. A sleigh ride had been planned, but the girls would not leave their father, so the guests departed early, and as morning gathered, the happy family sat together round the fire.

"Just a year ago we were groaning over the dismal Christmas we expected to have. Do you remember?" asked Jo, breaking a short pause which had followed a long conversation about many things.

"Rather a pleasant year on the whole!" said Meg, smiling at the fire, and congratulating herself on having treated Mr. Brooke with dignity.

"I think it's been a pretty hard one," observed Amy, thinking of all the hours she'd spent watching Aunt March sleep in her armchair.

"I'm glad it's over, because we've got you back," whispered Beth, who sat on her father's knee.

Mr. March looked with fatherly satisfaction at the four young faces gathered around him and talked at some length of how proud he was of them all. He complimented Meg on her torn gown for it meant she'd worked hard and learned to value steady employment over fleeting fashion. He pointed to Jo's straight collar and neatly laced boots as proof that she had finally outgrown her wild-girl ways and gracefully accepted the yoke of womanhood. He praised Amy's willingness to run errands for her mother and wait on everyone with patience and good humor, for his youngest daughter had learned subservience. And what of Beth? He was afraid to say much, for fear she would slip away altogether, though, he said, recalling the Great Change she had wrought in Mr. Laurence, she was not so shy as she used to be.

Jo closed her eyes and listened to the beautiful familiarity of her father's voice, his gentle and wise intonations. Having him home was a much-cherished present but even more precious was having the whole family together, all the Marches gathered sweetly under one roof, safe and protected from the bright of the day. She swore that she would keep them that way, that no harm would come to them, and that John Brooke would regret the day he decided to challenge her. She didn't doubt she would defeat him, for she was still that wild girl, despite her collars and laces. Tomorrow, she would begin the hunt, following her quarry, gathering evidence, and proving her case, but today was still Christmas and they would sing hymns at Beth's piano until long past noon.

Chapter Seventeen

AUNT MARCH SETTLES THE QUESTION

Like bees swarming after their queen, mother and daughters hovered about Mr. March the next night, neglecting everything to look at, wait upon, and listen to the new invalid, who was in a fair way to be killed by kindness. As he sat propped up in a big chair by Beth's sofa, with the other three close by, and Hannah popping in her head now and then "to peek at the dear man," nothing seemed needed to complete their happiness. But something was needed, and the elder ones felt it, though none confessed the fact. Mr. and Mrs. March looked at one another with an anxious expression as their eyes followed Jo, who had sudden fits of sobriety and was seen to shake her fist at Mr. Brooke's umbrella, which had been left in the hall. During their late night consultation on the subject of Jo's misconception (Mrs. March refused to call it a delusion, though that was precisely how she thought of it), Mr. March urged patience. So many events had happened in the course of the year, it was no surprise that even the most stalwart of their beloved daughters was feeling the effects. They discussed pulling her from Gentleman Jackson's salon, as her time there seemed to have aided and abetted her outlandish belief, but they didn't want to disturb her further.

Meg, who could not help but ponder Jo's lunatic notion, was absentminded, shy, and silent, started when the bell rang, and averted her eyes when John's name was mentioned. Amy said, "Everyone seemed waiting for something, and couldn't settle down, which was queer, since Father was safe at home," and Beth innocently wondered why their neighbors didn't run over as usual.

As she watched Meg, Jo plotted her next step. Convincing her parents of John's duplicity was important, but not as crucial as stopping him before he made another attempt on one of their lives. So far her family had escaped permanent damage but she didn't doubt that he would step up his attacks now that he knew his original scheme had failed.

Tracking a slayer came with an interesting set of challenges, as it could be done only after dark, the time when slayers were at their most alert. For generations, vampires had tried to create a sunbathing costume that would allow them to go abroad safely and discreetly during daylight hours but so far no such suit had been invented.[28] Jo, therefore, had to sneak into John's room, most likely while he was asleep, and risk discovery, although that risk was somewhat mitigated by her proficiency in skulking, which she had mastered at the salon. Her instructor had been much impressed with how easily she adopted the Berryman Technique[29] for gliding across the floor without seeming to move her legs.

Jo was biding her time until the small hours of the morning, when, at nine P.M., a modest tap sounded on the door, which she opened with a grim aspect that was anything but hospitable.

"Good evening. I came to get my umbrella, that is, to see how your father finds himself this night," said Mr. Brooke, getting a trifle confused as his eyes went from Jo's face to Meg's.

"It's very well, he's in the rack. I'll get him, and tell it you are here." And having jumbled her father and the umbrella well together in her reply, Jo ran out of the room to take immediate advantage of Brooke's vacated establishment.

The instant her sister vanished, Meg began to sidle toward the door, murmuring . . .

---

[28] See footnote 15.

[29] Created by Joseph Berryman (b. 1736), American magician-vampire whose deft performance of the Hovering Human trick led to the widespread rumor that vampires could levitate.

"Mother will like to see you. Pray sit down, I'll call her."

"Don't go. Are you afraid of me, Margaret?" and Mr. Brooke looked so hurt that Meg felt a fresh spurt of anger at Jo for planting absurd ideas in her head. Of course the man before her wasn't a slayer! He was everything that was lovely and kind and gentle. She was perfectly ridiculous for letting Jo's accusations affect her at all. Anxious to appear friendly and at her ease, she put out her hand with a confiding gesture, and said gratefully . . .

"How can I be afraid when you have been so kind to Father? I only wish I could thank you for it."

"Shall I tell you how?" asked Mr. Brooke, holding the small hand fast in both his own, and looking down at Meg with so much love in the brown eyes that her heart began to flutter, and she both longed to run away and to stop and listen.

"Oh no, please don't, I'd rather not," she said, trying to withdraw her hand, and looking frightened in spite of her denial.

"I won't trouble you. I only want to know if you care for me a little, Meg. I love you so much, dear," added Mr. Brooke tenderly.

This was the moment for the calm, proper speech she'd practiced ("Thank you, Mr. Brooke, you are very kind, but I agree with Father that I am too young to enter into any engagement at present, so please say no more, but let us be friends as we were"), but

Meg didn't make it. She forgot every word of it, hung her head, and answered, "I don't know," so softly that John had to stoop down to catch the foolish little reply.

He seemed to think it was worth the trouble, for he smiled to himself as if quite satisfied, pressed the plump hand gratefully, and said in his most persuasive tone, "Will you try and find out? I want to know so much, for I can't go to work with any heart until I learn whether I am to have my reward in the end or not."

"I'm too young," faltered Meg, wondering why she was so flustered, yet rather enjoying it.

"I'll wait. To be honest, I'm not quite ready at this very moment to become a vampire, as it's a rather significant life change and I would like some time to grow more accustomed to it. As well, I'm very fond of the sun and love to feel it beat down on my face. But in the meantime, you could be learning to like me. Would it be a very hard lesson, dear?"

"Not if I chose to learn it, but . . ."

"Please choose to learn, Meg. I love to teach, and this is easier than German," broke in John, getting possession of the other hand, so that she had no way of hiding her face as he bent to look into it.

His tone was properly beseeching, but stealing a shy look at him, Meg saw that his eyes were merry as well as tender, and that he wore the satisfied smile of one who had no doubt of his success. Struck by his easy confidence, she wondered again if Jo could have possibly been right. If he had targeted her whole family for destruction, then wouldn't he be excited at the thought of achieving his goal? Feeling an uncomfortable sense of impending doom, she said, "I don't choose. Please go away and let me be!"

Poor Mr. Brooke looked as if his lovely castle in the air was tumbling about his ears, for he had never seen Meg in such a mood before, and it rather bewildered him.

"Do you really mean that?" he asked anxiously, following her as she walked away.

"Yes, I do. I don't want to be worried about such things. Father says I needn't, it's too soon and I'd rather not."

"Mayn't I hope you'll change your mind by-and-by? I'll wait and say nothing till you have had more time. Don't play with me, Meg. I didn't think that of you."

"Don't think of me at all. I'd rather you wouldn't," said Meg.

He was grave and pale now, and looked decidedly more like the novel heroes whom she admired, but he neither slapped his forehead nor tramped about the room as they did. He just stood looking at her so wistfully, so tenderly, that she found herself doubting her own conclusion. What if he weren't a slayer but a genuine suitor? What would have happened next I cannot say, if Aunt March had not come hobbling in at this interesting minute.

The old lady couldn't resist her longing to see her nephew, for she had met Laurie as she took her airing, and hearing of Mr. March's arrival, drove straight out to see him. The family were all busy in the back part of the house, and she had made her way quietly in, hoping to surprise them. She did surprise two of them so much that Meg started as if she had seen a ghost, and Mr. Brooke vanished into the study.

"Bless me, what's all this?" cried the old lady with a rap of her cane as she glanced at the departing young gentleman.

"It's Father's friend. I'm so surprised to see you!" stammered Meg, feeling that she was in for a lecture now.

"That's evident," returned Aunt March, sitting down. "But what is Father's friend saying to make you look like a peony? There's mischief going on, and I insist upon knowing what it is," with another rap.

"We were only talking. Mr. Brooke came for his umbrella," began Meg, wishing that Mr. Brooke and the umbrella were safely out of the house.

"Brooke? That boy's tutor? Ah! I understand now. I know all about it. Jo blundered into a wrong message in one of your Father's letters, and I made her tell me. You haven't gone and accepted him, child?" cried Aunt March, looking scandalized.

"Shan't I call Mother?" said Meg, much troubled.

"Not yet. I've something to say to you, and I must

free my mind at once. This Cook is a vampire slayer and he's only interested in you as a means to kill me," said the old lady impressively.

Meg had thought very much the same thing only a moment before, but her aunt's vehement insistence made her reevaluate the validity of that conclusion. The paranoid old lady thought every maid, cook, valet, and butler in Concord was a vampire slayer; naturally, she would think the same of a lowly tutor (whom she seemed to have mistaken for a cook anyway). But like almost all maids, cooks, valets, and butlers in the city, he was merely a hardworking man struggling to make ends meet. Shame on Jo for making her think any differently.

"I shall sire whom I please, Aunt March," she said, nodding her head with a resolute air.

"Highty-tighty! Is that the way you take my advice, Miss? You'll be sorry for it by-and-by, when you're pulling a stake out of your chest."

"It can't be worse than having a conversation with you," retorted Meg.

Aunt March put on her glasses and took a look at the girl, for she did not know her in this new mood. Meg hardly knew herself, she felt so brave and independent, so glad to defend John and assert her right to love him, if she liked. Aunt March saw that she had begun wrong, and after a little pause, made a fresh start, saying as mildly as she could, "Now, Meg, my dear, be reasonable and take my advice. I mean it kindly, and don't want you to spoil your whole life by aligning yourself with a man who means to end it. This Rook[30] is a slayer and has dastardly plans to do you and your family—and by family, I of course mean myself—harm. I don't doubt that he's part of the group that's been trying to decapitate me since they removed the head from your poor uncle's body."

"Father and Mother don't believe John is a slayer."

"Your parents, my dear, have no more worldly wisdom than a pair of babies."

"I'm glad of it," cried Meg stoutly, although, of course, she would like them to be able to spot a slayer should one appear to court her.

Aunt March took no notice, but went on with her lecture. "I realize you are having your first romance and cannot thusly be relied on to be logical. You are, in fact, poor and young and silly, and I will not stand for this another moment. From this minute on, you are not to see any more of this Hook. He is banished forever, do you understand?"

"The only thing I understand is how egregiously you've misjudged Mr. Brooke, Aunt March. John is good and wise, he's got heaps of talent, he's willing to work and sure to get on, he's so energetic and brave.

---

[30] Unclear as to whether Aunt March means he is a chess piece or if the old lady is confused or if it's a mistake by the typesetter.

Everyone likes and respects him, and I'm proud to think he cares for me, though I'm so poor and young and silly," said Meg, looking prettier than ever in her earnestness.

"He knows you have got important relations, child. That's the secret of his liking. He wants to kill me in my coffin."

"Aunt March, how dare you say such a thing? John is above such meanness, and I won't listen to you a minute if you talk so," cried Meg indignantly, forgetting everything but the injustice of the old lady's suspicions. "My John wouldn't kill you, any more than I would. We are willing to work and we mean to wait. I'm not afraid of being poor, for I've been happy so far, and I know I shall be with him because he loves me, and I . . . "

Meg stopped there, remembering all of a sudden that she hadn't made up her mind, that she had told "her John" to go away and that he might be overhearing her inconsistent remarks.

Aunt March was very angry, for she hated her advice not to be heeded, especially on a topic as serious as her life and possible assassination. Clearly, she would have to increase her own security to balance the greater threat to her welfare. It was all she could do.

"Well, I wash my hands of the whole affair! You are a willful child, and you've lost more than you know by this piece of folly. No, I won't stop. I'm disappointed in you, and haven't spirits to see your father now. Don't expect anything more from me. I'm done with you forever."

And slamming the door in Meg's face, Aunt March drove off in high dudgeon. She seemed to take all the girl's courage with her, for when left alone, Meg stood for a moment, undecided whether to laugh or wail. Before she could make up her mind, she was taken possession of by Mr. Brooke, who said all in one breath, "I couldn't help hearing, Meg. Thank you for defending me, and Aunt March for proving that you do care for me a little bit."

"I didn't know how much till she abused you," began Meg.

"And I needn't go away, but may stay and be happy, may I, dear?"

Here was another fine chance to make the crushing speech and the stately exit, but Meg never thought of doing either. "Yes, John," she whispered and hid her face on Mr. Brooke's waistcoat.

Fifteen minutes after Aunt March's departure, Jo came rushing into the house, paused an instant at the parlor door, and hearing no sound within, knocked down the door, terrified that she might find the glutinous remains of her dear sister upon the carpet and sofa. Instead, she beheld the enemy serenely sitting on the sofa, with her soon-to-be-decapitated sister enthroned upon his knee and wearing an expression of the most abject submission. Jo gave a sort of gasp, as if the hot sun had suddenly shined on her, for such an unexpected turning of the tables actually took her breath away. At the odd sound the lovers turned and saw her. Meg jumped up, looking both proud and shy, but "that man," as Jo called him, actually laughed and said coolly, as he kissed the astonished newcomer, "Sister Jo, congratulate us!"

That was adding insult to injury. It was altogether too much, and making some wild demonstration with her hands, Jo leaped into the air and landed on Mr. Brooke's chest, propelling him to the floor, where he lay stunned for the merest moment before grabbing a small side table and smashing it over Jo's head. The table split with a resounding crack and wood shards rained on the carpet as Jo's fist connected with Mr. Brooke's chin. His head dropped but his back arched, and with a mighty heave, he rolled over, pressing Jo into the carpet with a gleeful chuckle.

"Filthy vamp," he muttered.

Jo raised her knee and applied forceful pressure on the part of a man that Gentleman Jackson described as "most vulnerable to injury" and heard his pained wail. She kicked him twice, then flipped him over, her arm against his throat, slowly depleting his weak human body of more air.

When the fight began, Meg vanished without a word. Rushing upstairs, she startled the invalids by exclaiming tragically as she burst into the room, "Oh, do somebody go down quick! Jo is acting dreadfully!"

Mr. and Mrs. March left the room with speed, hastened down to the parlor, where they found Jo slowly choking the life out of Meg's suitor. Mr. March immediately ordered his daughter to cease and desist, and although Jo was far too angry to respond the first time, she quit her occupation without delay when he threatened to leave her outside for one full hour in the bright midday sun.

Meg arrived in the room, followed by the other two girls.

Marmee helped a wheezing John to his feet and led him to the couch while Jo looked on with burning eyes. His assurance of health was sought and attained before anyone turned to her to inquire after her well-being. She tapped her toe impatiently as Meg tore off a piece of her skirt and dabbed at his bleeding lip and her father offered him a cigarillo.

When John was comfortably situated, her mother turned to her, her voice bathed in disappointment, for she had been so proud of Jo for controlling her bosom enemy and now this shocking display of unrestraint. "Jo, you may now explain to us how came you to attack John, a visitor in this house, and a dear and wonderful friend to all of us."

"As I've mentioned several times before, though you refuse to listen to me, Mr. Brooke is a vicious vampire slayer responsible for Father's and Beth's illness. I didn't have evidence before but now I have proof taken from his own room," she announced.

With a shake of her head, Marmee said, "Jo, I realize you are determined to pursue a career as a defender, but that doesn't excuse you from basic propriety. It is not suitable for a young lady to enter a gentleman's rooms unaccompanied, nor is it proper for her to rifle among his things."

Jo impatiently accepted her mother's criticism. Marmee was the best and goodest creature in the whole world, which was sometimes, only at the rarest times, of course, a little difficult to live with. "It was not my intention to rifle but to find evidence that would save all our lives. And I did," she explained, producing from her pocket a slip of paper which she passed to her mother for examination. "The recipe for the chilly death. I found it in a small case in his closet hidden under a false floorboard. I also discovered some of the formula itself but I destroyed it immediately, lest it do further harm."

While Marmee read the ingredients, Brooke laughed viciously. "You've stopped me. Oh, you have. I'm your prisoner now. But you'll never stop us all. I am one among many and we are legion, and we won't rest until we've wiped all you filthy demons, you grotesque abominations, you monstrous insults to God, from the face of the—"

His speech cut off suddenly as Meg dove for his throat, her fangs driving into his flesh as if trying to tear out his very soul. Intent on his rant, Brooke hadn't seen it coming, nor had any of the occupants in the room. Father took a step forward, to chastise or comfort, Jo did not know, but before he could do anything, Marmee squeezed his arm and shook her head. Their kind, wonderful, oh-so-very-good mother understood her daughter's intent before the girl herself even understood it, and she had no desire for her husband to interfere with the natural order of things.

Jo's heart cheered in joy at the slaying of their enemy, the man who had wrought so much damage and caused so much grief. But then her joy turned to misery as Meg cut open her vein and pressed Brooke's lips to her arm. "No!" cried Jo, rushing forward, but she, like her father, was intercepted by the gentle Mrs. March, who patted her daughter's arm and promised softly that everything would be all right. Meg was acting in a way most natural to a young girl in love who discovered her lover was not all he seemed. Of a certainty, she felt betrayed and was driven in part by a desire to punish him for his treachery by making him the thing he hated most. But a larger part of her simply wanted to keep him beside her for always. Marmee knew neither motivation was a bad thing. Many a satisfying union had begun with one spouse resenting the other for a premature death and unasked-for rebirth. She herself had borne a grudge against Mr. March for two whole days before she acknowledged that her new condition was wholly superior to her old one.

But her mother's confident assurances did little to calm Jo down. She saw the fear in Brooke's eyes as he, like so many weak humans before him, drank the blood of a vampire to survive. His terror was palpable, for clearly he had long ago resigned himself to a violent death at the hand of a vengeful vampire but had never come to terms with the possibility of change, of being turned into one of them: a filthy demon, a grotesque abomination, an insult to God.

Hannah came in to see what all the commotion was about and tsked disapprovingly at the damage done to the little room. The sound seemed to wake Meg from a stupor and she looked up at her parents, then down at her fiancé, then up at her parents again. For a moment, she seemed confused by her own actions, as if they were done by someone else, but then she smiled, blood dripping from the corners of her mouth, and said, "I know we were meant to wait three years, but this simply felt right."

Marmee quietly asked the girls to leave and with great reluctance they allowed themselves to be led out by Hannah. Nobody ever knew what went on in the parlor that evening, but a great deal of talking was done, and quiet Meg astonished her parents by the eloquence and spirit with which she defended her impulsive actions, pleaded her suit, told her plans, and persuaded them to arrange everything just as she wanted it. Mr. Brooke was unconscious and therefore unable to make his opinion of the situation known, but it was assumed that his sentiments had undergone a sweeping change with his own transformation into a demon and that he would be delighted to be accepted into one of Concord's oldest vampire families, that he would happily comply with their strict humanitarian diet, and that he would eagerly supply the names of his coconspirators.

The tea bell rang before she had finished describing the paradise which her fiancé would supply her, but the Marches left off their discussion to go into supper. Before they did, Marmee suggested they bury John in the back garden, where the transformation would be completed and where the whole family would gather the next night to greet him when he emerged from his grave, hungry and slightly discombobulated from the alteration.

After Mr. March dug a shallow grave and Meg tossed her beloved in, they went in for their meal, Meg looking so happy that Jo hadn't the heart to be angry or dismal. Amy was very much impressed by Meg's dignity, Beth beamed at her from a distance, while Mr. and Mrs. March surveyed their daughter with such tender satisfaction that it was perfectly evident

Aunt March was right in calling them as "unworldly as a pair of babies." No one ate much, but everyone looked very happy, and the old room seemed to brighten up amazingly when the first romance of the family began there.

"You can't say nothing pleasant ever happens now, can you, Meg?" said Amy, trying to decide how she would group the lovers in a sketch she was planning to make.

"No, I'm sure I can't. How much has happened since I said that! It seems a year ago," answered Meg, who was in a blissful dream lifted far above such common things as supper.

"The joys come close upon the sorrows this time, and I rather think the changes have begun," said Mrs. March. "In most families there comes, now and then, a year full of events. This has been such a one, but it ends well, after all."

"Hope the next will end better," muttered Jo, who found it galling to call a slayer brother. Perhaps if he hadn't so recently tried to kill Beth and her father, she could be calm about it, but he had, so she was not and she spent the entire meal brooding about the unhappy event.

The front door banged to admit Laurie, who came prancing in, overflowing with good spirits, bearing a great bridal-looking bouquet for "Mrs. John Brooke," and evidently laboring under the delusion that the whole affair had been brought about by his excellent management.

"I knew Brooke would have it all his own way, he always does, for when he makes up his mind to accomplish anything, it's done though the sky falls," said Laurie, when he had presented his offering and his congratulations, only noticing then his tutor's absence and drawing the logical conclusion that he had once again missed out on all the fun. "Is the old fellow in the backyard, then?"

Jo confirmed with a nod.

"You don't look festive, ma'am, what's the matter?" asked Laurie, following Jo into a corner of the parlor, whither all had adjourned to greet Mr. Laurence.

"I don't approve of the match, but I've made up my mind to bear it, and shall not say a word against it," said Jo solemnly. "You can't know how hard it is for me to welcome a slayer into the family. Just a few hours ago he wanted us all dead and now we're supposed to dance at his wedding," she continued with a little quiver in her voice.

"What's this? A slayer?" asked Laurie.

Jo realized then that her friend had not taken her concerns any more seriously than her family, though she had repeatedly aired them to him. Calmly, she related the series of events that had led to that evening's impromptu siring. Laurie was aghast and apologetic for bringing such a creature into their midst, for he would never have hired, let alone befriended, someone with such archaic views on demonry. "I was positive you had it wrong. He seemed like an enlightened gus like me."

Of course she didn't hold Laurie responsible in any way. How could she blame him for his doubt when she had been unable to convince her entire family? Her only concern had been for the safety of her family and, by extension, Mr. Laurence. But now, through her poor handling of the affair, her sister had changed John years before she was ready.

"It can never be the same again. I've lost my dearest friend," sighed Jo.

"You've got me, anyhow. I'm not good for much, I know, but I'll stand by you, Jo, all the days of my life. Upon my word I will!" and Laurie meant what he said.

"I know you will, and I'm ever so much obliged. You are always a great comfort to me, Teddy," returned Jo, gratefully shaking hands.

"Well, now, don't be dismal, there's a good fellow. It's all right you see. Meg is happy, Brooke will fly round and get settled immediately, Grandpa will attend to him, and it will be very jolly to see Meg in her own little house. We'll have capital times after she is gone, for I shall be through college before long, and then we'll go abroad on some nice trip or other. Wouldn't that console you?"

"I rather think it would, but there's no knowing

what may happen in three years," said Jo thoughtfully.

"That's true. Don't you wish you could take a look forward and see where we shall all be then? I do," returned Laurie.

"I think not, for I might see something sad, and everyone looks so happy now, I don't believe they could be much improved." And Jo's eyes went slowly round the room, brightening as they looked, for the prospect was a pleasant one.

Father and Mother sat together, quietly reliving the first chapter of the romance which for them began some 130 years ago. Amy was drawing the lovers, the present half of whom sat apart in a beautiful world of her own, the light of which touched her face with a grace the little artist could not copy. Beth lay on her sofa, talking cheerily with her old friend, who held her little hand as if he felt that it possessed the power to lead him along the peaceful way she walked. Jo lounged in her favorite low seat, with the grave quiet look which best became her, and Laurie, leaning on the back of her chair, his chin on a level with her curly head, smiled with his friendliest aspect, and nodded at her in the long glass which reflected them both.

So the curtain falls upon Meg, Jo, Beth, and Amy. Whether it ever rises again, depends upon the reception given the first act of the domestic drama called *Little Vampire Women.*

PART
TWO

Chapter Eighteen

GOSSIP

In order that we may start afresh and go to Meg's wedding with free minds, it will be well to begin with a little gossip about the Marches. And here let me premise that if any of the elders think there is too much "lovering" in the story, as I fear they may (I'm not afraid the young folks will make that objection), I can only say with Mrs. March, "What can you expect when I have four gay girls in the house, and a dashing young neighbor over the way?"

The three years that have passed have brought but few changes to the quiet family. The war is over, and Mr. March safely at home, busy with his books and the small parish which found in him a minister by nature as by grace, a quiet, studious vampire, rich in the wisdom that is better than learning, the charity which calls all humankind "brother," the piety that blossoms into character, making it august and lovely.

These attributes, in spite of poverty and the strict integrity which shut him out from the more worldly successes, attracted to him many admirable vampires, as naturally as sweet herbs draw bees, and as naturally he gave them the honey into which two hundred fifty years of hard experience had distilled no bitter drop. His good book was the holy bible, the exact one human ministers preached out of daily, and his lessons were the same: do unto others, love thy neighbor. His "humanitarian" philosophy of treating all people with respect was, just as John Brooke and his cohorts had feared, starting to spread and grow beyond the small "cult of humanity" community where it was founded.

To outsiders the five energetic women seemed to rule the house, and so they did in many things, but the quiet scholar, sitting among his books, was still the head of the family, the household conscience, anchor, and comforter, for to him the busy, anxious vampire women always turned in troublous times, finding him, in the truest sense of those sacred words, husband and father.

The girls gave their hearts into their mother's keeping, their souls into their father's, and to both parents, who lived and labored so faithfully for them, they gave a love that grew with their growth and bound them tenderly together by the sweetest tie which blesses life and outlives death.

Mrs. March is as brisk and cheery, and no more

grayer, as when we saw her last, and just now so absorbed in Meg's affairs that the hospitals and homes still full of wounded "boys" and soldiers' widows, decidedly miss the motherly missionary's visits.

John Brooke did his duty manfully, rising to the demands of his new life with all the enthusiasm his young fiancée could hope for. A fighter by nature, he eagerly traded one cause for another, happily adopting the vampire struggle as his own. His loyalty to Meg developed with equal swiftness, for he was profoundly grateful to her for bestowing on him invincibility and immortality. Though he'd found her insipid and gullible in life, in death he found her delightful and blissfully fell in with her plans for their future.

The adjustment wasn't without its challenges, for Brooke dearly loved the taste of human blood as well as the acquisition of it. But through Meg's patient instruction, for he was the student now, he learned to control his impulses and even gained an appreciation for deer's blood, which had some of the tang of the human variety. His progress during those three years was everything his prospective in-laws could be proud of and they happily cheered him on when he refused Mr. Laurence's more generous offers, and accepted the place of bookkeeper, feeling better satisfied to begin with an honestly earned salary than by running any risks with borrowed money. They were also proud of the way he named all his coconspirators in the plot to kill the Marches, and he abjectly apologized to Beth for causing her a moment's unease with the chilly death. He'd only targeted her for execution because she had so skillfully and so smoothly deflected the stake aimed at her sister's heart by Fred Vaughn, an observation that further enflamed Jo's resentment, for she hated to think of any sister being worthy of execution save herself.

Meg had spent the time in working as well as instructing her beloved in his new life, growing womanly in character, wise in housewifely arts, and prettier than ever, for love is a great beautifier. She had her girlish ambitions and hopes, and felt some disappointment at the humble way in which the new life must begin. Sallie Gardiner had just gotten married, and Meg couldn't help contrasting her fine house and carriage, many gifts, and splendid outfit with her own, and secretly wishing she could have the same. But somehow envy and discontent soon vanished when she thought of all the patient love and labor John had put into becoming the perfect vampire for her, and when they sat together in the twilight, talking over their small plans, the future always grew so beautiful and bright that she forgot Sallie's splendor and felt herself the richest, happiest girl in Christendom.

Jo never went back to Aunt March, for the old lady took such a fancy to Amy that she bribed her with the offer of drawing lessons from one of the best teachers going, and for the sake of this advantage, Amy would have served a far harder mistress. So she gave her evenings to duty, her overnights to pleasure, and prospered finely. Jo meantime devoted herself to her training at the salon, where she was in her third year as a cadet. Graduation loomed and with it the prospect of a job with a firm or agency devoted to the defense of vampires. With John's help, Gentleman Jackson caught all but one of his former plotters. The villain who had escaped, a fierce slayer who went by the nom de guerre Dr. Bang, had long since disappeared from the county.

Beth remained delicate long after the fever was a thing of the past. Not an invalid exactly, but never again the pale-faced, healthy creature she had been, yet always hopeful, happy, and serene, and busy with the quiet duties she loved, everyone's friend, and an angel in the house, long before those who loved her most had learned to know it.

Laurie, having dutifully gone to college to please his grandfather, was now getting through it in the easiest possible manner to please himself. A universal favorite, thanks to money, manners, much talent, and the kindest heart that ever got its owner into scrapes by trying to get other people out of them, he stood in great danger of being spoiled, and probably would have been, like many another promising boy, if he had not possessed a talisman against evil in the memory of the kind old man who was bound up in his success, the motherly friend who watched over him as if he were her son, and last, but not least by any means, the knowledge that four innocent vampire girls loved, admired, and believed in him with all their hearts.

Being only "a glorious human boy," of course he frolicked and flirted, grew dandified, aquatic, sentimental, or gymnastic, as college fashions ordained, hazed and was hazed, talked slang, and more than once came perilously near suspension and expulsion. But as high spirits and the love of fun were the causes of these pranks, he always managed to save himself by frank confession, honorable atonement, or the irresistible power of persuasion which he possessed in perfection. In fact, he rather prided himself on his narrow escapes, and liked to thrill the girls with graphic accounts of his triumphs over wrathful tutors, dignified professors, and vanquished enemies. The "men of my class" were heroes in the eyes of the girls, who never wearied of the exploits of "our fellows," and were frequently allowed to bask in the smiles of these great creatures, when Laurie brought them home with him.

Amy especially enjoyed this high honor, and became quite a belle among them, for her ladyship early felt and learned to use the gift of fascination with which she was endowed. Meg was too much absorbed in her private and particular John to care for any other lords of creation, and Beth too shy to do more than peep at them and wonder how Amy dared to order them about so, but Jo felt quite in her own element, and found it very difficult to refrain from imitating the gentlemanly attitudes, phrases, and feats, which seemed more natural to her than the decorums prescribed for young ladies. They all liked Jo immensely, but never fell in love with her, though very few escaped without paying the tribute of a sentimental sigh or two at Amy's shrine. And speaking of sentiment brings us very naturally to the "Dovecote."

That was the name of the little brown house Mr. Brooke had prepared for Meg's first home. Laurie had christened it, saying it was highly appropriate to the gentle lovers who "went on together like a pair of turtledoves, with first a bill and then a coo." It was a tiny house, with a little garden behind and a lawn about as big as a pocket handkerchief in the front. The house was furnished lovingly by Mrs. March and the girls, who went on many solemn shopping excursions to stock the house with all the amenities required by a new bride.

The linen closet was particularly well-stored, for Aunt March, having said she would have nothing further to do with Meg if she married "that book,"[31] was rather in a quandary when the former tutor became a valuable resource in the fight against slayers. She never broke her word, and was much exercised in her

---

[31] See footnote 30.

mind how to get round it, and at last devised a plan whereby she could satisfy herself. A dear family friend was ordered to buy, have made, and marked a generous supply of house and table linen, and send it as her present, all of which was faithfully done, but the secret leaked out, and was greatly enjoyed by the family, for Aunt March tried to look utterly unconscious, and insisted that she could give nothing but the old-fashioned pearls long promised to the first bride.

And now Beth was there, laying the snowy piles smoothly on the shelves and exulting over the goodly array and the house was complete and ready for the bride and groom to return home replete after their wedding tomorrow.

Chapter Nineteen

THE FIRST WEDDING

Meg did not want a fashionable wedding, but only those around her whom she loved, and to them she wished to look and be her familiar self. So she made her wedding gown herself, sewing into it the tender hopes and innocent romances of a girlish heart. Her sisters braided up her pretty hair, and the only ornaments she wore were the lilies of the valley, which "her John" liked best of all the flowers that grew.

"You do look just like our own dear Meg, only so very sweet and lovely that I should hug you if it wouldn't crumple your dress," cried Amy, surveying her with delight when all was done.

"Then I am satisfied. But please hug and kiss me, everyone, and don't mind my dress. I want a great many crumples of this sort put into it today," and Meg opened her arms to her sisters, who clung about her with April faces for a minute, feeling that the new love had not changed the old.

"Now I'm going to tie John's cravat for him, and then to stay a few minutes with Father quietly in the study," and Meg ran down to perform these little ceremonies, and then to follow her mother wherever she went, conscious that in spite of the smiles on the motherly face, there was a secret sorrow hid in the motherly heart at the flight of the first bird from the nest.

All three girls wore suits of thin silver gray (their best gowns for the summer), with blush roses in hair and bosom, and all three looked just what they were, pale-faced, happy-hearted girls, pausing a moment in their busy lives to read with wistful eyes the sweetest chapter in the romance of vampire womanhood.

There were to be no ceremonious performances, everything was to be as natural and homelike as possible, so when Aunt March arrived, she was scandalized to see the bride come running to welcome and lead her in, to find the bridegroom fastening up a garland that had fallen down, and to catch a glimpse of the paternal minister marching upstairs with a grave countenance.

"Upon my word, here's a state of things!" cried the old lady, taking the seat of honor prepared for her, and settling the folds of her lavender moiré with a great rustle. "You oughtn't to be seen till the last minute, child."

"I'm not a show, Aunty, and no one is coming to

stare at me, to criticize my dress, or count the cost of my luncheon. I'm too happy to care what anyone says or thinks, and I'm going to have my little wedding just as I like it."

But poor Meg did not get to have her little wedding just as she liked it, for no sooner were the words out of her mouth than an arrow sailed through the open window and struck her in the shoulder, enough inches away from her heart to do her no damage but close enough to disturb a fond bridegroom, who waved his hammer angrily.

"Attack!" he cried, running toward the window, right into the face of danger like a brave young vampire should do.

Meg jumped in front of her screeching aunt March, as Amy was not immediately present to provide protection, and extricated the arrow from her shoulder, bemoaning the tear that now rent her beautiful dress. Nasty, awful slayers to ruin a girl's most special day!

"The Pendergrast Offense,"[32] Jo called, dashing down the stairs as another arrow, this one alight with flames, crossed the room. "Attack during an important affair, for your targets are gathered and distracted. I should have seen this coming."

---

[32] From Chapter 14 of *Mr. Bloody Wobblestone's Scientifical Method for Tracking, Catching, and Destroying Vampire Slayers*, "Frequent Maneuvers and Easy Ways to Counter Them."

Mr. Laurence extinguished the fire before it had time to consume the carpet and urged his grandson, who was trying to help, to seek cover. Laurie protested that he was as able-bodied as any man present to defend hearth and home, but Jo interrupted his fine speech . . .

"Best listen, my boy. You have a dreadfully mortal human trick about you."

If there was anything a mortal human boy hated to be called, it was a mortal human boy, and Laurie, feeling the slight keenly, refused to move from his perch next to his grandfather.

Jo was inclined to press the matter, but with new arrows flying through the window in a constant stream, now wasn't the time. She ran to John at the window as Amy charged into the room to relieve Meg of her responsibility. The youngest sister tried to convince her to seek refuge in the linen closet to save her dress further damage, but the bride refused to be separated from her beloved on this, their wedding day, for she had promised, or, rather, had been prepared to promise, to remain true through better or worse.

"We need to take the fight to them," Jo said, well aware the enemy had the tactical advantage of being able to enter any establishment at will. Only vampires were handicapped by the need for an invitation.

Brooke nodded, for he knew their attacker could be only the nefarious Dr. Bang, a man whose methods his former collaborator knew much about and whose bravery extended only so far as a fast assault and a faster retreat. Bang preferred underhanded means such as the chilly death to direct confrontation, and that he was willing to risk this attack revealed how poorly he was thinking. His main goal, indeed his only goal, was to revenge himself on his undead former ally by ruining his wedding, for even if all the players survived, the perfect memory of this perfect night would be polluted by the battle.

It was a dastardly plan, for a wedding should be held sacred by both sides of the never-ending human-vampire struggle, but it left Bang, who wasn't an experienced field officer, on unfamiliar ground. "Now," Brooke cried, jumping through the window a mere second before Jo, the stench of his foe's spicy cologne filling his nostrils and clouding his vision until all he could see was his own hunger. Deer's blood was all very good for keeping one alive but it had nothing on the vibrant, red coursing blood of a sworn enemy.

Jo arrived at the catapult first, for Brooke was still a little shaky on his "vampire legs," and examined the mechanical device for clues, but the humans who had set it up were long gone. Try as she might, Jo could hear nothing but the rustling of the trees and her own family's faint distressful chatter. She closed her eyes and inhaled deeply but without her allium mask could not get passed the garlicky notes in Bang's cologne.

"A point for the slayers," she said as John kicked the contraption that had thrown arrow after arrow at the house. He should have known it would be a cowardly trick. Dr. Bang didn't have the cheek to risk a full-on attack.

Once Meg was assured of her bridegroom's safety, which, in truth, she never really doubted, for she had remarkable faith in his fighting skills, she handed him the hammer again and told him to get busy, for there was much more to repair now than mere fallen garlands.

There was no bridal procession, but a sudden silence fell upon the room as Mr. March and the young couple took their places under the green arch, their bride clothes no less beautiful for the rips, stains, and burns singed upon them. Mother and sisters gathered close, as if loath to give Meg up. The fatherly voice broke more than once, which only seemed to make the service more beautiful and solemn. The bridegroom's hand trembled visibly, and no one heard his replies. But Meg looked straight up in her husband's eyes, and said, "I will!" with such tender trust in her own face and voice that her mother's heart rejoiced and Aunt March sniffed audibly.

Jo did not relax, for she feared another attack, and Laurie stared fixedly at her, with a comic mixture of merriment and emotion in his wicked black eyes and she knew he would enact some revenge for her calling him a mortal human boy. Beth kept her face hidden on her mother's shoulder, but Amy stood like a graceful statue, with a most becoming ray of moonshine touching her white forehead and the flower in her hair.

It wasn't at all the thing, I'm afraid, but the minute she was fairly married, Meg cried, "The first kiss for Marmee!" and turning, gave it with her heart on her lips. During the next fifteen minutes she looked more like a carnation than ever, for everyone availed themselves of their privileges to the fullest extent, from Mr. Laurence to old Hannah, who, adorned with a headdress fearfully and wonderfully made, fell upon her in the hall, crying with a sob and a chuckle, "Bless you, deary, a hundred times! The blood ain't spilled a mite, and everything looks lovely."

Everybody cleared up after that, and said something brilliant, or tried to, which did just as well, for laughter is ready when hearts are light. After supper, people strolled about, by twos and threes, through the house and garden, enjoying the moonshine without and within. Meg and John happened to be standing together in the middle of the grass plot, when Laurie was seized with an inspiration which put the finishing touch to this unfashionable wedding.

"All the married people take hands and dance round the new-made husband and wife, as the Germans do, while we bachelors and spinsters prance in couples outside!" cried Laurie, promenading down the path with

Amy, with such infectious spirit and skill that everyone else followed their example without a murmur. But the crowning joke was Mr. Laurence and Aunt March, for when the stately old gentleman chasséd solemnly up to the old lady, she just tucked her cane under her arm, and hopped briskly away to join hands with the rest and dance about the bridal pair, while the young folks pervaded the garden like butterflies on a midsummer night.

When the impromptu ball drew to a close, people began to go.

"I wish you well, my dear, I heartily wish you well, but I think you'll be sorry for it," said Aunt March to Meg, adding to the bridegroom, as he led her to the carriage, "You've got a treasure, young man, see that you deserve it."

"Laurie, my lad, if you ever want to indulge in this sort of thing, get one of those little girls to help you, and I shall be perfectly satisfied," said Mr. Laurence, settling himself in his easy chair to rest after the excitement of the evening.

"I'll do my best to gratify you, Sir," was Laurie's unusually dutiful reply, as he carefully unpinned the posy Jo had put in his buttonhole.

The little house was not far away, and the only bridal journey Meg had was the quiet walk with John from the old home to the new. It sounded like a grand scheme at the time but now everyone worried that the happy couple would be set upon by slayers in the forest. John was arranging transport by carriage when Meg came down, looking like a pretty Quakeress in her dove-colored suit and straw bonnet tied with white. She immediately dismissed the new arrangement, citing her complete faith in her husband's ability to protect her as well as her own not inconsiderable skills as a fighter. Although neither her parents nor her sisters were satisfied by this argument, they acknowledged that the decisions were now Meg's to make and gathered about her to say "good-bye," as tenderly as if she had been going to make the grand tour.

"Don't feel that I am separated from you, Marmee dear, or that I love you any the less for loving John so much," she said, clinging to her mother, with full eyes for a moment. "I shall come every day, Father, and expect to keep my old place in all your hearts, though I am married. Beth is going to be with me a great deal, and the other girls will drop in now and then to laugh at my housekeeping struggles. Thank you all for my happy wedding night. Good-bye, good-bye!"

They stood watching her, with faces full of love and hope and tender pride as she walked away, leaning on her husband's arm, with her hands full of a pair of dueling pistols to fend off any attackers and the June moonlight brightening her happy face—and so Meg's married life began.

Chapter Twenty

CALLS

Like most other young matrons, Meg embarked on her married life with the determination to be a model housekeeper. John should find home a paradise, he should always see a smiling face, should fare sumptuously every day, and never know the loss of a button. She brought so much love, energy, and cheerfulness to the work that she could not but succeed, in spite of some obstacles. Her paradise was not a tranquil one, for John could not rest or relax now that Dr. Bang was back in Concord, and he frequently railed about his ineffectiveness in apprehending the great villain who threatened his family. The trail, which had grown cold three years ago, was suddenly hot again, and John would not stop until he'd drained every last drop of blood out of the former conspirator who had now taunted him.

Meg understood her husband's concern and tried to wait gently and patiently for him to overcome his wrath and settle calmly into married life like a new husband should. Instead, he spent hours prowling Concord, his nose flared, his eyes sharp, hunting for signs of his archenemy. In this way, the bride passed many nights in solitude, fearful of her husband, who was still a novice, despite his three years. She was, as well, in a large way intolerant of his seeming obsession, which prevented him from making a living as a book-keeper. He'd already lost two jobs because he refused to sit quietly in an office adding columns while Bang was on the loose.

"Oh, dear," thought Meg, on one such night, as she waited for her husband to return, "married life is very trying, and does need infinite patience as well as love, as Mother says." The word "Mother" suggested other maternal counsels given not long ago, and received with unbelieving protests.

"John is a good vampire, but he has his faults, and you must learn to see and bear with them, remembering your own. He is very decided, but never will be obstinate, if you reason kindly, not oppose impatiently. He is very accurate, and particular about the truth—a good trait, though you call him 'fussy.' Never deceive him by look or word, Meg, and he will give you the confidence you deserve, the support you need. He has a temper, not like ours—one flash and then all over—but

224

the white, still anger that is seldom stirred, but once kindled is hard to quench."

Taking her mother's wise words to heart, Meg sought out Jo and prevailed upon her to capture the vexing Dr. Bang, so she could finally begin married life as it ought to be. Jo consented immediately, for she was already on the hunt for Bang and his confederates. Like John, she couldn't rest calmly in her coffin while the man who had done so much damage to Beth was at liberty, for she saw that the knowledge of his return made her sister listless and nervous, a condition only alleviated by a one-month visit to the seaside, when she was able to put the vile slayer from her thoughts. Unlike John, Jo was a cadet at Gentleman Jackson's salon and a student of Wobblestone's scientifical method, so she began her search with the catapult which had assaulted them during the wedding. It revealed several clues, for it was made very precisely by an excellent craftsman, and the cologne thrown upon it was of a special brew, with its sharp undernotes of masking garlic. The evidence spoke of skill, sophistication, and wealth, indicating a well-off, well-placed member of Concord society, of which there were only a few humans.

In order to find the culprit, Jo needed to infiltrate the house of her suspects, and to infiltrate the house of her suspects Jo required Amy's assistance, for her youngest sister frequently paid social calls on the people in question.

"Come, Jo, it's time," said Amy, shortly after ten on the Thursday following. In order to stay current, many humans in polite society set aside at-home nights, when they were available for visits from their vampire neighbors.

"I've done a good many rash and foolish things in my life, but I don't think I ever was mad enough to say I'd make six calls in one night," Jo muttered, for she hated making calls of the formal sort.

"Jo March, you are perverse enough to provoke a saint!" cried Amy, who had been cajoled into this venture by her sister.

"You are right. Very well, I'll go if I must, and do my best. You shall be commander of the expedition, and I'll obey blindly, will that satisfy you?" said Jo, with a sudden change from perversity to lamblike submission.

"You're a perfect cherub! Now put on all your best things, and I'll tell you how to behave at each place, so that you will make a good impression. I want people to like you, and they would if you'd only try to be a little more agreeable. Do your hair the pretty way, and put the pink rose in your bonnet. It's becoming, and you look too sober in your plain suit. Take your light gloves and the embroidered handkerchief."

While Amy dressed, she issued her orders, and Jo obeyed them, not without entering her protest, however, for she sighed as she rustled into her new organdie, frowned darkly at herself as she tied her bonnet strings in an irreproachable bow, wrestled viciously with pins as she put on her collar, wrinkled up her features generally as she shook out the handkerchief, whose embroidery was as irritating to her nose as the present mission was to her feelings, and when she had squeezed her hands into tight gloves with three buttons and a tassel, as the last touch of elegance, she turned to Amy with an imbecile expression of countenance, saying meekly . . .

"I'm perfectly miserable, but if you consider me presentable, I die happy," she said, knowing her sister was right. If she was to find the enemy, then she had to blend in and not be conspicuous in her investigations.

"You're highly satisfactory. Turn slowly round, and let me get a careful view." Jo revolved, and Amy gave a touch here and there, then fell back, with her head on one side, observing graciously, "Yes, you'll do. Your head is all I could ask, for that white bonnet with the rose is quite ravishing. Hold back your shoulders, and carry your hands easily, no matter if your gloves do pinch. There's one thing you can do well, Jo, that is, wear a shawl. I can't, but it's very nice to see you, and I'm so glad Aunt March gave you that lovely one. It's simple, but handsome, and those folds over the arm are really artistic. Is the point of my mantle in the middle, and have I looped my dress evenly? I like to show my boots, for my feet are pretty, though my fangs aren't."

"You are a thing of beauty and a joy forever," said

Jo, looking through her hand with the air of a connoisseur at the blue feather against the golden hair. "Am I to drag my best dress through the dust, or loop it up, please, ma'am?"

"Hold it up when you walk, but drop it in the house. The sweeping style suits you best, and you must learn to trail your skirts gracefully. You haven't half buttoned one cuff, do it at once. You'll never look finished if you are not careful about the little details, for they make up the pleasing whole."

Jo sighed, and proceeded to burst the buttons off her glove, in doing up her cuff, but at last both were ready, and sailed away, looking as "pretty as picters," Hannah said, as she hung out of the upper window to watch them.

"Now, Jo dear, the Chesters consider themselves very elegant people, so I want you to put on your best deportment. Don't make any of your abrupt remarks, or do anything odd, will you? Just be calm, cool, and quiet, that's safe and ladylike, and you can easily do it for fifteen minutes," said Amy, as they approached the first place, having borrowed the white parasol and been inspected by Meg.

"Let me see. 'Calm, cool, and quiet,' yes, I think I can promise that." And it was true, for she planned to blend into the background so well her hosts wouldn't notice her peeking through their drawers.

Amy looked relieved but realized soon after they

arrived that she should have included "completely immobile" among her instructions, for Jo never stopped strolling about the room, examining cabinets and admiring shelves and on one particularly noteworthy occasion disappearing into the hall for a full minute.

"Try to be sociable at the Lambs' and for goodness' sake, do be still. You make everyone nervous with your pacing to and fro. Gossip as other girls do, and be interested in dress and flirtations and whatever nonsense comes up. They move in the best society, are valuable persons for us to know, and I wouldn't fail to make a good impression there for anything."

Jo promised to be agreeable, to gossip and giggle and have horrors and raptures over any trifle, but she didn't say a word about her mobility.

Amy felt anxious, as well she might, for when Jo turned freakish there was no knowing where she would stop. Amy's face was a study when she saw her sister skim into the next drawing room, kiss all the young ladies with effusion, beam graciously upon the young gentlemen, and join in the chat with a spirit which amazed the beholder.

"She rides splendidly," Lucretia said, by way of compliment to Amy. "Who taught her?"

"No one. She used to practice mounting, holding the reins, and sitting straight on an old saddle in a tree. Now she rides anything, for she doesn't know what fear is, and the stableman lets her have horses cheap because she trains them to carry ladies so well. She has such a passion for it, I often tell her if everything else fails, she can be a horse breaker, and get her living so," Jo said, roaming around the parlor as she imitated Amy riding a horse. She told several more stories about her sister's skill, each one a more dreadful blunder than the last. But there was still worse to come, when Jo frankly admitted that Amy painted many of their articles of clothing in order to make them lovely and fashionable, as they couldn't afford to buy anything new.

By the time she finished her anecdote about the March girls' thriftiness, she felt for sure the Lambs were not involved in the conspiracy, for she couldn't pick up a hint of the cologne sent at all and she'd carefully sniffed all the members during their giddy chat. "Amy, we must go. Good-bye, dear, do come and see us. We are pining for a visit. I don't dare to ask you, Mr. Lamb, but if you should come, I don't think I shall have the heart to send you away."

Jo said this with such a droll imitation of May Chester's gushing style that Amy got out of the room as rapidly as possible, feeling a strong desire to laugh and cry at the same time.

"Didn't I do well?" asked Jo, with a satisfied air as they walked away. Two suspects down, only four to go.

"Nothing could have been worse," was Amy's crushing reply. "What possessed you to tell those stories about my saddle, and the hats and boots, and all the rest of it?"

"Why, it's funny, and amuses people. They know we are poor, so it's no use pretending that we have grooms, buy three or four hats a season, and have things as easy and fine as they do." She didn't add that she had to talk to them about something if she was going to close enough to smell them properly.

"You needn't go and tell them all our little shifts, and expose our poverty in that perfectly unnecessary way. You haven't a bit of proper pride, and never will learn when to hold your tongue and when to speak," said Amy despairingly.

Poor Jo looked abashed, and silently chafed the end of her nose with the stiff handkerchief, as if performing a penance for her misdemeanors.

"How shall I behave here?" she asked, as they approached the third mansion.

"Just as you please. I wash my hands of you," was Amy's short answer.

At the Porters', Jo talked briefly with her hosts, then wandered off to find their three sons, a pretext that gave her leave to search the house unmolested. She inspected the study, library, and drawing room without discovering anything the least bit suspicious before stumbling upon three big boys and several pretty children who were getting ready for bed. She apologized for disturbing them in their nursery and quickly closed the door.

She returned to the parlor and discovered that Mr. Tudor happened to be calling likewise, which impressed Amy greatly, for his uncle had married an English lady who was third cousin to a living lord. Previously, Jo avoided Mr. Tudor because she didn't like him: He put on airs, snubbed his sisters, worried his father, and didn't speak respectfully of his mother. But now, as she caught a whiff of spicy garlic, her dislike turned to loathing and she leapt at him with all her strength, propelling him to the floor with a gasp of surprise. The ladies screamed, the gentlemen protested, and Amy said wearily, "You might treat him civilly, at least."

Jo bared her fangs as beads of sweat formed on Tudor's forehead but he managed to keep his voice smooth as he said, "Miss March, I must insist that you remove yourself from my person immediately."

Her only response was a snarl.

A drop of sweat trickled down the side of his face as he held his ground. "I realize this kind of behavior is commonplace among your sort but we in polite society do not physically accost unmarried gentlemen."

"Dr. Bang," she growled, low and menacing.

"Really," Mrs. Porter said, appalled by Jo's behavior. "You are guests in my home. I *invited* you in."

Jo growled again and brushed her fangs against Mr. Tudor's neck.

He coughed awkwardly. "Oh, very well. Yes, I am familiar with Dr. Bang. I don't think his country manners are quite the thing and he could stand to wash more often, but he runs an organization devoted to the eradication of vampires, to which I subscribe. I think it's detestable the way you lot own so much of the fertile land in the country. It's just plain rude to hoard all the good soil."

The last thing Jo cared about was Mr. Tudor's small-minded prejudices or petty hypocrisy, for he would have no problem if he himself owned all the good land. "Dr. Bang. Where is he?"

"I believe the old boy scuttled off to New York City after your sister's wedding. He was rather in a panic when he came to me looking for further funding." Now sweat streamed down his face. "I believe you could find him in Waverly Place. Ah, three eighteen, if I remember correctly."

Mrs. Porter rushed to apologize for her guest, whom she had no idea was a sympathizer, as Mr. Tudor begged Jo not to reveal the source of her information to Dr. Bang.

"It's no use trying to argue with you," Amy began.

"Not the least, my dear," said Jo smugly, removing herself from Tudor's person and allowing him to stand up while the magistrate was called for to apprehend him. She knew that the villain, being from one of the best families and related by marriage to a living lord, would suffer nothing worse than a slap on the wrist, but she couldn't very well eliminate him there in the Porters' drawing room, for, though her sister gave her no credit for manners, she did realize that was not precisely the thing.

Having completed her task, Jo tried to extricate herself from the rest of the visits, but Amy insisted they carry forward with their original plan. Luckily, the Phillipses were out and the young ladies in the fifth house were engaged. That left Aunt March, who Jo thought they should skip entirely, but Amy insisted they go, for her aunt liked them to pay her the compliment of coming in style and making a formal call.

They found the old lady preparing to pay a call on them, and grateful she wouldn't have to leave herself open to attack by stepping out of her house, she invited them to have a small rodent in her drawing room. After their grueling night, both girls eagerly accepted the snack, which Jo wolfed down and Amy sucked daintily at for fifteen minutes.

"Are you going to help about the fair, dear?" asked Aunt March.

"Yes, Aunt. Mrs. Chester asked me if I would, and I offered to tend a table, as I have nothing but my time to give."

"I'm not," put in Jo decidedly. "I hate to be patronized, and the Chesters think it's a great favor to allow us to help with their highly connected fair. I wonder you consented, Amy, they only want you to work."

"I am willing to work. It's for the freedmen as well as the Chesters, and I think it very kind of them to let me share the labor and the fun. Patronage does not trouble me when it is well meant."

"Quite right and proper. I like your grateful spirit, my dear. It's a pleasure to help people who appreciate our efforts. Some do not, and that is trying," observed Aunt March, looking over her spectacles at Jo, who sat apart, rocking herself, with a somewhat morose expression.

If Jo had only known what a great happiness was wavering in the balance for one of them, she would have turned dove-like in a minute, but unfortunately, extrasensory vampire powers do not extend to mind-reading, no matter what it says in some sensation-alistic French novels.[33] Better for them that they cannot as a general thing, but now and then it would be such a comfort, such a saving of time and temper. By her next speech, Jo deprived herself of several years of pleasure, and received a timely lesson in the art of holding her tongue.

"I don't like favors, they oppress and make me feel

---

[33] Most specifically the works of Madame de La Fayette, in whose stories vampires could transform into any animal, run faster than a horse, move small mountains, and, most fantastically, suffer only mild discomfort when out in the noonday sun.

like a slave. I'd rather do everything for myself, and be perfectly independent."

This was a very damaging statement indeed, as Jo had cause to learn a few moments later, when Aunt March announced that she would be taking Amy with her to Europe the next week. The advantages to the girl were obvious, Aunt March said, but she listed them again for Jo's benefit, including her excellent manners, docility, fluency in French, and her deft skills as a protectress, for she could see her niece was very disappointed by the information, though she admirably, and surprisingly, held her tongue until she got home.

"Oh, Mother!" Jo cried. "She's too young, it's my turn first. I've wanted it so long. It would do me so much good, and be so altogether splendid. I must go!"

"I'm afraid it's impossible, Jo. Aunt says Amy, decidedly, and it is not for us to dictate when she offers such a favor."

"It's always so. Amy has all the fun and I have all the work. It isn't fair, oh, it isn't fair!" cried Jo passionately.

As her mother pointed out all the ways in which the decision had been influenced by her daughter's poor performance, the girl thought of all she would be missing by not going to Europe. Oh, what a desperate tragedy! How she longed to travel and see new places and meet ancient vampires who lived in gloomy castles atop menacing cliffs!

" . . . no hope of it this time, so try to bear

it cheerfully, and don't sadden Amy's pleasure by reproaches or regrets," her mother said, concluding her little lecture on Jo's dreadful behavior, most of which its subject missed.

"Jo, dear, I'm very selfish, but I couldn't spare you, and I'm glad you are not going quite yet," whispered Beth, embracing her, basket and all, with such a clinging touch and loving face that Jo felt comforted in spite of the sharp regret that made her want to box her own ears, and humbly beg Aunt March to burden her with this favor, and see how gratefully she would bear it.

But the sight of Beth's sweet face reminded her of a more important journey she had to undertake, which that night's disappointments had driven entirely from her mind, further proof, she thought, that paying calls was nothing but a time-wasting faradiddle. Dr. Bang was still at large, and Beth would never be safe until the sworn enemy of all the Marches had been stopped and his evil plans thwarted once and for all. To accomplish that, Jo would follow him anywhere, to the ends of the earth or the bowels of hell if necessary, so New York City didn't seem very far to go at all.

Chapter Twenty-One

TENDER TROUBLES

"I want to go away somewhere this winter for a change," announced Jo to Marmee.

"Why, Jo?" and her mother looked up quickly.

With her eyes on her work Jo answered soberly, "I want something new. I feel restless and anxious to be seeing, doing, and learning more than I am. I brood too much over my own small affairs, and need stirring up, so as I can be spared this winter, I'd like to hop a little way and try my wings."

"Where will you hop?"

"To New York. I had a bright idea yesterday, and this is it. You know Mrs. Kirke wrote to you for some respectable young vampire to teach her children and sew. It's rather hard to find just the thing, but I think I should suit if I tried."

"My dear, go out to service in that great board-inghouse!" and Mrs. March looked surprised, but not displeased.

"It's not exactly going out to service, for Mrs. Kirke is your friend—the kindest vampire that ever lived—and would make things pleasant for me, I know. Her family is separate from the rest, and no one knows me there. Don't care if they do. It's honest work, and I'm not ashamed of it."

"Nor I. But your training?"

"All the better for the change. The salon has an affiliate in New York, and Gentleman Jackson has writ-ten a letter of introduction for me. I shall see and hear new things and get new ideas."

"I have no doubt of it, but are these your only rea-sons for this sudden fancy?"

"No, Mother."

"May I know the others?"

Jo looked up and Jo looked down, wondering how much to tell her, for Marmee had also noticed Beth's low spirits. The girl sat alone a good deal, didn't talk to their father as much as she used to, sang sad songs, and had a look in her eye that was hard to understand. Jo knew the strange behavior was on account of her fear of Dr. Bang, but she couldn't tell her mother that, for Marmee would never let her go to New York City if she suspected danger. But nor could she lie to her mother. "It may be vain and wrong to say it, but—I'm afraid—Laurie is getting too fond of me."

It was a convenient truth commandeered on the spot, but it was also a relevant one, she realized, recalling the odd mixture of anxiety and merriment in Laurie's face yesterday when she instructed him to devote himself to one of the "pretty, modest girls" whom he did respect, and not waste his time with the silly ones.

"Then you don't care for him in the way it is evident he begins to care for you?" and Mrs. March looked anxious as she put the question.

"Mercy, no! I love the dear boy, as I always have, and am immensely proud of him, but as for anything more, it's out of the question."

"I'm glad of that, Jo."

"Why, please?"

"Because, dear, I don't think you suited to one another. As friends you are very happy, and your frequent quarrels soon blow over, but I fear you would both rebel if you were mated for life. You are too much alike and too fond of freedom, not to mention hot tempers and strong wills, to get on happily together, in a relation which needs infinite patience and forbearance, as well as love."

"That's just the feeling I had, though I couldn't express it," Jo said, knowing it was true. She would never love someone so well that she would happily surrender that freedom she was so fond of. But she feared Laurie would never understand that. "I'm glad you think he is only beginning to care for me. It would trouble me sadly to make him unhappy, for I couldn't turn the dear old fellow into a vampire merely out of gratitude, could I?"

"You are sure of his feeling for you?"

Jo grew more uncomfortable as she answered, with the look of mingled pleasure, pride, and pain which young girls wear when speaking of first lovers, "I'm afraid it is so, Mother. He hasn't said anything, but he looks a great deal and you know how he's always wanted to be a vampire. I think I had better go away before it comes to anything."

"I agree with you, and if it can be managed you shall go."

Jo looked relieved, for she had no idea what she would do if Marmee didn't grant her permission to go to New York to find Dr. Bang, and after a pause, said, smiling, "Thank you. Let us say nothing about it to Laurie till the plan is settled, then I'll run away before he can collect his wits and be tragic."

The plan was talked over in a family council and agreed upon, for Mrs. Kirke gladly accepted Jo, and promised to make a pleasant home for her. The teaching would render her independent, and such leisure as she got might be made useful by training, while the new scenes and society would be agreeable. Jo was eager to be gone, for she could not rest comfortably in the home nest knowing it was threatened. As well, her restless nature and adventurous spirit loathed to be idle when there was work to be done. When all was settled, with fear and trembling she told Laurie, but to her surprise he took it very quietly. He had been graver than usual of late, but very pleasant, and when jokingly accused of turning over a new leaf, he answered soberly, "So I am, and I mean this one shall stay turned."

Jo was very much relieved that one of his virtuous fits should come on just then, and made her preparations with a lightened heart, for Beth seemed more cheerful, and knew she was doing the best for all.

"One thing I leave in your especial care," she said, the night before she left.

"You mean your books?" asked Beth.

"No, my boy. Be very good to him, won't you?"

"Of course I will, but I can't fill your place, and he'll miss you sadly."

"It won't hurt him, so remember, I leave him in your charge, to plague, pet, and keep in order."

"I'll do my best, for your sake," promised Beth, wondering why Jo looked at her so queerly.

When Laurie said good-bye, he whispered significantly, "It won't do a bit of good, Jo. My eye is on you, so mind what you do, or I'll come and bring you home."

Chapter Twenty-Two

JO'S JOURNAL

New York, March

Dear Marmee and Beth,

I'm going to write you a regular volume, for I've got heaps to tell about my situation, though I'm not a fine young vampire lady traveling on the continent like Amy. I enjoyed my journey with all my heart, and Mrs. Kirke welcomed me so kindly I felt at home at once, even in that big house full of strangers. She gave me a funny little sky parlor—all she had, but there is a stove in it, and a roomy coffin far from the window. The nursery, where I teach and sew, is a pleasant room next Mrs. Kirke's private parlor, and the two little girls are pretty children, rather spoiled, I fancy, but they took to me after telling them "The Seven Bad Pigs," and my days have already fallen into a familiar pattern of teaching, sewing, and training.

I have my meals with the children, for I'm too bashful

at present to eat with all the strangers at the great table, though no one will believe it. The children dine on rats, squirrels, and chicken, as do I, for Mrs. K. knows that I have been raised a devout humanitarian and would never want to undermine your teachings in any way.

The house is a mix of humans and vampires, which is an unusual combination and makes for some interesting interaction at sunrise and sunset, when there is the most dealings between the two. On the second evening, as I went downstairs after breakfast, two of the young human men were setting their hats before the hall mirror after a long day at work, and I heard one say low to the other, "Who's the new party?"

"Governess vampire, or something of that sort."

"What the deuce is she doing here?"

"Friend of the old lady's."

"Handsome head, but no style."

"Not a bit of it. Give us a light and come on."

I felt angry at first, and then I didn't care, for a governess is as good as a clerk, and I've got sense, if I haven't style, which is more than some people have, judging from the remarks of the elegant beings who clattered away, smoking like bad chimneys. I hate ordinary people!

The vampires in the house are much lovelier, for none of them are particularly plump in the pocket and have none of the airs of the wealthy. They are down-to-earth folk and very kind, even the ones who hunt their own food, and I've had many interesting conversations *with my fellow-boarders.*

One such pleasant vampire is Professor Friedrich Bhaer, whom I first saw taking a heavy hod of coal out of the hands of a human servant girl and saying, with a kind nod and a foreign accent, "It goes better so. The little back is too young to haf such heaviness."

Wasn't it good of him? I like such things, for as Father says, trifles show character, and so many vampires pay scant attention to humans, let alone ones who are maids and such.

Professor Bhaer is from Alba Iulia,[34] very learned and good, but poor as a church mouse, and gives lessons to humans to support himself. For some of his scholars, Mrs. K. lends him her parlor, which is separated from the nursery by a glass door, so while he arranged his books, I took a good look at him. He appears to be about forty years old but is almost six hundred in chronological years. A regular Transylvanian—rather stout, with brown hair tumbled all over his head, a bushy beard, good nose, the kindest eyes I ever saw, and a splendid big voice that does one's ears good, after our sharp or slipshod American gabble. His clothes were rusty, his hands were large, and he hadn't a really handsome feature in his face, except his beautiful fangs, yet I liked him, for he had a fine head, his linen was very nice, and he looked like a gentleman, though two buttons were off his coat and there

---

[34] Capital of Transylvania from 1541 to 1690.

*was a patch on one shoe. He looked sober in spite of his
humming, till he went to the window to turn the hyacinth
bulbs toward the moon.*

*Tina, the child of the Frenchwoman who does the fine
ironing in the laundry here, has lost her heart to Mr. Bhaer,
and follows him about the house like a dog whenever he is
at home, which delights him, as he is very fond of children,
though a "bacheldore." Kitty and Minnie Kirke likewise
regard him with affection, and tell all sorts of stories
about the plays he invents, the presents he brings, and the
splendid tales he tells. The younger vampire men quiz him,
it seems, call him Old Fritz, Lager Beer, Ursa Major, and
make all manner of jokes on his name. But he enjoys it like
a boy, Mrs. Kirke says, and takes it so good-naturedly that
they all like him in spite of his foreign ways.*

*I met him when he came into the parlor with some
newspapers for Mrs. Kirke. She wasn't there, but Minnie,
who is a little old woman, introduced me very prettily.*

"This is Mamma's friend, Miss March."

*"Yes, and she's jolly and we like her lots," added
Kitty, who is an "enfant terrible."*

*We both bowed, and then we laughed, for the prim
introduction and the blunt addition were rather a comical
contrast.*

*"Ah, yes, I hear these naughty ones go to vex you,
Mees Marsch. If so again, call at me and I come," he
said, with a threatening frown that delighted the little
wretches.*

I promised I would, and he departed, but it seems as if I was doomed to see a good deal of him, for the next day as I passed his door on my way out, by accident I knocked against it with my umbrella. It flew open, and there he stood in his dressing gown, with a big blue sock on one hand and a darning needle in the other. He didn't seem at all ashamed of it, for when I explained and hurried on, he waved his hand, sock and all, saying in his loud, cheerful way . . .

"You haf a fine night to make your valk. Bon voyage, Mademoiselle."

I laughed all the way downstairs, but it was a little pathetic, also to think of the poor man having to mend his own clothes. The Transylvanian gentlemen embroider, I know, but darning hose is another thing and not so pretty.

Although I don't have much time to spare, I was moved to offer my help, which he only accepted as an even exchange of services, so now I'm taking Transylvanian[35] *lessons. The Professor also teaches German, Romanian, and Hungarian but I chose Transylvanian because it is, as my tutor says, the hidden language of our ancestors. I'm somewhat reluctant about the endeavor, for as you know I have little skill when it comes to languages but the*

---

[35] Although mortal Transylvanians historically spoke either Romanian or Hungarian, vampires from the region had their own "secret" language by which they communicated during the Inquisition to confound spies and informers.

Professor is confident that I'll catch on quickly. I'm sure my first few lessons will go smoothly and then I will get stuck fast in a grammatical bog.

I've been so busy settling in, I haven't had much time to spend at Gentleman Jackson's New York affiliate, called the New Institute for Vampire-Slayer Hunting, but I have stopped by and introduced myself to the instructors, who are worldly and wise and somewhat rougher or harder than their Concord counterparts. No defender could be higher in my estimation than Gentleman Jackson, for he has been about this business for many centuries, even before our kind ceased to live in shadows, but the vampires here seem very experienced and knowing. I'm positive that, with their help, I'll learn a great many things.

I think that's enough information for one missive, for it's late now and I must go to my coffin if I am to get any rest at all this day. Please know that so far my big-city adventure is shaping up to be most happy and productive and yet I still miss you all dreadfully. I will promise not to get into any mischief if you will all promise to be well and not change. (That goes double for you, Bethy!) Send my love to Laurie, who I hope is happy and busy, that he has given up smoking and lets his hair grow. Read him bits of my letter. I haven't time to write much, and that will do just as well.

Bless you all! Ever your loving . . . Jo

Chapter Twenty-Three

FRIENDS

Though very happy in the social atmosphere about her, and very busy with the nightly work that earned her blood and made it sweeter for the effort, Jo was profoundly disappointed with her New York adventure, for she had made no progress in her objective to find Bang. She readily admitted to an initial hesitance, for being in a great, vast city and away from her family were two large changes that were entirely intimidating, and she wanted to first feel comfortable with them before bearding the lion in his den.

Perhaps she would have been a little braver had her first visit to the New York affiliate not been so unsettling, but she hadn't anticipated that the building would be so large and imposing. And yet the immense gray structure, smoked black with pollution and hemmed with bars, was a welcoming little cottage compared with its overseer, Mr. Dashwood, the smokiest gentleman in a room full of smokers. Carefully cherishing his cigar between his fingers, he advanced with a nod and a countenance expressive of nothing but sleep. Feeling that she must get through the matter somehow, Jo produced her letter of introduction and, growing more and more inarticulate with each sentence, blundered out fragments of the little speech carefully prepared for the occasion.

"A friend of mine desired me to come—some training—just a few weeks—would like your help—be glad to do more if it suits."

While she babbled and blundered, Mr. Dashwood had taken the letter, and was turning over the leaves with a pair of rather dirty fingers, and casting critical glances up and down the neat pages.

"Not a novice, I take it?" observing that Gentleman Jackson called her by her first name.

"No, sir. I've had some experience."

"Oh, have you?" and Mr. Dashwood gave Jo a quick look, which seemed to take note of everything she had on, from the bow in her bonnet to the buttons on her boots. "Well, you can fill out an application, if you like. We've more cadets than we know what to do with at present, but I'll run my eye over it, and give you an answer next week."

Now, Jo did not like to leave an application, for

applying for a program much like the one she'd already graduated from didn't suit her at all, but, under the circumstances, there was nothing for her to do but fill out a form and walk away, looking particularly tall and dignified, as she was apt to do when nettled or abashed. Just then she was both, for it was perfectly evident from the knowing glances exchanged among the gentlemen that a female aspiring to be a defender was considered a good joke, and a laugh, produced by some inaudible remark of the headmaster, as he closed the door, completed her discomfiture. Half resolving never to return, she went home, and worked off her irritation by stitching pinafores vigorously, and in an hour or two was cool enough to laugh over the scene and long for next week.

When she went again, Mr. Dashwood was alone, whereat she rejoiced. He was much wider awake than before, which was agreeable, and was not too deeply absorbed in a cigar to remember his manners, so the second interview was much more comfortable than the first.

"We'll take you, if you don't object to repeating a few classes," he said, in a businesslike tone.

"Thank you, sir. I appreciate the opportunity," she said, for repeating classes meant extra training, which translated into extra preparedness and to that she could have no objection. But her visit to New York, though interestingly educational in many ways, had a precise purpose from which she would not be swayed by other concerns. "I wonder, sir, if you've had any time to think about the matter Gentleman Jackson discussed in his letter."

"Eh?" asked Mr. Dashwood, frowning.

"Dr. Bang, sir. He's a pernicious slayer from up north who knows the formula for the chilly death. Perhaps you've heard of vampires dying, human-like, of a strange disease similar to scarlet fever?"

Mr. Dashwood shot up from his chair and called for his assistant, saying excitedly to her, "You know of this illness?"

"Yes, yes, my father and sister suffered from it."

"Good. Very good," he said, then immediately apologized for implying that it was good that her father and sister had suffered. "I meant only that it was good that you had information, for we've had one case and have been much puzzled by it."

The headmaster's assistant came into the room and took notes while Jo answered a dozen questions about the chilly death, explaining all she knew and detailing her pursuit of Dr. Bang. She could not recall the precise measurements for the antidote and strongly urged that he write immediately to Gentleman Jackson to discover the exact recipe.

When the interview was over, Mr. Dashwood stood again and offered his hand. "Thank you, ma'am, for coming in. With your help, we'll be able to stop this plague before it begins."

Jo assured them she was glad to help, then reiterated why she was there and requested his assistance in apprehending Dr. Bang at his Waverly Street residence.

The headmaster was surprised to hear that Miss March had such detailed information about their enemy and assured her they would take care of the matter right away. He pulled out his poison-dart gun, affixed it to his belt, and ordered his second in command to secure a warrant to provide them access to the establishment, for as vampires they could not enter without an invitation from the city. Then he called for his team to follow him to Waverly Place. He paused at the door for the address, which Jo, realizing now that she wasn't part of the squad even if she was a cadet, withheld, for it was her only bargaining chip and she refused to let them go without her.

Mr. Dashwood furrowed his brow and calmly explained the immodesty involved in a woman, a mere slip of a girl, really, pursuing such a dangerous course of action, but Jo, no mere slip of a girl, despite her girlishness, stood her ground and was soon issued a battle jacket[36] that the defenders in the city wore, a sort of

---

[36] Invented by Harken Hennings (b. 1803) in 1853 and very popular with defenders working in the modern urban crime environment. His first attempt at vampire armor, an iron neckerchief to protect one from decapitation, had to be recalled because sharp clasps of the garment inadvertently removed the wearer's head.

vest made of material impenetrable by wood.

Two hours later, Mr. Dashwood's team had swept the home, which was a four-story townhouse in an area known as Greenwich Village, and secured the perimeter, but the hideout had been recently deserted, for only a large family of rats remained to gorge on stale bread and cheese. The team questioned the neighbors using a potion that ensured that only the truth would be spoken, which Mr. Dashwood himself had invented. The interviews revealed Bang to be a secretive man who kept the blinds drawn and received visitors at all hours of the night and day.

"Other collaborators," Mr. Dashwood said. "Don't lose heart, Miss March, the trail is still hot. I will put a detail on this building in case he comes back and pursue all the clues left in the abandoned house."

Jo didn't lose heart, for she knew what he said was true, that the house was a treasure trove of leads to follow up on, and while the members of the New Institute for Vampire-Slayer Hunting searched for answers using all the resources at their disposal, she searched using all the resources at hers.

Eager to find material, any material at all, that might be relevant, she searched newspapers for reports of accidents, incidents, and crimes that might be linked to Dr. Bang. She excited the suspicions of public librarians by asking for works on poisons, seeking additional information about the chilly death. She studied faces in the street, and characters, good, bad, and indifferent, all about her, hoping that a greater understanding of humanity might give her insight into Bang's mind. She delved in the dust of ancient times to learn about tricks and ploys so old that they were as good as new, and introduced herself to folly, sin, and misery, as well as her limited opportunities allowed, by going to bars and taverns where Bang and his gang might frequent. She accompanied Mr. Dashwood and his team on raids of suspected headquarters and hideouts and received as compensation a nice stipend that she put toward taking Beth to the mountains next summer. She descended into the depths of the New Institute laboratory, where Dashwood's people ran tests on the slayers they'd captured. She thought she was prospering finely and acquiring new skills, but unconsciously she was beginning to desecrate some of the womanliest attributes of a woman's character. She was living in bad society, and though in the pursuit of good, its influence affected her terribly, for she was feeding heart and fancy on dangerous and insubstantial food, and was fast brushing the innocent bloom from her nature by a premature acquaintance with the darker side of life, which comes soon enough to all of us.

Jo told nobody in the house why she was so busy. If anyone in the boardinghouse noticed her distraction or that she seemed to always be on the go, always on the point of arriving somewhere or leaving somewhere else, he or she didn't say. She didn't share her occupation with Professor Bhaer because previous conversation with him led her to believe he would not approve. The Professor was a traditional gentleman vampire from Transylvania, centuries old and committed to the ancient ways, and she could tell from the disgust in his voice when he spoke of truth potions and poisoned darts that he didn't have much respect for vampires like Gentleman Jackson with their scientifical methods and their newfangled inventions.

After a month of acquaintance, Jo longed to confess her secret to the Professor, for she found him to be as attractive as a genial fire and as happy-hearted as a boy. The pleasant curves about his mouth were the memorials of many friendly words and cheery laughs, his eyes were never cold or hard, and his big hand had a warm, strong grasp that was more expressive than words. She had great respect for his intellect, for she knew that in his native city he had been a vampire much honored and esteemed for learning and integrity.

She had a chance to witness his impressive intelligence and integrity one night when, in the course of an evening at a philosophical symposium, she heard him defend religion with all the eloquence of truth against those who would reason it into nothingness and replace God with intellect. She began to see that character is a better possession than money, rank, intellect, or beauty, and to feel that if greatness is what a wise vampire has defined it to be, "truth, reverence, and good will,"[37] then her friend Friedrich Bhaer was not only good, but great.

She valued his esteem, she coveted his respect, she wanted to be worthy of his friendship, and just when the wish was sincerest, she came near to losing everything. It all grew out of a cocked hat, for one evening the Professor came in to give Jo her lesson with a paper soldier cap on his head, which Tina had put there and he had forgotten to take off.

Jo said nothing at first, for she liked to hear him laugh out his big, hearty laugh when anything funny happened, so she left him to discover it for himself, and presently forgot all about it, for to hear a Transylvanian read Sălaj[38] is rather an absorbing occupation. After the reading came the lesson, which was a lively one, for Jo was in a gay mood that night, and the cocked hat kept her eyes dancing with merriment. The Professor didn't know what to make of her, and stopped at last to ask with an air of mild surprise that was irresistible . . .

---

[37] Quotation from American vampire-philosopher Emerson Walter (1703–2002), who led the New Hunger movement of the mid-1800s, which introduced the notion, radical in its time, that a vampire must be more than his appetite. The quote is from his essay "On the Spiritual Disadvantages of the Fully Tummy and the Empty Soul."

[38] Szekler Sălaj (1143–1577), vampire-poet whose epic trilogy about the Dacian Wars is the only known poem to exist in the Transylvanian language.

"Mees Marsch, for what do you laugh in your master's face? Haf you no respect for me, that you go on so bad?"

"How can I be respectful, Sir, when you forget to take your hat off?" said Jo.

Lifting his hand to his head, the absentminded Professor gravely felt and removed the little cocked hat, looked at it a minute, and then threw back his head and laughed like a merry bass viol.

"Ah! I see him now, it is that imp Tina who makes me a fool with my cap. Vell, it is nothing, but see you, if this lesson goes not vell, you, too, shall vear him."

But the lesson did not go at all for a few minutes because Mr. Bhaer caught sight of a picture on the hat, and unfolding it, said with great disgust, "I vish these papers did not come in the house. They are not for children to see, nor young people to read. It is not vell, and I haf no patience with those who make this harm."

Jo glanced at the sheet and saw a pleasing illustration composed of a lunatic, a corpse, a vampire, and a viper. She did not like it, but the impulse that made her turn it over was not one of displeasure but fear. For a minute she fancied the article that accompanied the picture, which was the image the New Institute used to represent itself, might mention her, for the press often reported on, and sensationalized, the frequent raids into the lairs of suspected slayers carried out by the Dashwood Dozen, as journalists liked to call the band of devoted defenders. It did not, however, and her panic subsided as she remembered that there was nothing to connect her. She had betrayed herself, however, by a look, for though an absent vampire, the Professor saw a good deal more than people fancied. He knew that Jo was in town to accomplish a very important task, and had met her down among the streets in the unsavory part of town more than once, but as she never spoke of it, he asked no questions in spite of a strong desire to know more about her work. Now it occurred to him that she was doing what she was ashamed to own, and it troubled him. He did not say to himself, "It is none of my business. I've no right to say anything," as many people would have done. He only remembered that she was young and poor, a girl far away from mother's love and father's care, and he was moved to help her with an impulse as quick and natural as that which would prompt him to put out his hand to save a baby from a puddle. All this flashed through his mind in a minute, but not a trace of it appeared in his face, and by the time the paper was turned, and Jo's needle threaded, he was ready to say quite naturally, but very gravely . . .

"Yes, you are right to put it from you. I do not think that good young girls should see such stories, which turn these Dashwooders into heroes. You should be protected from such sordid filth."

"All may not be bad, you know. Groups like the Dashwood Dozen serve a purpose. Someone must rid society of slayers or we are all at risk," said Jo, scratching gathers so energetically that a row of little slits followed her pin.

"Visky sellers satisfy a need for liquid, but I think you and I know that's not the vay to quench a thirst. Slayers must be captured, yes, but not using these scientifical methods which erode our natural abilities. A vampire who relies on a serum of truth loses the ability to glamour and control minds. Ve are not meant to vear masks to filter out garlic. Ve haf the natural ability, but vhy learn and study if you can buy an instrument at the store? The old vays are dying and vith it our identity. The new ones see these stories about the Dashwooders and their ilk and think this is vhat it means to be vampire. They don't learn to develop their powers. Ve are holy creatures. Humans are damned. If ve continue to become more like humans, ve vill be damned, too."

Mr. Bhaer spoke warmly, and walked to the fire, crumpling the paper in his hands. Jo sat still, looking as if the fire had come to her, for her mortification remained long after the cocked hat had turned to smoke and gone harmlessly up the chimney.

Jo had never encountered a vampire who felt as he did, for the reliance on potions, instruments, and scientifical investigation was hailed by many, if not all, of her acquaintances as a breakthrough in slayer hunting. Employing the very tools on slayers that slayers used on them was seen as a way of leveling the playing field. The old method of relying on instinct and honing natural abilities had been deemed a failure by Bloody Wobblestone, and she had believed it. But now she had to reconsider her beliefs, for she respected the Professor's intellect far too much to dismiss his words. They stayed with her during her lesson and, after another unsuccessful raid on Bang's supposed hideout, she asked the Professor to elaborate on his philosophy so that she herself might come to share it.

He did not look surprised by her request, which proved to her that he knew everything, even though she had spoken none of it. "Ve are vampires," he said, echoing his words from the earlier evening but with a new emphasis and pride. "Ve can do many things which these humans cannot and that is how ve catch our enemies. Not by the vials and potions. Dashwood and his dozen vant glory, not justice." He launched then into such a fantastic account of the ways vampires had evolved through millennia to survive among humans, charmorization[39] and transmogrification among them, that Jo felt as though she was listening to a tale from one of Madame de La Fayette's books.

"Can you really change into a bat?" she asked excitedly.

---

[39] A type of glamour spell that permanently "charms" its victim into believing something contrary to fact. A standard glamour spell lasts only as long as its creator stares into the eyes of his victim.

"Yes, yes, of course," he said solemnly.

"Can you do it here? Right now?" Her enthusiasm was such that she charged forward with her request, never once considering the propriety of it, and it was only when he looked slightly abashed that she realized it might seem to him as if she considered the great wonder a mere parlor trick. "I didn't mean . . . I'm sorry . . . " she stuttered.

The kindly gentleman smiled, revealing those beautiful fangs, shook his head gently, and disappeared into thin air, reappearing a moment later as a furry, winged creature a few inches above her head. And it looked as if to be grinning at her!

Proper or not, Jo clapped her hands, for it seemed like the most glorious thing she'd ever seen. "How marvelous," she shouted, for she knew nothing of a bat's ability to hear and its ears were so small.

A second later, Mr. Bhaer was back before her, somber black suit and all. "This is how ve are to track our enemies, not on the back of a stupid horse or, vorse, being pulled by one. Ve have spent so many years living openly among humans that ve think ve are human. Before, vhen ve had to hide, ve knew vhat ve vere."

He spoke so gravely, Jo felt silly to be excited, and she turned down the full boil of her enthusiasm to a soft simmer so that she could listen and learn as much as she could.

The Professor was an eager instructor, grateful for

a pupil who sincerely understood and appreciated the old ways. As Bhaer shared his knowledge, she shared the true purpose of her visit and confessed everything about her association with the Dashwood Dozen, Gentleman Jackson, and Mr. Wobblestone. Her kind friend could find no real fault with her behavior, for Jo was still young yet and had not the breadth of experience that a man of his centuries might. No one among her acquaintance esteemed the old ways as he did, but none, he suspected, had been around long enough to know them well.

"Don't vorry," he said, patting her soft hand. "Ve vill capture this villain who did such harm to your sister."

Jo believed him, and in the days and weeks that followed, she saw how his old-fashioned way of tracking slayers was vastly superior to the so-called modern scientific method. Mr. Bhaer had no need for potions, for he could charm humans into telling him the truth and many whom he questioned about Bang simply volunteered the information he required. Likewise, he could hear, see, and smell things happening a great distance farther away than Jo had ever imagined. Garlic was no deterrent to him, for he could filter out specific layers of smell, among them allium, to identify the particular odor he was in search of.

His abilities held Jo in awe, for it seemed to her that he could do anything, but when she would lie quietly in her coffin on the edge of sleep at day, she would admit that his abilities didn't amaze her at all. These talents were no greater or lesser than his other vast talents such as kindness and intellect and good humor. She paid attention, studied hard, and made fair progress in the acquisition of skills, none of which she mastered but all of which she aspired to, and at sunrise on the day she was to leave, for every piece of evidence indicated Bang had departed New York for parts north, she tried one last time to turn herself into a bat, following his instructions carefully to close out her surroundings and see nothing but star-dappled velvet sky.

The result was its own sensation, for the very head that imagined the dark blue night changed into a bat but the rest of her remained bipedal and earthbound.

"Half bat, half girl, wholly adorable," Mr. Bhaer said, with his big hearty laugh. But his mood soon turned serious, for he sat silently pulling his beard a long while. His hair stuck straight up all over his head, for he always rumpled it wildly when disturbed in mind.

She was going early, so she bade him good-bye before he went to sleep, saying warmly, "Now, Sir, you won't forget to come and see us, if you ever travel our way, will you? I'll never forgive you if you do, for I want them all to know my friend."

"Do you? Shall I come?" he asked, looking down at her with an eager expression which she did not see.

"Yes, come next month. Laurie graduates then, and

you'd enjoy commencement as something new."

"That is your best friend, of whom you speak?" he said in an altered tone.

"Yes, my human boy Teddy. I'm very proud of him and should like you to see him."

Jo looked up then, quite unconscious of anything but her own pleasure in the prospect of showing them to one another. Something in Mr. Bhaer's face suddenly recalled the fact that she might find Laurie more than a "best friend," and simply because she particularly wished not to look as if anything was the matter, she began to become awkward, and the more she tried to relax, the more uncomfortable she grew. Fortunately Mrs. Kirke called out to her from the stairs above, so she managed to distract herself for an instant, hoping the Professor did not notice. But he did, and his face changed again from that momentary anxiety to its usual expression, as he said cordially . . .

"I fear I shall not make the time for that, but I vish the friend much success, and you all happiness. God bless you!" And with that, he shook hands warmly and went away.

But after everyone went to sleep, he sat long before his fire with the tired look on his face and the "heimweh," or homesickness, lying heavy at his heart. Once, when he remembered Jo as she sat with the little child in her lap and that new softness in her face, he leaned his head on his hands a minute, and then roamed about the room, as if in search of something that he could not find.

"It is not for me, I must not hope it now," he said to himself, with a sigh that was almost a groan. Then, as if reproaching himself for the longing that he could not repress, he went and kissed Tina's tousled head as she played in the parlor, took down his seldom-used meerschaum, and opened his Plato.

He did his best and did it manfully, but I don't think he found that a rampant girl, a pipe, or even the divine Plato, were very satisfactory substitutes for wife and child at home.

Early as it was, he was at the station that twilight to see Jo off, and thanks to him, she began her solitary journey with the pleasant memory of a familiar face smiling its farewell, a bunch of violets to keep her company, and best of all, the happy thought, "Well, my sojourn's over, and I haven't captured Bang, but I've made a friend worth having and I'll try to keep him all my life."

Chapter Twenty-Four

HEARTACHE

Whatever his motive might have been, Laurie studied to some purpose that year, for he graduated with honor, and gave the Latin oration with the grace of a Phillips[40] and the eloquence of a Demosthenes,[41] so his friends said. None of the Marches could attend the ceremony, since it occurred during the bright of the day on a swath of exposed grass in the middle of a commons, but he repeated his speech for them later that evening in

---

[40] Wendell Phillips (1811–1884), famous orator from Boston who, though involved in abolitionism, had no discernable ties to the vampire-rights movement, making his reference here confusing.

[41] Another famous orator (384–322 B.C.), from Athens, without any connection to vampires. It has been suggested that these two references are an attempt by the author to establish a vampire-free space for Laurie on such an important day.

the front garden. They were all there, his grandfather—oh, so proud—Mr. and Mrs. March, John and Meg and Jo and Beth, and all exulted over him with the sincere admiration which boys make light of at the time, but fail to win from the world by any after-triumphs.

They had supper in his honor, a grand feast of roasted duck and seared lobster and crispy salmon in vegetable broth piled so high that the table dipped from the weight. It was far too much for one person to eat, let alone a giddy young graduate who had so many things he wanted to talk about. But he did his best out of consideration for the others and tried to eat everything they passed, despite his full belly. In the end, he could finish only a quarter of the generous repast, and enough leftovers remained to feed half of Concord. His friends, he realized wryly, had been vampires for so long, they were completely incapable of gauging a human boy's appetite.

"You'll come and meet me later, Jo?" Laurie asked, as the family left together at the end of the evening.

"I'll come, Teddy, rain or shine, and march before you, playing 'Hail the conquering hero comes' on a Jew's harp."

Laurie thanked her with a look that made her think in a sudden panic, "Oh, deary me! I know he'll say something, and then what shall I do?"

Morning meditation and evening work somewhat allayed her fears, and having decided that she wouldn't be vain enough to think people were going to propose when she had given them every reason to know what her answer would be, she set forth at the appointed time, hoping Teddy wouldn't do anything to make her hurt his poor feelings. A call at Meg's still further fortified her for the tête-à-tête, but when she saw a stalwart figure looming in the distance, she had a strong desire to turn about and run away.

"Where's the jew's-harp, Jo?" cried Laurie, as soon as he was within speaking distance.

"I forgot it." And Jo took heart again, for that salutation could not be called lover-like.

She always used to take his arm on these occasions, now she did not, and he made no complaint, which was a bad sign, but talked on rapidly about all sorts of faraway subjects, till they turned from the road into the little path that led homeward through the grove. Then he walked more slowly, suddenly lost his fine flow of language, and now and then a dreadful pause occurred. To rescue the conversation from one of the wells of silence into which it kept falling, Jo said hastily, "Now you must have a good long holiday!"

"I intend to."

Something in his resolute tone made Jo look up quickly to find him looking down at her with an expression that assured her the dreaded moment had come, and made her put out her hand with an imploring, "No, Teddy. Please don't!"

"I will, and you must hear me. It's no use, Jo, we've got to have it out, and the sooner the better for both of us," he answered, getting flushed and excited all at once.

"Say what you like then. I'll listen," said Jo, with a desperate sort of patience.

Laurie was a young lover, but he was in earnest, and meant to "have it out," if he died in the attempt, so he plunged into the subject with characteristic impetuosity, saying in a voice that would get choky now and then, in spite of manful efforts to keep it steady . . .

"I've loved you ever since I've known you, Jo, couldn't help it, you've been so good to me. I've tried to show it, but you wouldn't let me. Now I'm going to make you hear, and give me an answer, for I can't go on so any longer."

"I wanted to save you this. I thought you'd understand . . . " began Jo, finding it a great deal harder than she expected.

"I know you did, but girls are so queer you never know what they mean. They say no when they mean yes, and drive a man out of his wits just for the fun of it," returned Laurie, entrenching himself behind an undeniable fact.

"I don't. I never wanted to make you care for me so."

"I worked hard to please you, and I gave up everything you didn't like, and waited and never complained when Beth turned my grandfather and Meg turned John, for I hoped you'd love me and change me, though being human I know I'm not half good enough . . . " Here there was a choke that couldn't be controlled, so he decapitated buttercups while he cleared his "confounded throat."

"You, you are, you're a great deal too good for me. I love your humanity, it makes you so wonderful and special and I can't for a moment contemplate the thought of taking it away. I don't know why it feels so wrong but it does and I can't change the feeling."

"Really, truly, Jo?"

He stopped short, and caught both her hands as he put his question with a look that she did not soon forget.

"Really, truly, dear."

They were in the grove now, close by the stile, and when the last words fell reluctantly from Jo's lips, Laurie dropped her hands and turned as if to go on, but for once in his life the fence was too much for him. So he just laid his head down on the mossy post, and stood so still that Jo was frightened.

"Oh, Teddy, I'm sorry, so desperately sorry, I could stake myself. I wish you wouldn't take it so hard, I can't help it. You know it's impossible for a vampire to transform someone who they don't want to transform," cried Jo inelegantly but remorsefully, as she softly patted his shoulder, remembering the time when he had comforted her so long ago.

"They do sometimes," said a muffled voice from the post.

"I don't believe it's the right sort of transformation,

and I'd rather not try it," was the decided answer.

"You'll get over this after a while, and find some lovely accomplished human girl, who will adore you, and make a fine mistress for your fine house. I shouldn't. I'm homely and awkward and odd and old, and you'd be ashamed of me, and we should quarrel—we can't help it even now, you see—and I shouldn't like elegant society and you would, and you'd hate my slayer hunting, and I couldn't get on without it, and you'd resent me for changing you because you couldn't go in the sun anymore and you'd miss the warmth of it on your face, I know you would because after all these years, I still miss it, we should be unhappy, and wish we hadn't done it, and everything would be horrid."

"I'll tell you what's horrible, being the only human among your own acquaintance. To have to eat long boring meals by yourself and go to sleep when everyone's having fun and be weaker than your elderly grandfather, who can pick you up bodily and toss you across the conservatory as if you were lighter than a feather. It's not fair!" with a stamp to emphasize his passionate words.

"I know it seems bad now but you'll see that I'm right, by-and-by, and thank me for it . . . " she began solemnly.

"I'll be hanged if I do!" and Laurie bounced up off the grass, burning with indignation at the very idea.

"Yes, you will!" persisted Jo. "And I don't believe I shall ever turn anyone. I'm happy as I am, and love my liberty too well to be in a hurry to give it up for any mortal man."

"I know better!" broke in Laurie. "You think so now, but there'll come a time when you will care for somebody, and you'll love him tremendously, and live and die for him and you won't be able to stand that he's not eternal like you. I know you will, it's your way, and I shall have to stand by and see it," and the despairing lover cast his hat upon the ground with a gesture that would have seemed comical, if his face had not been so tragic.

"You're wrong. I won't ever make someone a vampire. No human will ever make me love him in spite of myself," cried Jo, losing patience with poor Teddy. "I've done my best, but you won't be reasonable, and it's selfish of you to keep teasing for what I can't do. I shall always be fond of you, very fond indeed, as a friend, but I'll never turn you, and the sooner you believe it the better for both of us—so now!"

That speech was like gunpowder. Laurie looked at her a minute as if he did not quite know what to do with himself, then turned sharply away, saying in a desperate sort of tone, "You'll be sorry some day, Jo."

"Oh, where are you going?" she cried, for his face frightened her.

"To the devil!" was the consoling answer.

For a minute Jo's heart stood still, as he swung himself down the bank toward the river, but it takes much folly, sin, or misery to send a young man to a violent death, and Laurie was not one of the weak sort who are conquered by a single failure. He had no thought of a melodramatic plunge, but some blind instinct led him to fling hat and coat into his boat, and row away with all his might, making better time up the river than he had done in any race. Jo unclasped her hands as she watched the poor fellow trying to outstrip the trouble which he carried in his heart.

He didn't manage to outstrip it but after consultation with his grandfather, who had business in London that needed attending to by a human, he took it with him to Europe.

Being an energetic immortal, Mr. Laurence arranged all the details within a week, and before the blighted being recovered spirit enough to rebel, they were off. During the time necessary for preparation, Laurie bore himself as young gentlemen usually do in such cases. He was moody, irritable, and pensive by turns, lost his appetite, neglected his dress and devoted much time to playing tempestuously on his piano, avoided Jo, but consoled himself by staring at her from his window, with a tragic face that haunted her dreams by day and oppressed her with a heavy sense of guilt by night. Unlike some sufferers, he never spoke of his unrequited passion, and would allow no one, not even Mrs. March, to attempt consolation or offer sympathy. On some accounts, this was a relief to his friends, but the nights before his departure were very uncomfortable, and everyone rejoiced that the "poor, dear fellow was going away to forget his trouble, and come home happy." Of course, he smiled darkly at their delusion, but passed it by with the sad superiority of one who knew that his fidelity like his love and desire to be vampire was unalterable.

When the parting came he affected high spirits, to conceal certain inconvenient emotions which seemed inclined to assert themselves. This gaiety did not impose upon anybody, but they tried to look as if it did for his sake, and he got on very well till Mrs. March kissed him, with a whisper full of motherly solicitude. Then feeling that he was going very fast, he hastily embraced them all round, not forgetting the afflicted Hannah, and ran downstairs as if for his life. Jo followed a minute after to wave her hand to him if he looked round. He did look round, came back, put his arms about her as she stood on the step above him, and looked up at her with a face that made his short appeal eloquent and pathetic.

"Oh, Jo, can't you?"

"Teddy, dear, I wish I could!"

That was all, except a little pause. Then Laurie straightened himself up, said, "It's all right, never mind," and went away without another word. Ah, but it wasn't all right, and Jo did mind, for while the curly head lay on her arm a minute after her hard answer, she felt as if she had stabbed her dearest friend, and when he left her without a look behind him, she knew that the human boy Laurie never would come again.

Chapter Twenty-Five

BETH'S SECRET

When Jo came home from her stay in New York, she had been struck with the change in Beth. No one spoke of it or seemed aware of it, for it had come too gradually to startle those who saw her daily, but to eyes sharpened by absence, it was very plain and a heavy weight fell on Jo's heart as she saw her sister's face. It was no brighter and but little thinner than when she left, yet there was a strange, transparent look about it, as if the immortal had been refined away, and the divine was shining through the frail flesh with an indescribably pathetic beauty. Jo saw and felt it, but said nothing until Laurie was gone, then proposed a mountain trip; Beth thanked her heartily, but begged not to go so far away from home. Another little visit to the seashore would suit her better, so Jo took Beth down to the quiet place, where she could live much in the open air, and let the fresh sea breezes blow a little color out of her rosy cheeks.

It was not a fashionable place, but even among the pleasant people there, the girls made few friends, preferring to live for one another. Beth was too shy to enjoy society, and Jo too wrapped up in her to care for anyone else. So they were all in all to each other, and came and went, quite unconscious of the interest they excited in those about them, who watched with sympathetic eyes the strong sister and the feeble one, always together, as if they felt instinctively that a long separation was not far away.

Jo did feel it, yet didn't speak of it, for she couldn't understand the situation well enough to explain it; her sister seemed to be dying, and dying profoundly, of nothing in particular, as if life itself were killing her. It made no sense and defied the laws of nature, for vampires didn't die except through violent means, but as much as she wanted to blame Dr. Bang and his associates, she knew this was no chilly death. Beth remained lucid, conscious, and calm, nothing ached, yet she was slowly drifting away from her.

"Jo, dear, I'm glad you know it. I've tried to tell you, but I couldn't," Beth said, looking at her so tenderly that there was hardly any need for her to say anything. "I've known it for a good while, dear, and now I'm used to it, it isn't hard to think of or to bear. Try to see it so and don't be troubled about me, because it's best, indeed it is."

"Is this what made you so unhappy before I left for New York, Beth? You did not feel it then, and keep it to yourself so long, did you?" asked Jo, refusing to see or say that it was best, and surprised to discover that anxiety about Dr. Bang had no part in Beth's trouble.

"Yes, I gave up hoping then, but I didn't like to own it. I tried to think it was a sick fancy, and would not let it trouble anyone, for it is still incomprehensible to me even now how it could be happening. But when I saw you all so well and strong and full of happy plans, it was hard to feel that I could never be like you, and then I was miserable, Jo."

"Oh, Beth, and you didn't tell me, didn't let me help you? How could you shut me out, bear it all alone?"

Jo's voice was full of tender reproach, and her heart ached to think of the solitary struggle that must have gone on while Beth learned to say good-bye to health, love, and life, and take up her cross so cheerfully.

"Perhaps it was wrong, but I tried to do right. I wasn't sure, no one said anything, and I hoped I was mistaken. It would have been selfish to frighten you all when Marmee was so anxious about Meg, and Amy away, and you so happy with Laurie—at least I thought so then."

"I can't do without you, Beth. You must get well!"

"I want to, oh, so much! I try, but every day I lose a

little, and feel more sure that I shall never gain it back. It's like the tide, Jo, when it turns, it goes slowly, but it can't be stopped."

"It shall be stopped. Something dreadful is causing this. Vampires don't die from some vague, unnamed wasting disease. It's not possible. There's an explanation for what's happening, another dread potion, and we must find it. I'll work and pray and fight against it. I'll keep you in spite of everything. There must be ways, it can't be too late. God won't be so cruel as to take you from me," cried poor Jo rebelliously, for her spirit was far less piously submissive than Beth's.

Simple, sincere people seldom speak much of their piety. It shows itself in acts rather than in words, and has more influence than homilies or protestations. Beth could not reason upon or explain the faith that gave her courage and patience to give up life, and cheerfully wait for death. Like a confiding child, she asked no questions, but left everything to God and nature, Father and Mother of us all, feeling sure that they, and they only, could teach and strengthen heart and spirit for this life and the life to come.

By and by Beth said serenely, "You'll tell them this when we go home?"

"I think they will see it without words," sighed Jo, for now it seemed to her that Beth changed every day.

"Perhaps not. I've heard that the people who love best are often blindest to such things. If they don't see it, you will tell them for me. I don't want any secrets, and it's kinder to prepare them. Meg has John to comfort her, but you must stand by Father and Mother, won't you, Jo?"

"If I can. But, Beth, I don't give up yet. I'm going to find what's causing this and save you," said Jo.

Beth lay a minute thinking, and then said in her quiet way, "I have a feeling that it never was intended I should live long. I'm not like the rest of you. I was never supposed to be made immortal. I never made any plans about what I'd do when I grew up. I never thought of being married, as you all did. I couldn't seem to imagine myself anything but stupid little Beth, trotting about at home, of no use anywhere but there. I never wanted to go away, and the hard part now is the leaving you all. I'm not afraid, but it seems as if I should be homesick for you even in heaven."

Jo could not speak, and for several minutes there was no sound but the sigh of the wind and the lapping of the tide. A white-winged gull flew by, with the flash of moonlight on its silvery breast. Beth watched it till it vanished, and her eyes were full of sadness. A little gray-coated sand bird came tripping over the beach "peeping" softly to itself, as if enjoying the moon and sea. It came quite close to Beth, and looked at her with a friendly eye and sat upon a warm stone, dressing its wet feathers, quite at home. Beth smiled and felt comforted, for the tiny thing seemed to offer its small friendship and remind her that a pleasant world was still to be enjoyed.

"Dear little bird! See, Jo, how tame it is. I like peeps better than the gulls. They are not so wild and handsome, but they seem happy, confiding little things. I used to call them my birds last summer, and Mother said they reminded her of me—busy, Quaker-colored creatures, always near the shore, and always chirping that contented little song of theirs. You are the gull, Jo, strong and wild, fond of the storm and the wind, flying far out to sea, and happy all alone. Meg is the turtledove, and Amy is like the lark she writes about, trying to get up among the clouds, but always dropping down into its nest again. Dear little girl! She's so ambitious, but her heart is good and tender, and no matter how high she flies, she never will forget home. I hope I shall see her again, but she seems so far away."

"She is coming in the spring, and I mean that you shall be all ready to see and enjoy her. I'm going to have you well by that time," began Jo, feeling that the talking change was a wonderful sign, for it seemed to cost no effort now. Perhaps the ease with which she spoke indicated the start of a recovery, for the sea air, bracing and brisk, had reinvigorated her before.

"Jo, dear, don't hope anymore. It won't do any good. I'm sure of that. We won't be miserable, but enjoy being together while we wait. We'll have happy times, for I don't suffer much, and I think the tide will go out easily, if you help me."

Jo leaned down to kiss the tranquil face, and with that silent kiss, she dedicated herself soul and body to saving Beth.

She was right. There was no need of any words when they got home, for Father and Mother saw plainly now what they had prayed to be saved from seeing. Tired with her short journey, Beth went at once to her coffin, saying how glad she was to be home, and when Jo went down, she found that she would be spared the hard task of telling Beth's secret. Her father stood leaning his head on the mantelpiece and did not turn as she came in, but her mother stretched out her arms as if for help, and Jo went to comfort her without a word.

Chapter Twenty-Six

THE VALLEY OF
THE SHADOW

When the first bitterness was over, the family accepted the inevitable, and tried to bear it cheerfully, helping one another by the increased affection which comes to bind households tenderly together in times of trouble. They put away their grief, and each did his or her part toward making the time she had left happy.

The pleasantest room in the house was set apart for Beth, and in it was gathered everything that she most loved, flowers, pictures, her piano, the little worktable, and the beloved dolls. Father's best books found their way there, Mother's easy chair, Jo's desk, Amy's finest sketches. Every day Meg entertained her with tales of domesticity, and John quietly set apart a little sum, that he might enjoy the pleasure of keeping the invalid supplied with the kittens she loved and longed for. Old Hannah never wearied of fussing around her, straightening the coffin sheets and fluffing her pillow.

Oh, yes, everyone graciously acknowledged the truth except Jo, who ranted and railed nightly against the morbidity of treating a living girl like she was a household saint in its shrine. This was the true sick fancy, she thought, as there sat Beth, tranquil and busy as ever, for nothing could change the sweet, unselfish nature, and even while preparing to leave life, she tried to make it happier for those who should remain behind.

As much as she wanted to spend every waking minute with her sister, Jo could not stand by and watch her family blithely welcome death into their home. Beth's illness was an anomaly, an impossibility, a glitch in the normal function of demonry, and Jo knew it had to be caused by some logical event. Brooke swore he knew of no potion or formula that could create a wasting disease such as this in any vampire, but she felt in her soul that his former associate Dr. Bang was responsible for the strange illness and would not rest until she proved it.

Although she no longer believed so stridently in the scientifical method, Jo consulted with Gentleman Jackson, for she would leave no stone unturned in her hunt and he had many masons at his disposal. By day she haunted the salon's library and by night she haunted the countryside, napping only briefly and finally achieving full transmogrification when she was tired enough to empty her mind of everything save the star-dappled velvet sky. As a bat, she covered many miles, making her way clear to Boston but discovering nothing of interest there or anywhere in the nearest hundred miles.

And then one night she figured it out. Beth bit into a beloved kitten, her feeble fangs draining it as the creature softly mewed, but she was far too tired to have more than half and insisted Jo finish it.

As the cost of kittens was dear, the consuming of them remained Beth's special province and she dined on them almost exclusively now, for everyone wanted her to be as happy as possible. But Jo welcomed the leftover, a sweet delicacy and a genuine treat. As soon as she finished it, she felt overcome with exhaustion, as if the hours she'd been keeping to find Beth's killer had caught up to her all at once, and she left her sister's side to seek her own coffin. She slept long and hard that day, waking up several hours past sunset with a strange feeling of desolation, for it hardly seemed worth rising from her casket if it meant watching her sister's frail body sink inexorably into nothingness. It was far better to stay there, wrapped in oblivion, far away from a battle that was already lost, even if the little soldier had yet to leave the field.

She woke many hours later, still lethargic but determined to shake off the fatigue that clung to her like a frightened child, for the weariness shamed her. Her nights of late had been a frenetic mix of traveling, studying, and nursing but she happily did it all for her dear sister and wouldn't complain about it for a moment. Her constitution, like all vampires, was robust and strong and capable of withstanding a great deal of abuse, so much so that it seemed to her now that the tiredness had an out-of-body feel to it, as if a large, heavy weight had been pressing down on her chest. The feeling of hopelessness about Beth was also strange, for in that moment she had given up entirely on her sister, and that was something she would never in her right mind do.

With that thought, she threw off the last vestige of sleep and, clearheaded once more, realized that she *hadn't* been in her right mind. Something had affected her and changed her behavior. She recalled the strange period of exhaustion and despair and tried to remember what preceded it, a deep sleep, certainly, but a symptom, not the cause, and before that the kitten.

The kitten!

Jo bounded out of her coffin, the conspiracy so clear to her now that she couldn't believe she hadn't seen it sooner, for it was written plainly on every paw of the indulgence Beth loved. Her brief recovery at the seaside and her seeming improvement during this most recent trip affirmed her dark suspicion that her sister was consuming poisoned kittens. How? she thought, scrambling down the hall, her legs blurring with speed, as she tried to imagine the science that made such a hideous thing possible, and hideous indeed it was, for it had attacked Beth on two fronts, one physical, the other metaphysical. Now her sick fancy that she was always meant to die made perfect sense, for Jo herself had felt the same despair after only a small taste. Poor Beth had been consuming her darling kittens for months.

She recalled the many times she found Beth reading in her well-worn little book, heard her singing softly, to beguile the sleepless day, or saw her lean her face upon her hands, while sobs wracked her frail body, and Jo would watch her with grief as deep as the sea, feeling that Beth, in her simple, unselfish way, was trying to wean herself from the dear old life, and fit herself for the life to come, by sacred words of comfort, quiet prayers, and the music she loved so well.

Seeing this had done more to anger Jo than any action of Bang's, for Beth gave death the upper hand with this attitude of surrender, although consistent with the uneventful, unambitious beauty of her life, full of the genuine virtues which "smell sweet, and blossom in the dust," the self-forgetfulness that makes the humblest on earth remembered soonest in heaven.

But now she understood that it wasn't frail, meek Beth who had handed over the keys to her soul but an evil potion that had made her abandon all hope.

In her room, Jo rushed to Beth's coffin, expecting to find her asleep.

"Not asleep, but so happy, dear. I've been much to you, haven't I, Jo?" she asked, with wistful, humble earnestness.

"Oh, Beth, so much, so much!" and Jo's head went down upon the pillow beside her sister's.

"Then I don't feel as if I'd wasted my life. I'm not so good as you think me, but I have tried to do right. And now, when it's too late to begin even to do better, it's such a comfort to know that someone loves me so much, and feels as if I'd helped them."

"It's not too late, dear. It's not. I've learned that I won't lose you, that you'll be more to me than ever, and death can't part us, though it seems to. It's just poison making us think that. Hold on a little longer and you will be healthy and strong."

"I know death cannot, and I don't fear it any longer, for I'm sure I shall be your Beth still, to love and help you more than ever. You must take my place, Jo, and be everything to Father and Mother when I'm gone. They will turn to you, don't fail them, and if it's hard to work alone, remember that I don't forget you, and that you'll be happier in doing that than hunting slayers or seeing all the world, for love is the only thing that we can carry with us when we go, and it makes the end so easy."

"You don't have to go, Beth. You're being poisoned

but that's over now. You're going to get better, I swear it," cried Jo.

But indeed it was too late, for the potion that had wrought so much misery, wrought one more and ended the dear girl's life. As Beth had hoped, the "tide went out easily," and in that desperate moment, as Jo gripped her hand and willed her to live, whatever life remained in her vampire body ceased to be a force.

Jo wailed and howled at the stupidity of it all, a young vampire girl tricked into mortality, willing herself to death to satisfy some unknown ambition. Her parents rushed to her side, their grief as profound as hers but gentler in its understanding that even this, too, had a purpose. Marmee counseled acceptance but Jo could not comply, for she knew there was no divine plan to her sister's passing. No, a human hand had done this thing, one that Jo was determined to remove from its body, as well as its arms, legs, head, and entrails. She promised her sister's death would not go unavenged.

With prayers and tender hands, Mother and Meg made Beth ready for the long sleep that pain would never mar again, seeing with grateful eyes the beautiful serenity that soon replaced the pathetic patience that had wrung their hearts so long, and feeling with reverent joy that to their darling death was a benignant angel, not a phantom full of dread.

While her mother and Meg thanked God that Beth

was well at last, Jo tracked down the kitten supplier, a Mr. Cleaver who ran a warehouse on the outskirts of town. He was a tall man, a great hulking beast of a human, and the second she unfurled herself from bat form, he attacked, knocking Jo to the ground and ramming her head into the bricks. Her vision blurred; her ears roared. Cleaver pounded his fist into her face, laughing as she struggled to gather her wits. He punched her again, but rather than disorient her further, the act snapped her scattered mind into focus. She pooled her strength into her arms and tossed him off her as if he were a twig instead of a log.

His laughter grew louder as he hurled insults: beast, abomination, animal, atrocity, scum. From somewhere, he grabbed an ax and ran toward her, swinging in a wide arc, left, right, left, right. Although she wanted to run, Jo planted her legs and waited. Left, right, left, right. Then, when the blade was a hair's breadth from her neck, she jumped, her body soaring up, up, up to the rafters. She flipped once and landed, only a split second later, behind Cleaver. Before he could even register shock, she held the ax against his throat.

"Who?" she asked lowly.

"So it worked then?" Cleaver asked, grinning despite the threat.

She pressed the blade closer. "Who?"

"He said it would. Start with the weak one, he said, just to make sure the new formula worked."

Jo moved the ax an inch to one side, cutting his skin. Blood trickled down his throat. She could smell his fear. "Who?" she asked again. She would not leave until she had the name of the man who had given him the potion that he'd fed daily to the cats.

He laughed but it wasn't like before. Now it was a hollow sound trying to mask the terror. Jo drove the ax into his skin again. "Tell me, or die"—she made another incision—"slowly."

Silence followed. Jo waited, absorbing the smell of human blood. How sweet it was.

Finally, he stuttered, "S . . . S . . . Simpson. Henry Simpson."

"And where can I find this Henry Simpson?" she said softly.

"Market Lane. Third house."

Market Lane was near the old Backbird farm, only two miles from there. She could be at the man's door in less than fifteen minutes. Satisfied, she took a half-step back and lowered the ax. Seeing an opportunity, Cleaver swung out a leg. Jo stumbled, then fell, the ax landing with a clatter a few feet away. He pulled a stake, long and vicious, from his pocket, hurled it at her with all his might. It sped through the air, quicker than a bullet, and landed in her arm. She didn't even notice, as she threw herself on him and knocked him to the ground, her eyes kindling as the scent of blood pervaded her nostrils.

She had meant to leave him there, bleeding but alive, to hunt the next victim and the next victim until she finally held Dr. Bang's life in her hands. But now she had the smell of blood in her nose, a smell too sweet to resist and she didn't see why she should. She owed this man nothing, not her parents' humility, not Beth's goodness, not her own abstention. If anything, the debt ran the other way, and in exchange for her sister's life, she would take his and feed her own soul on the vibrant red blood that, in sustaining him, sustained her.

Chapter Twenty-Seven

ALL ALONE

It was easy to swear eternal vengeance when drinking the blood of your enemy, and anger and ire were purified by sweet purpose. But when the desperate pleas of your foe were silent, the beloved victim gone, and nothing remained but loneliness and grief, then Jo found her promise very hard to keep.

How could she track down a heartless killer when her own heart ached with a ceaseless longing for her sister? She tried in a blind, hopeless way to do her duty, secretly rebelling against it all the while, for it seemed unjust that her few joys should be lessened, her burdens made heavier, and life get harder and harder as she toiled along. Some people seemed to get all moonlight, and some all shadow. It was not fair, for she tried more than Amy to be good, but never got any reward, only disappointment, trouble, and hard work.

Poor Jo, these were dark days to her, for something like despair came over her when she thought of spending her whole life chasing Dr. Bang down the same endless alley. "I can't do it. I wasn't meant for a life like this, and I know I shall break away and do something desperate if somebody doesn't come and help me," she said to herself, when her first efforts failed and she fell into the moody, miserable state of mind which often comes when strong wills have to yield to the inevitable.

But the inevitable wasn't wholly inevitable, she told herself during those terrible days, when she lay in her coffin unsleeping and some part of her spirit held on to hope. The clue the kitten farmer had given her yielded no results, for there was no such human as Henry Simpson who existed in Concord or Massachusetts. She had been misled by a lie, and there was nothing she could do about it now. In her moment of weakness she had destroyed her only source of information. Oh, was there any more fitting retribution for her slip from grace than this! She could not admit to her parents that she had strayed from the humanitarian path, for she was too ashamed to have given her bosom enemy such rein as to devour a man.

If the folly extended only to the death of the villain, then she might have confessed all and sought absolution, but its ramifications reached far beyond that and showed a sinful lack of foresight in not considering for a moment that information obtained under duress might in fact be wrong information. She understood now why Mr. Dashwood so faithfully applied his truth-telling serum, for what vampire save herself was foolish enough to accept the word of a human? Humans promised honesty and delivered lies, their fluid mortal brains pulling last-minute facts from the air like rabbits from a magician's hat. If only she had held on to her temper or called upon some of Beth's innate sweetness, she would have handled the situation more astutely, perhaps successfully executing Professor Bhaer's charm method to elicit the much-desired lead. But she had been reckless and incautious and now had nothing to act upon.

These thoughts tortured her as she went about Beth's humble, wholesome duties and delights, plying the brooms and dishcloths that Beth had presided over. As she used them, Jo found herself humming the songs Beth used to hum, imitating Beth's orderly ways, and giving the little touches here and there that kept everything fresh and cozy, which was the first step toward making home happy, though she didn't know it till Hannah said with an approving squeeze of the hand . . .

"You thoughtful creeter, you're determined we shan't miss that dear lamb ef you can help it. We don't say much, but we see it, and the Lord will bless you for't, see ef He don't."

As comfortable as a well-tended home was it could never be a substitute for well-executed retribution, and she felt rebuked by Beth's housewifely spirit that seemed to linger around the little mop and the old brush, never thrown away. "I have to do something," said Jo, knowing there were other Beths in the world who would need rescuing, for what villain would destroy a potion as powerful as the one that killed Beth after employing it so perfectly? A new chilly death was in the air and it made Jo feel cold just thinking about it.

So she returned to Gentleman Jackson's salon and presented herself to the vampire gentleman himself early one evening in hopes of regaining her purpose. Although she no longer wholeheartedly subscribed to his methods, she profoundly believed in his mission and knew she had something to offer in return for all the help provided in the past and all the help he would provide in the future. As she spoke, she could hear the whisper of Beth's angel wings and knew she was doing the right thing.

Gentleman Jackson listened to her proposal with quiet interest, confining himself to an uncritical nod when she confessed to eating an information source before confirming the integrity of the data. He knew each generation was the same and every member had to experience something for herself before learning the lessons of her elders. So be it, he thought, surprised again by the young vampire woman before him, who seemed to encapsulate all that one desired in a salon cadet save for her gender, which couldn't be helped. He didn't know how his instructors would take to her proposal, but when she demonstrated her skills for herself, skills he'd thought long lost to previous generations, like the Transylvanian language itself, he could not deny the necessity of giving it a try. Every year the slayers grew more pernicious, every year they invented new ways of killing them, as if fire, stake, and decapitation weren't enough, and every year the salon took measure and adapted. This was merely another adaptation.

Jo taught her first class in transmogrification with her parents' blessing, for they were happy to see her preparing lesson plans at her desk, scratching away, with her black pinafore on, and an absorbed expression. Her students weren't as pleased to receive the lessons, for she was a slip of a girl who had never given instruction before and in the beginning she didn't know how to go about it. She stood in the front by the blackboard reading her notes, which caused their attentions to wander and soon all sixteen cadets were engaged in a loud debate about the dubious benefits of toad blood. To regain their attention, she turned into a bat and flew high above them and even landed a small grayish-green missile on the head of the student who had started the conversation.

After that little demonstration, they were putty in her hands and she deftly taught them how to transform themselves into bats. Few of the other instructors believed she would be able to succeed in her endeavor and they stood in the doorway transfixed as Mr. Arnold Petrie shook a pair of black wings from his back and turned his feet into tiny claws. Then her teaching schedule doubled, as she added a second course for instructors, as it was deemed unseemly for students to have a skill that the teachers lacked. In exchange for the lessons, they pursued the cat breeder link, providing Jo with fresh leads she knew she didn't deserve. But she was grateful for them and she followed them smartly, using all the resources at her disposal and keeping her temper firmly in check. She chased one name after another until finally she knew her villain to be the dastardly Dr. Bang. She'd assumed it was he all along but it was still a shock to have it confirmed, for to hear his name was to be instantly overcome with regret. If she had apprehended him in New York as she'd set out to do, then Beth would still be alive. It was futile, she knew, to brood over things she couldn't change, but it was nearly impossible to let them go. So she struggled nightly with her regret and devoted herself fully to capturing the evil Dr. Bang, whom she knew she would apprehend this time, for she was older and wiser. In the interim, she taught her students and kept home and spent time with her family and remembered Beth.

Working at the salon kept Mr. Bhaer foremost in her mind, for every time she talked of the star-dappled sky, she thought of him, and when she stumbled across a bundle of old exercise books, she turned them over, and relived that pleasant time at kind Mrs. Kirke's. She had smiled at first, then she looked thoughtful, next sad, and when she came to a little message written in the Professor's hand, her lips began to tremble, the books slid out of her lap, and she sat looking at the friendly words, as they took a new meaning, and touched a tender spot in her heart.

"Wait for me, my friend. I may be a little late, but I shall surely come."

"Oh, if he only would! So kind, so good, so patient with me always, my dear old Fritz. I didn't value him half enough when I had him, but now how I should love to see him, for everyone seems going away from me, and I'm all alone."

And holding the little paper fast, as if it were a promise yet to be fulfilled, Jo laid her head down on a comfortable rag bag, and cried, as if in opposition to the rain pattering on the roof.

Was it all self-pity, loneliness, or low spirits? Or was it the waking up of a sentiment which had bided its time as patiently as its inspirer? Who shall say?

Chapter Twenty-Eight

SURPRISES

Jo was alone in the twilight, lying on the old sofa, looking at the fire, and thinking. It was her favorite way of spending the hour of dusk. No one disturbed her, and she used to lie there on Beth's little red pillow, planning lessons, dreaming dreams, or thinking tender thoughts of the sister who never seemed far away. Her face looked tired, grave, and rather sad, for tomorrow was the six-month anniversary of Beth's death and she was thinking how fast the time went and how little she seemed to have accomplished.

Jo must have fallen asleep, for suddenly Laurie's ghost seemed to stand before her, a substantial, lifelike ghost, leaning over her with the very look he used to wear when he felt a good deal and didn't like to show it. But, like Jenny in the ballad . . .

"She could not think it he,"

and lay staring up at him in startled silence, till he stooped and kissed her. Then she knew him, and flew up, crying joyfully . . .

"Oh my Teddy! Oh my Teddy!"

"Dear Jo, you are glad to see me, then?"

"Glad! My blessed boy, words can't express my gladness," she said, her arms tightly around him, then pulling back to look at him, just look, for it had been such a long time, and she noticed the difference right away. It wasn't merely in his complexion, which was now an unearthly white, and the fangs that hung like branches, but in his manner and bearing and the glow that seemed to blaze from within. In her joy for him she felt a speck of sadness for herself, for the innocent human boy was gone and in his place this worldly vampire.

She knew in that instant that Amy was back, too, for only she could have wrought such a huge change in her dear friend. Knowing as she did how Laurie had rushed to Nice to comfort Amy when news of Beth's death reached them, she still never imagined that things had progressed so far so fast. But her mother had hoped for it, ever since Amy wrote to say she had refused a rich Englishman's proposal of marriage. Marmee had felt sure then that something better than what Jo called the "mercenary spirit" had come over her youngest daughter, and a hint here and there in her letters made her suspect that love and Laurie would win the day.

And clearly they had.

Lucky Laurie, to have finally achieved his lifelong goal of becoming a vampire and to have found his soul mate along the way! Jo didn't doubt for a moment that the two young lovers were perfectly suited.

"Where's Amy?"

"Your mother has got her down at Meg's. We stopped there by the way, and there was no getting my wife out of their clutches."

"Your what?" cried Jo, for Laurie uttered those two words with an unconscious pride and satisfaction which betrayed him.

"Oh, the dickens! Now I've done it," and he looked so guilty that Jo was down on him like a flash.

"You've gone and got married!"

"Yes, please, but I never will again," and he went down upon his knees, with a penitent clasping of hands, and a face full of mischief, mirth, and triumph.

"Actually married?"

"Very much so, thank you."

"Mercy on us. What dreadful thing will you do next?" and Jo fell into her seat with a gasp. Married after mere weeks as a vampire, perhaps a few months at the most? It was unheard of. She couldn't believe Amy had moved so quickly. Usually a year passed at least while the novice gained control of his new impulses and desires.

"A characteristic, but not exactly complimentary, congratulation," returned Laurie, still in an abject attitude, but beaming with satisfaction.

"What can you expect, when you take one's breath away, creeping in like a burglar, and letting cats out of bags like that? Get up, you ridiculous boy, and tell me all about it."

"Not a word, unless you let me come in my old place, and promise not to barricade."

Jo laughed at that as she had not done for many a long day, and patted the sofa invitingly, as she said in a cordial tone, "The old pillow is up garret, and we don't need it now. So, come and 'fess, Teddy."

"How good it sounds to hear you say 'Teddy'! No one ever calls me that but you," and Laurie sat down with an air of great content.

"What does Amy call you?"

"My lord."

"That's like her. Well, you look it," and Jo's eye plainly betrayed that she found her boy comelier than ever.

The pillow was gone, but there was a barricade, nevertheless, a natural one, raised by time, absence, and change of species. Both felt it, and for a minute looked at one another as if that invisible barrier cast a little shadow over them. It was gone directly however, for Laurie said, with a vain attempt at dignity . . .

"Don't I look like a married man and the head of a family?"

"Not a bit, and you never will. You've grown paler and fangier, but you are the same scapegrace as ever."

"Now really, Jo, you ought to treat me with more respect," began Laurie, who enjoyed it all immensely, for the first time ever he felt on equal footing with her.

"How can I, when the mere idea of you, vampired and settled, is so irresistibly funny that I can't keep sober!" answered Jo, smiling all over her face, so infectiously that they had another laugh, and then settled down for a good talk, quite in the pleasant old fashion. The change wasn't nearly as radical as Jo thought it would be.

"It's no use your going out to get Amy, for they are all coming up presently. I couldn't wait. I wanted to be the one to tell you the grand surprise."

"Of course you did, and spoiled your story by beginning at the wrong end. Now, start right, and tell me how it all happened. I'm pining to know."

"Well, I did it to please Amy," began Laurie, with a twinkle that made Jo exclaim . . .

"Fib number one. Amy did it to please you. Go on, and tell the truth, if you can, sir."

"Now she's beginning to marm it. Isn't it jolly to hear her?" said Laurie to the fire, and the fire glowed and sparkled as if it quite agreed. "It's all the same, you know, she and I being one. We did it up proper, I assure you, none of this rackety business of Meg and John, doing it on the fly in a fit of anger. Oh, no, we planned it for days before we actually took the plunge. We did it at the American consul's, in Paris, they have the loveliest garden and they planted me there under a rose bush. It was a quiet biting, of course, for even in our happiness we didn't forget dear little Beth."

"Did it hurt?"

"Only for a moment and Amy was very gentle with me and I knew what I was getting so I didn't mind one bit. I can't believe I'm finally one of you. There's no keeping me out of anything, now, dear. I'm going to become a defender, too, and learn everything you know and help Grandfather run the business. I feel strong and invincible and can't wait to get started."

Jo was little surprised by his attitude, for immortality had always suited the good fellow, but granting it never suited her. She couldn't say what about the act felt so repellent to her but there it was and it was no use denying it: You couldn't give eternal life without taking something away and she couldn't bear to take anything from anyone.

As if he guessed her thoughts Laurie held her hand, and said, with a manly gravity she had never seen in him before . . .

"Jo, dear, I want to say one thing, and then we'll put it by forever. I understand now what it means and why you couldn't do it. You never had the heart for it, for it's such an important thing, and of course Amy could do it. I think it worked out the way it was meant to be, and would have come about naturally, if I had waited, as you tried to make me, but I never could be patient, and so I got a heartache. I was a boy then, headstrong and violent, and it took a hard lesson to show me my mistake. For it was one, Jo, as you said, and I found it out, after making a fool of myself. Will you believe it, and go back to the happy old times when we first knew one another?"

"I'll believe it, with all my heart, but, Teddy, we never can be boy and girl again. The happy old times can't come back, and we mustn't expect it. We are man and woman now, with sober work to do, for playtime is over, and we must give up frolicking. I'm sure you feel this. I see the change in you, and you'll find it in me. I shall miss my human boy, but I shall love the vampire man as much, and admire him more, because he means to be what I hoped he would. We can't be little playmates any longer, but we will be brother and sister, to love and help one another for all eternity, won't we, Laurie?"

He did not say a word, but took the hand she offered him, and laid his face down on it for a minute, feeling that out of the grave of a boyish passion, there had risen a beautiful, strong friendship to bless them both. That he'd fulfilled his lifelong dream to be a vampire helped the matter along considerably.

By and by, Amy's voice was heard calling, "Where is she? Where's my dear old Jo?"

In trooped the whole family, and everyone was hugged and kissed all over again, and after several vain attempts, the three wanderers were set down to be looked at and exulted over. Mr. Laurence, hale and hearty as ever, was quite as much improved as the others by his grandson's transformation, for he could now be assured that the boy would never leave him as his granddaughter and Beth had.

The minute she put her eyes upon Amy, Meg became conscious that her own dress hadn't a Parisian air, that young Mrs. Moffat would be entirely eclipsed by young Mrs. Laurence, and that "her ladyship" was altogether a most elegant and graceful woman. Jo thought, as she watched the pair, "How well they look together! I was right, and Laurie has found the beautiful, accomplished girl who will become his home better than clumsy old Jo, and be a pride, not a torment to him."

"Blest if she ain't in silk from head to foot; ain't it a relishin' sight to see her settin' there as fine as a fiddle, and hear folks calling little Amy 'Mis. Laurence!'" muttered old Hannah, who could not resist frequent "peeks" through the slide as she set the table in a most decidedly promiscuous manner.

Mercy on us, how they did talk! first one, then the other, then all burst out together—trying to say everything in half an hour. It was fortunate that blood was at hand, to produce a lull and provide refreshment—for they would have been faint with hunger if they had gone on much longer. Such a happy procession as filed away into the little dining room! Mr. March proudly escorted Mrs. Laurence. Mrs. March as proudly leaned on the arm of "my son." The old gentleman took Jo, with a whispered, "You must be my girl now," and a glance at the empty corner by the fire, that made Jo whisper back, "I'll try to fill her place, sir."

Just then there came a knock at the porch door. Jo opened with hospitable haste, and started as if another ghost had come to surprise her, for there stood a tall bearded gentleman, beaming on her from the darkness like a midnight sun.

"Oh, Mr. Bhaer, I am so glad to see you!" cried Jo, with a clutch, as if she feared the night would swallow him up before she could get him in.

"And I to see Miss Marsch, but no, you haf a party," and the Professor paused as the sound of voices and the tap of dancing feet came down to them.

"No, we haven't, only the family. My sister and friends have just come home, and we are all very happy. Come in, and make one of us."

Though a very social man, I think Mr. Bhaer would have gone decorously away, and come again another day, but how could he, when Jo shut the door behind him, and bereft him of his hat? Perhaps her face had something to do with it, for she forgot to hide her joy at seeing him, and showed it with a frankness that proved irresistible to the solitary vampire, whose welcome far exceeded his boldest hopes.

"If I shall not be Monsieur de Trop,[42] I will so gladly see them all. You haf been sad, my friend?"

He put the question abruptly, for, as Jo hung up his coat, the light fell on her face, and he saw a change in it.

"Sorrowful. We have had trouble since I saw you last."

"Ah, yes, I know. My heart was sore for you when I heard that," and he shook hands again, with such a sympathetic face that Jo felt as if no comfort could equal the look of the kind eyes, the grasp of the big, warm hand.

"Father, Mother, this is my friend, Professor Bhaer," she said, with a face and tone of such irrepressible pride and pleasure that she might as well have blown a trumpet and opened the door with a flourish.

If the stranger had any doubts about his reception, they were set at rest in a minute by the cordial welcome he received. Everyone greeted him kindly, for they had heard a great deal about him, and the elder Marches in particular were eager to meet the man who had taught their daughter how to transform into a bat. They thought it was the most marvelous thing that Jo could fly, and she had been instructing her parents in transmogrification for months now, with varying degrees of success. Marmee hadn't gotten the hang of it yet, for, her daughter could tell, she resisted the notion

[42] Literally *Mr. Too Many*. From Helena Olyphant's 1792 Gothic novel, *The Hidden Fangs of Udolpho,* in which the vampire protaganist calls his victims Monsieur de Trop.

of turning into a bat. She wanted to be a more amiable bird like a cardinal or blue jay.

The Professor stayed a little while, for the company was genial and kind, but soon after he saw Laurie, whom he'd known to have recently been a human boy, he announced he had to leave. Jo was caught off guard by the abruptness of the declaration and tried to think of a reason to stall him, for she didn't want him to go now that he was finally there.

But the Professor wouldn't be swayed from his purpose and immediately took up his umbrella, for it was raining outside and being a vampire didn't protect one against soggy drops in one's eyes. He bid a proper good night to everyone, lingering longest over Mr. March, with whom he felt he could have many splendid long conversations, and walked determinedly to the porch.

Jo followed with a growing unease, for somehow she knew if he left now, she would never see him again. "Are you absolutely sure you have to go right away?" she asked, as he swung open the door. "We were just about to eat."

"Yes, yes," he said, backing away and stumbling unceremoniously on the package he'd brought with him, which was the reason for his visit.

Jo looked down, astonished. "Christopher Columbus!" she said, falling back into the old slang she hadn't used in years. "It's Dr. Bang."

Mr. Bhaer regained his balance awkwardly, stepping

on the doctor's elbow, then crushing his fingers, then kicking his knee. The victim couldn't protest this abuse, for a white handkerchief was stuffed in his mouth and ropes bound his arms and legs. All he could do was look at Jo with fear and loathing in his eyes. "Ah, yes, I haf captured him for you," the Professor stated, finally reaching for the door for stability when all else failed. Gingerly, he walked around the prisoner and felt steady again on his feet.

Her amazement was such that she couldn't think of anything to say. Here, wrapped like a present and offered like a gift, albeit a forgotten one left on the front porch, was the man she'd been hunting for over a year, the elusive author of all her sorrows. She rapped him once in the knee so recently injured but was otherwise bereft of a response.

The Professor explained. "When I heard what happened to your sister, I know this man is to blame. I found him and brought to you. He is yours. Do vhat you please."

Overwhelmed, Jo insisted that he come in again so that her family could properly thank him for the thoughtful service. "You're a hero. Please come back inside and let us drink a toast to you."

"No, no," he said, turning to go and tripping once more over his quarry. The doctor let out a large *ooph* as Bhaer's shoe connected with his stomach. Jo followed him into the rain, and he opened his umbrella like the gentleman he was, insisting now that she return to the party, for Laurie must be waiting for her.

"Laurie?" she repeated, confusion in her voice as she tried to figure out why he would think of that person above all others.

"Your best friend. The boy who is a vampire now."

"Yes, my sister . . . " she began, then broke off as the meaning of his words struck her, and she laughed with relief and delight and something else she couldn't put a name to. "He married my sister. He's Amy's husband. She turned him, not I."

"Oh, my God, that is so good!" cried Mr. Bhaer, managing to clasp his hands in spite of the umbrella. "Jo, I haf nothing but much love to gif you. I came to see if you could care for it, and I waited to be sure that I was something more than a friend. Am I? Can you make a little place in your heart for old Fritz?" he added, all in one breath.

"Oh, yes!" said Jo, and he was quite satisfied, for she folded both hands over his arm, and looked up at him with an expression that plainly showed how happy she would be to walk through life beside him, even though she had no better shelter than the old umbrella, if he carried it.

It was certainly proposing under difficulties, for even if he had desired to do so, Mr. Bhaer could not go down upon his knees, on account of the mud, and Dr. Bang was only a few feet away, alternately groaning in pain, struggling to break free and listening with interest.

"Friedrich, why didn't you . . . "

"Ah, heaven, she gifs me the name that no one speaks since Mama died!" cried the Professor, regarding her with grateful delight as they stood in a puddle.

"I always call you so to myself—I forgot, but I won't unless you like it."

"Like it? It is more sweet to me than I can tell," said Mr. Bhaer, more like a romantic student than a grave professor.

"Why didn't you tell me all this sooner?" asked Jo bashfully.

"Now I shall haf to show you all my heart, and I so gladly vill, because you must take care of it hereafter. See, then, my Jo—ah, the dear, funny little name— I had a vish to tell something the day I said good-bye in New York, but I thought the handsome friend vas betrothed to thee, and so I spoke not."

"Laurie's just a friend. That's all he's ever been."

"But how do I know? And now you gifest me such hope and courage, and I haf nothing to gif back but a full heart and these empty hands," cried the Professor, quite overcome.

Jo never, never would learn to be proper, for when he said that as they stood in the rain, she just put both hands into his, whispering tenderly, "Not empty now," and reaching up, kissed her Friedrich under the umbrella. It was dreadful, but she would have done it if there had been a dozen Dr. Bangs lying on the porch, for she was very far gone indeed, and quite regardless of everything but her own happiness. Though it came in such a very simple guise, that was the crowning moment of both their lives, when, turning from the night and storm and loneliness to the household light and warmth and peace waiting to receive them, with a glad "Welcome home!" Jo led her lover in, shut the door, and immediately announced to her entire family that she and the Professor were getting married.

"And Beth's killer is on the doorstep trussed up like a turkey," she added to the already exultant crowd. They were so moved by both pieces of news, the much-wished-for happy and the long-mourned sad, that there was nothing to be done but bring Dr. Bang in immediately, lay him on the dining room table, and feast on him, despite the bruises that were beginning to smart along his arms and legs. Everyone was in a festive mood, and it warmed Jo's heart to see her beloved among her family, for he seemed at home. It appeared others felt the same way, particularly Meg, because she suggested that Jo and Friedrich turn Aunt March's home into a school for vampire defenders to teach the old ways like Jo had been doing at the salon. Aunt March would no longer be needing her home, as the dear ancient had been staked just last week by Amy's replacement. It seemed a worldwide cabal had indeed been imminent all those years, and Aunt March had the keen satisfaction of knowing she was right, which, as for so many paranoids who come to violent ends, almost made up for the end itself.

The idea was met with universal approval, and Marmee and Father, deeming the occasion was special enough and the chosen meal sinful enough, made an exception to their devout humanitarianism and dined, like the rest, on Dr. Bang.

"We must have our sing, in the good old way, for we are all together again once more," said Jo, feeling that a good shout would be a safe and pleasant vent for the jubilant emotions of her soul.

They were not all there. But no one found the words thoughtless or untrue, for Beth still seemed among them, a peaceful presence, invisible, but dearer than ever, since death could not break the household league that love made dissoluble. The little chair stood in its old place. The tidy basket, with the bit of work she left unfinished when the needle grew "so heavy," was still on its accustomed shelf. The beloved instrument, seldom touched now, had not been moved, and above it Beth's face, serene and smiling, as in the early days, looked down upon them, seeming to say, "Be happy. I am here."

"Play something, Amy. Let them hear how much you have improved," said Laurie, with pardonable pride in his promising pupil.

But Amy whispered, with full eyes, as she twirled the faded stool, "Not tonight, dear. I can't show off tonight."

But she did show something better than brilliancy or skill, for she sang Beth's songs with a tender music in her voice which the best master could not have taught, and touched the listener's hearts with a sweeter power than any other inspiration could have given her. The room was very still, when the clear voice failed suddenly at the last line of Beth's favorite hymn. It was hard to say . . .

Earth hath no sorrow that heaven cannot heal;

and Amy leaned against her husband, who stood behind her, feeling that her welcome home was not quite perfect without Beth's kiss.

"Now, we must finish with Mignon's song, for Friedrich sings that," said Jo, before the pause grew painful. And Mr. Bhaer cleared his throat with a gratified "Hem!" as he stepped into the corner where Jo stood, saying . . .

"You vill sing vith me? Ve go excellently vell together."

A pleasing fiction, by the way, for Jo had no more idea of music than a grasshopper. But she would have consented if he had proposed to sing a whole opera, and warbled away, blissfully regardless of time and tune. It didn't much matter, for Mr. Bhaer sang like a true Transylvanian, heartily and well, and Jo soon subsided into a subdued hum, that she might listen to the mellow voice that seemed to sing for her alone.

The song was considered a great success, and the singer retired covered with laurels, and Amy put on her bonnet, and Laurie began to make their good-byes. But before anyone could leave, for the hour was late and the sun would soon rise, Mrs. March stretched out her arms, as if to gather children to herself, and said, with face and voice full of motherly love, gratitude, and humility . . .

"Oh, my girls, however long you may live, I never can wish you a greater happiness than this!"

LOUISA MAY ALCOTT

(1832–1888) was an American novelist best known for *Little Women*. The story is loosely based on her own childhood experience growing up in Concord, Massachusetts, with three sisters. Unlike Jo March, the protagonist of her famous novel, Alcott never became a vampire.

LYNN MESSINA

is the author of *Fashionistas*, *Tallulahland*, *Mim Warner's Lost Her Cool*, and *Savvy Girl*. When she's not writing about girls growing up—or girls growing up as *vampires*—she works as a freelance copy editor for various New York magazines.